*Here's to all of the LGBTQI+ love stories that
I wish I had read as a young gay kid.*

Fin &
Rye &
Fireflies

HARRY COOK

First published in 2020 by Ink Road
INK ROAD is an imprint and trademark
of Black & White Publishing Ltd

Black & White Publishing Ltd
Nautical House, 104 Commercial Street
Edinburgh, EH6 6NF

1 3 5 7 9 10 8 6 4 2   20 21 22 23

ISBN: 978 1 78530 247 3

A CIP catalogue record for this book is available from the British Library.

Typeset by Iolaire Typesetting, Newtonmore
Printed and bound by CPI Group (UK) Ltd, Croydon CR0 4YY

1

Fin

We arrive in Lochport on a Friday. A crappy day, a few days before my otherwise favourite holiday of the year, Halloween. We've been driving for about eight hours, which in teenage years equates to about a week. As we exit the highway and drift across Kettle Bridge, my first glimpse of our new home below reminds me of the It's a Small World ride at Disneyland.

Old rust-coloured barns and maple trees line the street. The house, a two-storey monstrosity with a red double door and high arched windows (windows that I have an intense feeling I'll want to throw myself out of before the day is over), sits leering at us.

"Fin, take your headphones out when I'm speaking to you," Dad says, his forehead narrowing into his regular furrowed crisscross. Mum shuffles in her seat and looks across at him, the air suddenly immensely stuffy and uncomfortable.

"Sorry," I mumble, fumbling with my earbuds and stuffing them into the backpack at my feet.

"I asked you to go and open the door for your mother," Dad almost barks. "Manners maketh the man, Fin."

Not quite sure what the hell he's talking about, but also not surprised by the cold tone in his voice, I get out of the car and greedily gulp in the fresh sea air from the harbour nearby. I wander around to Mum's side, opening the door for her and standing back. She looks up at me sheepishly, a brush of embarrassment lingering in her smile as she steps out. I smile back, retrieving a stick of sour grape gum from my jeans pocket as Dad joins us.

"So, what do we think?" he asks, his eyes switching between Mum and me, as if he's a carnival clown and we're about to throw a hoop at him to win an inflammable soft toy as a prize.

"It's ... the – it's nice. H-homely." Mum sounds like she's trying to convince herself more than Dad.

I give a thumbs-up, popping the piece of gum in my mouth before I turn to head inside.

So, I guess now is probably a good a time as any to explain how the hell I found myself upheaved to a brand-new town and into a creepy old house that resembles the set of *The Texas Chainsaw Massacre*.

Well ... It started with a kiss ... as most love stories often do.

2

Fin

Jesse Andrews worked at the Retro, a bowling alley in the centre of Pittford, and he had the arms of a Greek god. He was a senior, eighteen months and four days older than me (I know, I counted), and was a leading light of the track team. My best friend Emily and I spent most Friday nights bowling (poorly) and watching him like the besotted superfans of a boyband, as we sat scoffing extra-large milkshakes and chilli cheese fries.

The night of our kiss fell on a Friday. I left Mr Glasson's science class the second the bell rang and wandered over to the school car park to wait for Emily. Emily's car, a 1963 VW Bug, was always open as the lock was broken, so I sat among the various knick-knacks, pretzel wrappers and old car-fresheners until she finally arrived.

"Mrs Wilton has about as much sense as a can of tuna."

"Nice to see you too," I said, avoiding her backpack which came hurtling at my feet, landing with a flump as a pack of cigarettes and a deodorant stick rolled out across the rubber car mats.

"Ew. Seriously, Em, you smoking again?"

"Absolutely not," she said as she leaned over, grabbing one and lighting it quickly. Her purple-nail-varnished fingers held her cigarette like Audrey Hepburn while her wild mane of dusty blonde hair gave her a Courtney Love vibe. Who knows why Em hung out with me; not only is she seventeen, a year older than me, but she's one of the coolest people I've ever met. Effortlessly cool. Like those vintage Polaroids you see of sixties' rock stars who look like they've just rolled out of bed. I'm not complaining, though. I'm so happy to know her. My life would be a lonely place without her.

"Wilton gave me an F on my history report and I just – Fin. Are you even listening to me?"

I'd zoned out as we pulled into the bowling alley car park. I couldn't avert my eyes from Jesse who was leaning into the bonnet of his car, checking something out in the engine.

"Fin, you are about as helpful to my current situation as a dog-shit bag with a hole in it," came Emily's voice, knocking me out of my inappropriate fantasies.

"Hmm? What? Right. Mrs Wilton. Gotcha. That's so annoying."

"Wow, Fin, so convincing," Emily said, clocking on to what I was looking at – Jesse's buns, to be frank – and butting out her cigarette in the pull-out ashtray.

We got out of the Bug and wandered over to Jesse, my stomach fluttering like the propellers of a helicopter as he leaned back and smiled at us, pleased to remove himself from whatever issue was going on with his old Holden.

"My two favourite Friday-night patrons are here at last," he said, generating a mock cheer with his fists.

"I was just telling Fin about Mrs Wilton's vendetta against me, but he was more interested in checking out your ..."

I shot Emily a look that read, *I'll key your car if you say another word*, and she stopped herself.

"…your car," she finished.

"No way," Jesse said, turning his caramel-coloured eyes to me and sending his dimples upwards into a grin. "I didn't know you liked cars."

Neither did I.

"Uhhh, yeah. I love them. Total petrolhead. Huge fan. Especially the … Well, the engines and … Yeah, sure, mostly the engines I guess."

What in the fresh hell was I talking about?

"Well, maybe you could come back to my place tonight after my shift? I think it's a spark plug issue but I'm not sure. It'd be awesome if you could take a look at it for me?"

I forced my face into a smile that must have made me seem like I was pumped full of Botox and gave Emily the best glare I could without Jesse noticing.

"Sure … Yeah. Sure," I said, nodding like a bobble-head as Emily led me inside, down past the bowling lanes to the diner section, finding a booth near one of the vintage jukebox machines.

The walls lining the booth were covered in retro signs that read "5c Soda Pop" and "Chocolate Sundae just 59c!" with pictures of cartoon teenagers eating and laughing next to their colourful fifties cars. The light was dim and shadows bounced around the room, giving it a slightly sleazy downtown bar vibe.

Emily saddled into the booth and opened a menu, taking her chewing gum from her mouth and sticking it behind her ear like a savage.

"I'm starving, are you?"

"Not anymore."

"What, why?"

"Because you *destroyed* me back there."

"I *destroyed* you? Jesus, Fin. Could you be any more dramatic?"

"No seriously, what was that about? You might as well have told Jesse I wanted to mount him right there in the street!"

The waiter, a girl with short purple hair and a tattoo of Jack Skeleton on her upper arm, arrived at our table, holding her notepad and forcing her face into her idea of a welcoming smile.

"I'll get a burger and a large banana milkshake. I'm talking really large."

"Gotcha," came our waiter's reply who, on further inspection, I saw was named Tina. The badge on her regulation cotton shirt was coloured in with black and purple permanent markers: her one act of rebellion against working in such a retro utopia as this.

"No, I'm talking like enormous. I need so much banana milkshake in me I want to walk out of here looking like a banana. Ya get me? Like a bucket of banana mil–"

"She gets it, Em," I said, my rescue attempt for poor Tina a success as I made my order of cheese fries and a medium cream soda.

Before long, our food was devoured and dessert was served in the form of Jesse, who was now doing a thorough job of polishing the bowling balls behind the counter. I couldn't take my eyes off him as I speared a leftover cheese fry with my fork, pushing it around my plate with no intention of eating it at all.

"You should be careful of Jesse, you know," came Emily's voice over the sound my sad fry was making on the plate.

"And you, Queen of Nicotine, should quit smoking."

"No, I'm serious, Fin. He's a douche canoe. Both him and Jake

Mathers make the juniors' lives a living hell at school and I don't trust him as far as I can throw him."

"First of all, Jake Mathers is a douche, yes, but Jesse has been nothing but nice to me. Secondly, you won bronze at the inter-school athletics meet at pole vaulting, so I'm guessing you've the upper body strength to throw him relatively far. Hence your argument is invalid."

"Did you just say hence?"

"Alas, yes I did."

"Alas? My *god*, you're like a librarian."

"But with great eyebrows."

"True." She clinked her frothy milkshake glass against mine and winked.

"In all seriousness though, Em, I need you to help me get out of going to his place after here tonight. I have no idea what I'm talking about when it comes to cars. I don't even know how to drive manual. Obvs, given I've not got my licence."

She waved at the air, brushing my worries aside as if they were a mosquito.

"It's easy. Look at the engine, pretend to fiddle with it and then say, 'Oooh, yeah, looks like you might need a professional.' Play cool, you know?"

I rolled my eyes so far back in my head I felt they would detach and plop out of my face.

"Ah yes, *cool*. The trait I am best known for."

I put two toothpicks under my upper lip like fangs and crossed my eyes, sending Emily into a snort-laugh that scared the child in the booth across from us so much that he started to cry.

"Thaaaat's my cue to leave," Emily said, tucking a peroxide blonde curl behind her ear and licking ketchup from her index finger.

She ruffled my hair and slapped a twenty-dollar bill down on to the bill dish, throwing a casual "see you tomorrow" over her shoulder as she strode off, leaving me alone in the booth waiting for Jesse. He mouthed the words "won't be long" and gave me a wink that sent sparks through my heart and set my skin tingling.

"S-sure. Yeah," I murmured, suddenly feeling extremely self-conscious. (No way would I have chosen to wear a holey, moth-eaten sweater for a trip to Jesse's.)

I gulped the last bit of cream soda from my glass and ambled over to the arcade near the exit; race car simulators and dinosaur adventure games lined a small room. One of the neon lights overhead was broken and flickering in an attempt to give everybody in the arcade a chronic migraine.

Jesse's voice appeared from behind me as smooth as chocolate syrup on an ice-cream sundae.

"So! Sorry it took me a while to leave. All set?"

3

Fin

The ongoing screech from the car bonnet filled the awkward silence like a dolphin from hell.

Jesse's house wasn't far from the Retro and we didn't say a word to one another for the entire drive. His parents were apparently out of town until the following morning, which was perhaps why he felt no need to throw his cigarette away as we pulled into his garage. He got out and walked to the front of the car, clicking open and swinging up the bonnet, which creaked like the timbers of a sinking ship.

He looked up at me and smiled, a smile that had a hint of nervousness across its edges.

"So, I've been trying to figure out why it's making that ridiculous noise for about a week now. Any help and I will love you for ever."

I felt my knees pop and I steadied myself against the car door. *I will love you for ever.* Good god, can I get that in writing?

I slowly made my way to face the giant chunk of hot machinery below the bonnet.

"Uhh ..."

What was I thinking, you ask? No idea. There was no way I was going to be able to stay cool, calm and collected.

"It ... um ... looks like you uhh ..."

I realised Jesse was right next to me. I could smell his cologne and fresh sweat mingling with the smell of the greasy engine. His eyes were burning into the side of my face as I swallowed to avoid choking on my own tongue.

"It looks like you ... Could probably use a professional's opinion. I ... I would have to say that it –"

"You're not great with cars, are you?" came Jesse's voice, soft as velvet. "Not such a petrolhead after all ..."

I glanced up to see him place a mint on his tongue. He was smiling at me with a look that said, *It's all good, relax.*

I shook my head, stifling a giggle as I felt my face burn red.

"Nope."

We both started laughing, but my heart was pounding like I'd just done the loop-the-loop on the Demon rollercoaster at the fair that pitched up in town every summer.

"Well ... I am."

"You're what?" I asked, wiping the sweat from my upper lip as nonchalantly as I could.

"I am good with cars. But I ... I guess I wanted you to come and hang out with me."

It was as if, in that moment, the concrete floor beneath my feet turned to quicksand. As I struggled to keep myself upright, I took a breath, slowly letting my eyes focus on his.

"You ... You did?"

He took a step towards me.

"I like you, Fin," he murmured. He was close enough that I

could smell the mint on his breath, mixed with the ashy remnants of his last cigarette.

Without thinking, without even daring to second guess myself, I leaned in and kissed him, hard on the lips. As I pulled away, I stared into his eyes as if looking for pennies at the bottom of a well. Terrified, yet ridiculously elated about the feel of my lips on those of this man-babe before me, I stood motionless; each second that ticked by felt like an hour.

It was right at that moment, when my body thrummed with alive-ness, the moment when I felt the universe click into place, when everything felt like it finally made sense, that the world broke apart and the words I've since tried to forget, pierced the silence of that dark garage:

"What the *fuck?*"

Suddenly, out of nowhere, there stood Jake Mathers. His scrawny body and ratty face were hunched in horror; he looked stunned, like he'd just witnessed a murder. In one hand he held a can wrapped in a brown paper bag (I presumed it was beer), and his left sock didn't match his right one – it's amazing the things you notice in times of such incomprehensible weirdness.

The silence that followed seeped into my body through my very pores as we all stood waiting for someone, anyone, to say something.

"You're a ..." Jake was searching his foggy, useless head for a word like an explorer searches a map. "A *fag.*"

I felt the word leave Jake's mouth, travel through the air and slap me hard across the face. What came next was the back-hander that followed the initial wallop.

Jesse turned to me with a grin on his face like someone who'd just pulled the lever on one of those water-dunking games at a carnival. Jake came over and the two of them did a stupid hand-fist bump thing, which looked more like two people attempting to shake hands in the dark while drunk, and it all became crystal clear: I'd been set up. These two jokers were on a mission to uncover the Homosexual of Pittford High.

"My my *my*. Fin the fag," came Jake's whiny voice. "It kinda has a ring to it, huh?"

I stared into Jesse's eyes, desperate to see what I was sure had to be in there somewhere. A hint of compassion. A dash of decency. But there was nothing. Just malice. Just darkness.

And that was when I left that car, that garage and those two twisted jerks still celebrating their evening's sport.

4

Fin

"Mr and Mrs Whittle. We regret to inform you of your son's unnatural tendencies."

Muffled laughter.

"We have evidence that you are raising a pervert ..."

By the time I got home less than half an hour later, that was the message that some "worried parents" had left on our home phone.

Mum and Dad weren't entirely convinced by Jesse and Jake's acting skills, but still they asked me if I was "really a queer" to which I responded "yes".

This simple, honest answer made my mum cry and my dad's face turn the colour of the beetroot salad we were having for dinner. After which, their fits of outrage escalated throughout the evening. It's true that both my parents were raised by stalwarts of the Irish Catholic community; however, in my opinion, all this catastrophising seemed dramatic and extremely unnecessary. More to the point, I knew they weren't as concerned about religious principles so much as they were worried about their friends finding out they had a gay son – a son who, in their eyes, is no longer "normal".

After pacing the house for a solid twenty-four hours without sleep, they packed me off on a clapped-out old bus to stay with Aunt Carla out in the middle of nowhere while they arranged the "relocation" to Lochport. One that they assured me they were "forced into", thanks to *moi*. Bad news for *moi* that my dad's job as an engineering adjuster means he can pull off this kind of move.

Who knows what – if anything – they told my older brother Elliot about the commotion. He's been backpacking his way around the world for the past few months. I miss him, but can't face trying to contact him. No headspace. Elliot's always been the "normal" one of the Whittle brothers. And, being "normal" – whatever that actually means – is incredibly important to my parents.

Which brings us to the fun-filled here and now.

*

This upheaval to Lochport is my parents' idea of giving me a "fresh start" and "removing" me from any "distractions" that I might succumb to back in our old town. If only I'd known I was living in such a gay mecca I could've set my sights higher than kissing that weasel Jesse.

I take a breath and collect our bags from the car before trudging my way back up into our new abode. The house itself is bigger than any other house I've ever set foot in before. I have no idea how we can afford it; however, my one good guess is that it's one of those murder houses that make their way onto the market cheap after some horrendous crime. The floors are solid oak and the light fixtures are crystal. My room, I've decided, is the loft on the third floor. It's one of the smallest in the entire house, but it's perfect. One giant window seat as comfy as my bed sits atop an inbuilt bookcase; the view above of nothing but our new garden and the woods beyond.

Dad spared no time or expense in packing us up as quickly as possible, and so all our furniture arrived the day before yesterday. My parents hired movers, notified schools, arranged work stuff with lightning speed, citing a "family emergency", all before collecting me from Aunt Carla's on their way along the highway. The fact I survived even a day at Aunt Carla's is a total miracle. I can't stand cats, so when Dad told me I would be temporarily living with her (a woman who's homed not one, not two, but *eight* ex-stray felines), I was certain it was an assassination attempt.

With my bed neatly fitted in the corner of my new room, various boxes labelled "School", "Books", "Clothes", "Toiletries" sit squashed together near the wardrobe, but the mere thought of unpacking it all really does make me want to throw myself out of my third-storey window. Instead, I collapse onto the window seat, and stare morosely out at the view. I get the feeling this new town isn't going to be any more welcoming than our old one. Emily was my only real friend back in Pittford and she was different. One in a million. To top it off, "fresh start" or not, I know my parents definitely won't like my sexuality here any more than they did in Pittford.

Great stuff.

5

Fin

On the morning of Halloween, I finally muster the energy to leave our new house and explore. Apart from some serious "get me out of here" messages to Emily, I've barely spoken to anyone; Mum and Dad have been busy cleaning and unpacking and organising the house and any conversations we've had have been tense ... and that's putting it mildly.

As I head out the front door, I hear Dad's voice.

"Uhh-uhh, hold up, Fin," he says, coming out of the kitchen. "Where do you think you're going?"

"To explore."

"I think we need to have a talk."

"Dad, come on. I've been stuck in house for *two* days. Can't I go have a look around?"

Honestly, what does he think I'm up to – a chem-sex hook-up?

He stares at me. Clearly he's not going to let me out the front door until he's given me a talking-to, but strangely enough, both he and Mum seem to have calmed somewhat while I've been at Aunt Carla's. My guess is either Valium or Xanax.

"Fin, listen. I know this must seem like a lot to you. You might not understand it now, but one day you will recognise that what we have done is for the best. Your mother and I believe that a change of scenery, a fresh start will remove any … unnatural temptations. Otherwise, life could be an extremely difficult road for you." He takes a deep breath before delivering his killer line. "We – We just want the best for you, Fin. For you to have the same opportunities, the same lifestyle as we – and your brother – have. A normal life. Do you understand?"

I nod, desperate for the chandelier above my head to detach and crush me. There's that word again: normal.

Dad stares at me for a second before saying shortly: "Okay. Good. Be home no later than seven."

It's eleven o'clock in the morning. He's gifted me a solid eight hours of exploring. Perfect.

I wander down the street, the sky the colour of honey and the trees full of acorns. I have to hand it to Lochport; the town itself is pretty cute. I stroll into the centre, which takes about five minutes from our place, and find it full of maple and oak trees, rustic old buildings with shop signs like "Smith's Candies" and "McElroy's Fish & Chippie" and a wooden dock that looks like it's from the set of *JAWS*. A bright yellow bike with a pink seat leans against the window of McElroy's. It has a scribbled sign that reads "Free to a good home" followed by another sign underneath that reads: "Just kidding. $50. Pay within for the key." The bike's wheels are locked with a chain. I have a small wad of savings, $150 to be precise, from my job at a coffee store back in Pittford, and I figure a bike of this kind – especially that pink seat – is a sensational investment. I open the door and let myself in, a bell jingling somewhere out back. The smell of fish overpowers me like a chemical attack.

"Hello?" I say, calling into the abyss. "I … I'd like to buy the bike."

A rummaging noise comes from behind the plastic curtain and a woman wearing a yellow rain mac, high-top wellies and a fisherman's hat comes out to greet me; she's plump with big kind eyes and a button nose.

"Sorry, love. We just got a new delivery in and my hearing ain't what it used to be. You been waiting long? What can I get for ya?"

I smile. Her warmth is contagious.

"I was … I'm new here," I say. "I was actually hoping to buy that bike out front?"

"Oh that?" she says. "Oh, take it. You'd be doing me a favour! My daughter, Poppy, she put that fifty-dollar sign out front under mine. She calls herself a 'hustler'."

The door behind me swings open and cool air tickles the back of my neck.

"Speak of the devil. We were just discussing your hustling skills, darling."

Poppy, dark hair with piercing green eyes, leans over the counter next to me and gives her mother a kiss on the cheek.

"Poppy McElroy," she says, offering me her hand to shake. I can't help but notice that it's emblazoned with a ring on nearly every finger.

"Fin Whittle," I reply.

"And I'm Isla," Poppy's mother says, walking around to the front of the counter with a key on a pompom fob. "They call me a local treasure."

"Yeah, right. I take it you didn't get the fifty dollars for my bike?" Poppy asks, a crease in her forehead the size of the Grand Canyon.

"Mr Whittle here is kindly giving your old bike a new home," Isla says with a grin as we follow her out on to the street. "I refuse to take money from a new neighbour," she continues, unlocking the bike and presenting it to me like it's a showroom-fresh Mercedes S Class.

"Thank you so much," I say, glancing at Poppy who rolls her eyes and gives me the hint of a smile.

The three of us stand silently for a moment, the only noise coming from the splash of the ocean against the dock just across the street.

"I see Rye still hasn't caught anything," Poppy says, giving a nod to where a guy roughly my age is sitting on an upturned bucket with a fishing rod bobbing up and down in the grey sea. Next to him squats an English Bulldog, drool pooling under its cheeks.

"Not a thing," Isla says with a giggle. "Your friend's a terrible fisherman." And with that she heads back into the store to serve a customer.

Poppy turns to look me up and down.

"Fin, was it?"

I nod.

"Cool name," Poppy says, flashing me a grin which just as suddenly fades as something behind me catches her eye.

I follow her gaze across to the wharf.

Two guys and two girls are now standing a little way off from Poppy's friend Rye and laughing. At first I pay no attention to anything other than the adorable English Bulldog, but then I hear the word.

"Fag" rises up from the wharf's wooden slats. The air seems to echo with it; it's painted the sky the shade of hate and now it rains down like poison on the entire town.

Poppy doesn't miss a beat. "Come on!" she instructs me as she storms across the street and onto the wharf. I attempt to keep up, my new bike squeaking like a wheelbarrow as I push it across the road after her while simultaneously making a mental note to buy some WD40.

"Right, which one of you bastards said that?"

The four break apart from their huddle next to Rye and stare daggers at Poppy. I'm painfully aware of the ear-piercing squeaky noises my bike is making and I'm relieved when I can finally lean it against the wharf.

"I said, *which one of you*?" Poppy repeats.

The air is still, and the fisherman – Rye – has stood up, ready to defend himself if he has to. Tall, with dark skin and eyes like rock pools in summer, he's ridiculously handsome. So much so that he actually takes my breath away. His bulldog is snoozing next to him, completely unaware of the drama unfolding around her.

The difference between Rye and the two other guys is stark. They both look like they've never seen sunlight. The taller of the two is gangly and practically translucent, while the guy next to him stands rooted to the spot like the trunk of a tree. The girls are dull and model-esque in that catwalk, high fashion model/alien/vampire kind of way. Together, the four of them look like the undead or an incarnation of the Manson family.

"It was me, what of it?" the paler of the two girls says. Her hair is practically white; the dark circles under her eyes create the impression of a chronic case of anaemia.

"Seriously, Paisley?" Poppy snaps. "You think you can go around calling other people names with a name like that?"

Paisley scoffs, taken aback by Poppy's brazen response. "I'm the fourth Paisley in a long line of –"

"Couches? Old people couches? Is that what you were about to say?"

The girl next to Paisley looks ready to retaliate on her behalf when Poppy goes on: "And don't get me started on you, Bronwyn. It's impossible to take you seriously while you stand there looking like you've been struck by lightning. Seriously, do you not own a straightener? Or at the very least, an iron? You look like you've been trapped in Jumanji for the past decade."

Bronwyn takes a sharp inhale and cups her mouth with her hand. Poppy's right: her try-too-hard tousled hair is a sad and wispy bird's nest.

"And *you* two!" Poppy's really getting going now. "Mark? Hugh?"

I grip my bike handlebars and stare at her, feeling both impressed and slightly terrified to witness this woman I've only just met in all her gladiator fury.

"Yeah, you two. Tweedle Dee and Tweedle Dumber. Since when did you leave your caves before nightfall? Shouldn't you be collecting sticks?"

The two Tweedles take a moment to understand what she's actually saying. Eventually they figure it out but are too late to respond, as Poppy has already moved on.

"Now, I would love to stay and chat with you all, but I have a pleasant evening planned with my friend Rye here and my new friend Fin."

I feel my cheeks glow as she gestures to me.

"It's Halloween after all," Poppy goes on, "and we still need to figure out our costumes. Do you lot have any suggestions? I take it you've gone with *The Hills Have Eyes* theme this year, no?"

Dumbfounded silence. Mouths hanging open.

"No? Right, well … Away you go," Poppy says with a flick of her wrist.

The four of them turn on their heels and stomp off, still muttering under their breath.

Poppy spins around to smile at Rye and then me. "All good?" she says, fumbling in her pocket for a packet of gum and offering us a piece.

"Thanks, Pops," Rye says.

"That was … That was amazing." I can't help it. I'm in total awe of her.

She curtsies and bows like a circus performer and Rye lets out a laugh before turning to me with his hand outstretched.

"Rye," he says.

Those eyes. That smile.

"Fin," I say, my tummy doing a thousand backflips.

He's cute. Far too cute. Maybe the cutest damn thing I have ever laid eyes on. But I'm not about to be fooled again. Nope. No-sir-ee. I'm not stepping on that bear trap again.

Well, that's what I think until his eyes meet mine and he says three little words that hit me like a truck.

"Fin? Cute name."

Here we go again.

✴

Arriving home a few hours later, I bound up the stairs two at a time, race across the landing and up the ladder to my room. Mum texted earlier to let me know she is out buying groceries and I can hear Dad somewhere downstairs rummaging through the boxes scattered across the floor.

For the first time ever, I didn't fluff the chance at making new friends. I'm not far from doing a private dance of victory round my room.

Poppy invited me to join her and Rye at the local diner tonight and I have about an hour to figure out what I'm going to tell Dad, as well as figuring out a costume to wear for my first Halloween in this new town. I want to come across as cute but not too innocent; hot but not to the point of desperado.

"You okay?" comes Dad's voice drifting up from halfway up the ladder.

"All good," I reply, trying to sound casual.

"Whose bike is that outside?"

"It's. I … uh. I met some people …"

My face cringes into a shape that cannot be described.

"Some people?"

Dad has popped his head through the hatch now and is leaning on his forearms, trying to seem nonchalant.

I really didn't want to start off my "fresh start" with a whopping great lie, but I know how difficult – by which I mean impossible – it will be to explain that I've already fallen for the very first guy I've met in Lochport.

"A girl. Just a girl down at the fish shop. I … I bought this bike off of her and –"

Dad's master plan is taking shape before his very eyes. "A girl?"

His whole face lights up. I wouldn't be surprised if he could hear wedding bells.

"Yeah. She invited me to the diner in town tonight. It's got a dress-up theme and –"

"Say no more. I have just the thing."

I release a giant breath of air, my lungs relaxing after holding my breath for what feels like an eternity. Thirty seconds later, Dad is back with a tattered football jersey (shoulder pads included), shorts and helmet.

"It's … Halloween," I hear myself saying without much of an idea at what's going on.

"*Exactly*," Dad says, grinning like an idiot. "Zombie football player! You can wear my old uniform, rip it up a bit, add some fake blood."

"But …" I'm speechless. Elliot has always been the footballer, the one who bonded with Dad over sport. Like Elliot, my dad was captain of the school football team – and it's still a huge part of who he is. "Don't you want to save that? You know, pass it on to Elliot?"

"Elliot's got his own gear. Besides, I want you to have it. Take it from me. Girls love this kind of thing."

"They do?" I ask, baffled at the workings of heterosexual desire.

"Absolutely. Girls like to feel protected."

"By zombies?" I reply, attempting not to laugh in his face. The whole thing is absurd, but I'm glad he's speaking to me normally again, even if it is about girls and football. We haven't exactly been spending much quality time together since the whole thing blew up back at our old home.

He winks. "Be back no later than midnight."

He gets halfway down the ladder then springs back up like a Jack-in-the-Box.

"Oh, one last thing –"

I raise my eyebrows.

"What's her name?"

"Poppy," I reply while Rye's face floats blissfully into my mind.

"Poppy," Dad repeats with a grin. Yep, he's definitely hearing church bells. Possibly christening his grandkids.

As he disappears down the ladder and out of sight, my phone buzzes.

Poppy: Still all good for later?

Me: Yep. Can't wait.

Poppy: Great. Wear something spooky.

Me: If you insist.

6

Fin

I look like a mix between Daryl Dixon after a heavy day doing his *Walking Dead* thing and one of the zombies from the *Thriller* video.

I scan Penny's Diner until I see Poppy and Rye in a booth at the back of the room. I wish I could eloquently describe their costumes, but the only words that come to mind are "freakin' hilarious". Poppy's outfit consists of a giant box of Tampax and Rye is dressed head to toe in a red onesie-type thing that at first I think is supposed to be fire. Then, after putting two and two together, I realise they have literally gone as san-pro and menstrual blood.

Strong. Nailed it.

I laugh so hard it sounds like a honk and then quickly cover my mouth with my hand. Poppy spots me and waves me over.

I scoot into the booth and take them both in in all their glory.

"Jesus," I say, mostly to myself.

"You like? It was this or a cat and a litter box," Poppy says while swirling her metal straw in her soda.

"You look awesome!" Rye says as he leans over and touches the fake blood on my arm. "Very *Walking Dead* meets *Friday Night Lights*."

"Thanks," I say with a blush. "That was the plan."

Just then a waitress comes over and sits herself down in our booth.

"June-bug!" Poppy says as she budges up and pushes her plate of fries over to her.

"Hey," June says as she takes a fry with a manicured hand and bites half of it.

"Fin, June, June, Fin." Rye does the introductions with a neat little wave between the two of us.

"Nice to meet you," I say, reaching my hand across the table.

June takes it and kisses the top of it like a starlet in one of those old black and white movies.

"Mwah," she says with a wink.

Rye simply does this half-smile thing that manages to make me feel all tingly and then motions to June.

"June here is the leader of the queer-straight alliance at school, a pro at *Call of Duty 3* and also the first trans gal to ever play Audrey in *Little Shop of Horrors*."

"*And* the first *brown* trans gal in Lochport, period," June replies with a giggle. "Well, the first that we know of to flourish like I have."

She glowers over my shoulder and mouths the words "I'm bloody getting to it", then looks back at us and sighs.

"What are you guys after?" she says.

"Uh... Did you just swear at your manager?" Poppy says, wide-eyed.

"Ugh, Luke is such a douche." She rolls her eyes. "Plus, I

mouthed it. There was no sound. It's like farting on an aeroplane. It doesn't count."

I produce a less intense version of my earlier honk laugh and Rye giggles to himself. I feel my stomach drop as June and Poppy both burst out laughing.

"You are insanely cute, Mr Fin," June tells me, as she takes out her waitressy notepad and pen.

I notice Rye look between June and me and shift in his seat. When I meet his eye, he smiles and keeps looking right back at me.

"I'll get the waffles and cheese fries," he says, briefly breaking eye contact with me to address June.

"Make that two," says Poppy.

"Three," I chime in.

June stands, then leans against the side of the booth and read-justs her gorgeous long hair underneath her red and white hat.

"I finish my shift soon and I have Dad's car while he's away on business." She slaps her back pocket, which makes a jingling sound.

"Nice. We'll wait for you," Poppy says as June looks over at her manager and rolls her eyes again.

"Your food will be with you shortly," she says in an extremely over-exaggerated voice. "Lovely to meet you, Fin." June smiles and heads to the kitchen, her manager staring at her grumpily.

Rye, Poppy and I all sit quietly for a moment. The only noise is coming from the overhead speakers that are blasting Fleetwood Mac; it sounds like vinyl, which is the only respectful way to listen to such musical genius.

Our food is brought over shortly after and our giant buckets of "Screaming Soda" are adorned with marshmallow ghosts on sticks and fake jelly fingers. It looks pretty rad, I must admit. As we scoff everything down our food, Poppy offers Rye and me a swig of vodka from a hip flask, which we both happily accept. It's not usually my thing at all – the vodka – but, when in Rome …

"So, where did you say you were from?" Rye asks.

I swallow a bite of an extra cheesy fry. "Pittford?" I tell him. "It's about –"

"*No*. You do *not* come from Pittford," Poppy chimes in, her mouth a perfect "O" shape.

"I … Yep. I do," I say, the back of my neck suddenly very warm.

"My cousin Brad lives there. He used to go to Pittford High but graduated about three years ago."

"Cool," I say, racking my brain to think if I'd ever encountered anyone with the name Brad.

"Yeah, he's desperate to leave. Says there's nothing there but old white people and Jesus freaks. Isn't Pittford where that fanatical Westplain Baptist Church is? He told me about some crazy parade they have every year. Called the um … The –"

"The Birth of Jesus Parade? Yeah … That's a thing," I say, unsure how to veer the conversation away from the very last thing I want to talk about.

"What happens?" Rye says, seeming a little apprehensive.

"It's just a giant parade every Christmas where people dress up as biblical characters instead of your usual Santa or Rudolph," I say. Hearing it aloud makes it sound even dumber than I remember. "They're pretty anti-Santa Claus over in Pittford. Anything that isn't about the true meaning of Christmas, you know, doing exactly what they think the Bible says or burning for eternity in hell, is strictly forbidden."

Poppy laughs and says "I like him" to Rye.

"What did you go as?" Rye asks, genuinely intrigued.

"Santa Claus," I say, which sends them both into fits of giggles.

"I like you, Fin," Rye says, echoing Poppy's words. His perfect teeth are smiling at me below his perfect eyes set in his perfect face.

As I'm about to reply – to say what, I really don't know – a behemoth of a guy slides into the booth next to Rye with a flump.

"Hey, babe," Rye says, leaning over to give the guy a kiss.

But the guy swats Rye away like he's been shovelling crap all day.

"Not in public, Rye. Seriously."

Rye fidgets for a second but then seems to centre himself with Buddha-like zen.

"And what the hell are you wearing?" The rude dude sitting in front of me stares at Rye and Poppy's costumes, obviously trying, and failing, to figure them out.

"Um … So, Fin, this is Eric. Rye's boyfriend," Poppy says cautiously, looking between the three of us as if she's gauging what kind of mood Eric is in – or maybe to see how I'll respond to this turn of events.

Of course he has a boyfriend.

"Nice to meet you," I say, as friendly as I can. I lean over and outstretch my hand for Eric to shake.

He does a weird slap thing to it and then makes a fist which I assume I'm supposed to bump with my own. I'm almost certain he's drunk.

"Likewise, Tim," Eric says.

"No, it's … It's F–" I attempt to correct him, but he's already whispering something in Rye's ear.

Poppy leans over to me and whispers, "Just pretend I'm talking to you."

I sit like an idiot for what feels like an eternity until Rye looks up.

"What are you doing, you goof?" he says to Poppy, a grin on his face.

"Oh, sorry. I thought it was a whispering kinda night. I'm just telling Fin here how pretty his ear is."

Eric looks up. I don't know if he's sure whether Poppy is being pissy or having a joke.

"You're funny," Eric says.

"I know," Poppy says, taking out her hip flask and pouring another slug of vodka in both mine and Rye's drinks, avoiding Eric's recently purchased grape slushee.

"Um, thanks," he says, half joking.

"You're of legal age. Buy your own. This stuff is hard to get a hold of when one is in one's youth." Poppy snaps the cap back on and takes a sip from her bucket. "Plus, you stink of booze and your left eye is having trouble keeping up with your right. I think you've had enough already."

Rye keeps looking over at me and, maybe I'm imagining it, but whenever I look at him, I think I see a hint of a nervous smile on his lips. I feel like he's embarrassed by Eric and unsure of what direction his random behaviour might go in.

"And your costume is shithouse," Poppy says, motioning to Eric's half-assed attempt at a Fred Flintstone costume. He is wearing an orange T-shirt with permanent-marker black dots all over it. There's a stick, which I guess he just found outside, sitting in front of him on the table. I'm assuming that's his "club".

"So, Tim," Eric says as he takes a bite out of one of the jelly fingers from Rye's drink. "Are you ready for a game of rapid fire?"

"It's Fi– ... Rapid ... Rapid what?" I ask, baffled yet intrigued.

"Fire. It's where we ask you a bunch of questions and you have to answer without thinking. Any question you hesitate on you need to take a gulp of your drink. Hesitate too much and you're wasted and throwing up behind the bins outside. Right, Pops?"

"Correct," Poppy says with a wink, but she doesn't look exactly enthusiastic. "Not a great sight. But don't feel like you have to. It's a dumb jock game that acts as a mask when it comes to getting to know people, but I suspect it's actually a ploy to kill someone via alcohol poisoning."

I half laugh but secretly want to leave. I don't mind drinking, I really don't. I'm not against it. It's just not my favourite activity. (I know that's weird coming from a sixteen-year-old, but it really isn't.)

"Um ... Sure," I say, suddenly realising I have torn a cardboard coaster into about a million pieces.

"Remember, if you feel like you're going to barf, aim that way," Poppy says, pointing to Eric, who flips her the bird.

"Three," Eric begins.

"Two."

"One."

"Go."

"Name?"

"Fin."

"Age?"

"Sixteen."

"Shoe size?"

"Ten."

"Siblings?"

"One."

"Brother or sister?"

"Brother."

"Older, younger?"

"Older."

"Favourite food."

I go blank. "Uh. Pizza." I've no idea why I said that.

"Drink."

I take a drink.

"Ready again?" Eric's eyes are glowing like this is the most fun he's had in years.

"Three."

"Two."

"One."

"Favourite drink?"

"Water."

"Chocolate or strawberry?"

"Chocolate."

"Banana or raspberry?"

"Banana."

"Gay or straight?"

Has someone sucked all the air out of the room?

"Woaah, Eric. Easy there, big fella. We've only just met the guy," Poppy chimes in.

"What? Like I care. I'm with this dope, aren't I?" Eric says, motioning to Rye, who can't meet my gaze.

"I …" My body doesn't seem to know how to process anything right now.

"Or bi? Maybe bi? Pan? Asexual? Trans? *Les-bi-an?*" Eric is enjoying himself. "Or just boring straighty-one-eighty?"

"Gay."

For a second I feel like somebody else has spoken. It takes a beat to realise it was me. Poppy looks up and smiles awkwardly. I'm struggling to believe the words have actually left my mouth. I don't know whether I've ever said it out loud before.

"Well, ain't that something," Eric says, looking over at Rye. "Who knows where he's sprung from, but you've managed to make friends with the first new gay guy Lochport has seen in years. I'm impressed."

"Don't be a dick, Eric," Poppy snaps, adding to the tension bristling around us.

"No one dialled your number, Popsicle," Eric says back with a cold smile.

"I ... I didn't mean to c-cause –" This is excruciating. My words aren't working.

"No, buddy. Totally fine. We gotta go now anyway." Eric stands and puts his coat on. "Right, Rye?"

"Yeah. We're um ... I think we're gonna go," Rye says, avoiding our eyes like we're the Medusa or something.

"That was quick," Poppy says, a sharp hint of irritation in her voice.

"Yeah ... We. It's getting late and Eric needs to be up pretty early for practice, so –"

"Sure. Catch you tomorrow," Poppy says, eyes fixed on her drink as she swirls her straw around.

"Up top, Tim," Eric says as he throws his hand above his head.

"Fin. My ... It's Fin." I slap his hand.

"Whatever," he says, laughing, before leading the way out, Rye trailing behind him.

Poppy and I sit opposite one another. The low-hanging lights above our heads make a humming sound and the smell of coffee and caramel fudge that wafts past us as a waiter walks by lets us know that it's getting to the dessert stage of the evening.

"Sorry about him," she says with an eye roll.

I twist a piece of thread from the tablecloth around my finger. "Is ... Is he always like that?"

Poppy nods. "I hate that you had to do that."

"Do what?" I ask, my finger turning blue as I twist the thread tighter.

"Come out to us. Well. Like that I mean. It's shitty. It's a shitty thing he did. He's shit."

"It's okay." I smile, trying to reassure both her and myself. "I guess it's one less awkward conversation out the way that I don't need to have anymore."

"I think it's a flaming bag of crap that you even *have* to come out. Straight people don't have to. Why do people just *assume* you're straight-down-the-line hetero-flaming-sexual unless proven otherwise?"

I shrug, letting the blood return to my finger as I unwind the snake-like death grip the piece of thread has on it. I can't believe how easy Poppy is making this. Talking about being gay. The only other person I've ever chatted like this with is Emily and it took me *months* to get up the courage to tell her. I'm starting to wonder what in the fresh hell my parents were thinking bringing me *here* of all places. It's surely not quite what they had in mind. So far, it's like gay utopia – I seem to have fallen in with my tribe – though, to be fair, Pittford was pretty big on its identity as a homophobic hell hole. Whatever the go is, I'm kind of revelling in my new-found friends and the confidence they've given me.

"I have no idea what Rye sees in him," Poppy continues. She

cups her chin in her palm and stares ahead, clearly lost in her own thoughts. "Rye is *such* a decent guy. And Eric ... He's – Well, he's not ... that decent I guess and ... I dunno. It just – It just makes no sense to me."

I sit quietly. I'm not sure if she wants me to respond. I also don't really want to. Privately, I agree that he doesn't seem that cool but I don't know the guy ... Or the situation.

A Katy Perry song starts playing over the speakers, which sends Poppy's eyes into her forehead as June comes over and squeezes back into the booth with us.

"Where'd Rye go?" she asks, taking one of Poppy's fries and delicately chewing it to avoid smudging her perfectly glossed lips.

"Home with that ass-hat of a boyfriend of his," Poppy says.

June shakes her head sadly. "I'll be finished in five. You guys wanna come over to mine?"

I look at my phone: 10:18 p.m.

"Abso-frickin'-lutely," Poppy says. "Fin, you in?"

I nod. Curfew isn't until midnight.

7

Fin

We arrive at June's house, a nice bungalow right on the water, and immediately I'm pulled into an embrace by her mum, Regina, who gives me the warmest smile ever and offers me the leftover Halloween candy that hasn't been eaten by the neighbourhood kids or June's little sister, Rita.

After the introductions we head to June's room, which has more fairy lights adorning the walls than Disney World, and also a back door which leads down to one of two docks behind their house. I'm assuming the small fishing boat, which is bobbing up and down in the darkness at the end of the boardwalk, is their own personal row-boat.

"So, Fin. Mister Fin. The Finster. Fin for the Win! Fin of Finland!" Poppy is on a roll.

"Enough. My *god*. Are you drunk?" June is laughing as she throws her bag in a corner and sinks into a giant beanbag near the window.

"That would be wonderful. But sadly, no," Poppy says as she spins on June's desk chair.

I take in my surroundings. Old Hollywood movie posters line the walls and Broadway playbills are collaged across the ceiling.

"This place is amazing," I say. "So, do you go to Lochport High?"

"We do. And lucky for you, you have made friends with two of the most amazing gals you'll find at that old concrete dump," Poppy says, wandering over to the window and leaning out to look at the stars, which are truly spectacular, their reflections sparkling across the water.

"Rye is pretty special, too," June says as she lets her head sink back into the bean bag and closes her eyes.

"That he is," Poppy says.

I check my phone: 11:11 p.m.

"Eleven-eleven. Make a wish," I say.

"I wish Eric wasn't such a jerk-off," Poppy says, chewing on a loose strand of her hair.

I go to say something, but she's not finished.

"– and I wish Rye didn't put up with his shit and I wish good people found other good people and that guys like Eric weren't so dense and tone deaf, and I wish he hadn't forced you into coming out within the first five minutes of being –"

"Wait, he did what?" June says, sitting bolt upright.

The room is quiet for a moment; the lips on the *Rocky Horror Picture Show* poster on the wall seeming to glow red.

"That dumb Rapid Fire game," Poppy says.

"That boy is about as subtle as a dumpster fire," June says, heading to her closet and rummaging around in a bag on the floor.

"Here," she says, handing me a leaflet on which the letters "QSA" are framed by a rainbow flag and the slogan "Keep Calm, It's Just a Toilet" is stamped along the edge: "QSA: Queer

Straight Alliance. We have a meeting tomorrow, right after fifth period in the music rooms in C-block. You should come. We're planning a counter-protest against discrimination of bathroom usage at school." Her nails glint as she points to the slogan. "We're always looking for new members."

Suddenly I feel really warm. The air in the room thins, like there's an oxygen shortage. Activism might be too big a step right now.

"Sure," I say, my voice sounding squeaky.

I know that moving here is my parents' way of giving me a fresh start. I know that QSA meetings and QSA friends are exactly what they are trying to avoid by us being here, but in my heart I also know how stupid it is for them to want me to change. In my heart I *know* there is absolutely nothing wrong with me. My eyebrows alone are proof of that.

I take the flyer, fold it up and put it in my pocket.

"Thanks for a great Halloween," I say, standing. "I should probably head home."

"I'll drive you," June says, grabbing the keys from her desk. Poppy gets up too and before I know it we are all in the car and heading for my place.

We park outside and I can see that the light in the top right window is on. Mum and Dad are still up.

Poppy, June and I say goodnight and I head for the front door. When I'm inside I make for the stairs. I'm two rungs up the ladder to my room when I hear Dad's voice.

"Eleven fifty-four. Cutting it fine, Fin."

I close my eyes and swallow. As I climb back down and face him, I feel like a liar. I want to be anywhere but here right now.

"Poppy like your costume?"

I nod.

He nods back.

"It's good to make new friends, Fin…" Dad goes on, clearly wanting more enthusiasm from me. His previous good mood seems to have disappeared. Instead his face is void of any expression and his voice neutral. "Please just – Just don't make the same mistakes twice, okay?"

Did he follow me tonight or something?

"I know, Dad," I say, my stomach tightening and my upper body becoming heavy.

"Just a reminder, that's all," Dad says, the ice in his tone suddenly turning the air around him cold and unfriendly.

Yes, no doubt about it, he's in one of his moods.

"Well, I got it," I say, turning to the ladder. Then I head up through the hatch in the ceiling into my new room. The moonlight's casting a silver glow on my bed through the windows, as I close the hatch behind me.

Thank god he can't read my mind.

8

Fin

I wake early to the smell of pancakes, coffee and burnt toast. I can hear Mum humming along to the golden oldies radio station in the kitchen.

Dad's car is gone from the drive, so I know he's left for work and it's just me and Mum at home.

She looks up and smiles as I enter the kitchen, handing me a plate of syrup-drenched pancakes and giving me a kiss on the cheek.

"Thanks," I say, taking a seat on the kitchen bench and pouring myself an orange juice.

"How was your night?" Mum asks.

"Good. My costume was a hit," I say.

Mum smiles. "And … And Poppy?" she asks. She looks nervous. Like Poppy is my only chance at "normal". As if, without her, I might start belting out show tunes and shooting rainbows from my fingers.

"She's good." I don't really know what to say. I'm not going to lie and say we are a "thing" because we're not a thing. And it would be ridiculously fast work if we were.

Rye, on the other hand, refuses to leave my mind. I haven't stopped thinking about him since we met on the dock and, to be honest, it's driving me insane. I'm also extremely pissed that he has a boyfriend. More so because his boyfriend is a giant ass-hat and one hundred per cent unworthy of him.

I finish breakfast, give Mum a kiss goodbye before grabbing my bag and heading for the door. I'm three steps away when the phone in the hallway rings.

"Hello?" I say into the receiver. In the corner of my eye I see Mum walk out from the kitchen.

On the other end of the line there's static. Then –

"Dad? Is that – H-Hello?"

"Elliot, it's me!" I yell, excitedly.

"Fin?"

I smile. I haven't spoken to Elliot in ages. He's been travelling to every possible remote place with zero Wi-Fi/reception, which means we only hear from him when he's slumming it in a city somewhere.

I've missed speaking to him. Before he went away, we'd spend our weekends together, hiking, chilling or at the arcade. He would always be front and centre at every school performance I was in and, before he left school, I was safe from anyone like Jesse or Jake because Elliot was captain of the football team and they wouldn't dare touch me. We're close. Well, we *were* close. I'm wondering if that will still be the case when he finds out about the events of the last few weeks.

"Where are you?" I ask, holding the receiver away from Mum who is attempting to pry it out of my hands.

"Borneo!" he says. "The rainforest!"

"Are you kidding me?" I say, grinning to myself. Elliot's the type of guy who I can totally imagine in an ancient rainforest. It wouldn't surprise me if he was living up a tree with an orangutan by now.

"Yeah!" Elliott laughs. "It's awesome. I've got so much to tell you! But you guys moved?! How's Dad's new promotion? How are you liking Lochport?"

I'm guessing that's what Mum and Dad have told him. That we moved for Dad's work.

"Yeah, it's … It's all good," I lie.

We talk for a bit about his travels and I quickly distract him when he asks anything to about my life or what's been going on. We focus instead on his adventures out in the world far away from here; how he has been living on two-dollar noodles and rice for who knows how long and washing his clothes in waterfalls.

"I gotta go," I say, wrapping up the conversation as I feel it heading in the direction of what I'm desperate to avoid talking about: me. "Chat soon. Here's Mum." I hand the receiver over and head out the front door.

I take a deep breath and let the salty air from the harbour calm me. The leaves under my feet crackle and crunch like the sound of a mouth full of Corn Flakes as I make my way down our street and head for my new school.

I have the QSA flyer in my back pocket. I'm surprised at myself that I kept it. If Dad found it, I'm certain he would be in the car like a shot, racing towards the next town, and I'd be back on that clapped-out bus to Aunt Carla's, nursing a near-fatal asthma attack from her four thousand feral cats.

*

I arrive just as the first bell of the day goes and head for the reception area. A woman stands behind the reception desk chewing a pen ferociously like she's trying to bite it in half. Her eyes seem wild and I wonder if she's okay. With her swishy bangs, she reminds me of Taylor Swift – if Taylor Swift was into smoking heavy-duty bath salts.

"I … It's my first day," I say, walking up tentatively as if she might lunge over the counter and maul me.

She snaps out of her trance and smiles this toothy smile that's sweet but kind of terrifying too.

"Name?" she asks.

"F-Fin. Fin Whittle. I just moved here fr–"

"From Pittford. Yes. Here is your welcome pack." She hands me a manila folder with a weird sticky bow on it. "Your locker number is one-five-four and your textbooks are inside. Your timetable is in the folder towards the back, but your first class is geography. A-block. Room four-zero-one." She smiles that big insane smile again and then goes back to biting the hell out of her pen.

"Thanks," I say.

I turn to leave and find my way to a row of lockers, slowly walking along until I get to 154. My combination is on the back of the manila folder: 13-03-19. I open it up, grab my geography book, dump the giant folder onto the shelf and head off with a jog towards A-block.

The school is kinda nice looking (as far as schools go). Lots of archways and trees and benches to sit on. The cafeteria is enormous. Our tiny little hall in Pittford is like a dog kennel in comparison. I scan the buildings, B-block, C-block.

A-block. Perfect. I locate room 401 easily enough and, thankfully, I'm not the last one to arrive. I find myself a seat near the back and scan the room for any sign of Poppy, June or Rye. Mostly Rye. But nada. Nothing. Zip. The class is still void of my new friends by the time our teacher, Miss Chenoweth, arrives and closes the door behind her.

Note to self: resist the urge to ask Miss Chenoweth if she is any relation to Kristen Chenoweth. Resist. The. Urge.

The class whizzes by fairly quickly and, again thankfully, I'm not asked to stand and introduce myself or any of that other dumb-assery that teachers find it appropriate to make new people do. I realise I left my timetable in the folder which is in my locker, so I head back in that direction. The halls are buzzing with chatter and energy and when I get to my locker I see a ripped piece of paper sticking out from one of the ventilation slats.

Hope your first day is going good? Come have lunch with us.
You'll find us easily enough.
Love, Rye and Poppy

My heart skitters and I feel like a thousand butterflies are dancing in my tummy. *Love, Rye and Poppy.* Which one wrote it? Rye's name is first, so him? Now I can't stop thinking of that ridiculously cute smile and his curly hair. And then the fact that he has a human excuse for a toilet as a boyfriend slaps me across the face.

*

I have another period before lunch and, after checking my time-table, I realise it's advanced maths. Strangely enough, I don't mind maths. I guess I'm kinda good at it too, hence the whole "advanced" bit. And yes, I said hence. Emily would be rolling her eyes, keeping me right as always. I can't help but really miss that girl ...

The class is in D-block and somehow I've managed to get there just as our teacher does, making me the last one through the doors with her. Miss Delecki is seriously impressive. Her dark hair's in an immaculate bob and she has some awesome heels going on. I'm talking hot red ankle boots with a metal zip. An absolute boss.

The only seat left is one at the front. As I sit down, I notice that the two girls from the wharf yesterday – the ones who were tormenting Rye – are sitting together and staring at me. I know one of them was called Bronwyn but I can't think of the other one's name. Poppy likened her to a couch in an old person's house, but I can't for the life of me think of –

"Paisley –" Miss Delecki snaps. *That's it.* "– open your textbook and come back to the room, please. Daydreaming is one thing, but honestly, you look comatose."

Paisley does as she is asked and sighs loudly, as if resigned to a fate worse than death. Then her brain clicks into gear and she evidently decides to really throw me under the bus and reverse over my face.

"Of course, miss, but don't you think the new guy should introduce himself?"

Miss Delecki glances over to me and then back at Paisley. "Or, we could all introduce ourselves to him."

"Hmm. I think I'd rather he do it. Otherwise we won't be able to enjoy your wonderful class if we're all talking about each and every one of us."

Ooh. Paisley is good for a couch.

I stand, turn and death stare her with a look that says, *I will find you and I will kill you* in Liam Neeson's *Taken* voice.

"I'm Fin Whittle. I just moved here from Lochport. I like video games, ice cream, musicals and running, but not in that order, and I'm really happy to be here." Those last few words I add extra cheese to and then sit down and face the front.

Seemingly impressed at my effort, Miss Delecki gives me a little nod.

"And you like dudes, right?"

I flinch like someone just punched me in the chest.

"Paisley, Mr Whittle's sexuality is his own business and I –"

"Um, you're acting like it's something that should be hidden, miss," Paisley says with a faux smile that makes me want to vomit. Murmurs of stifled laughter and chatter blanket the air and I'm finding it impossible to breathe. "It's just that I saw Fin with Rye down at the wharf yesterday and I guess I put two and two together.' She pauses and puts that bus into reverse. "No doubt he'll join the QSA with that 'June' and become another one of those campaigners –"

I can't believe her finger quotes. I go to say something, anything, but no words come out.

"Enough, Paisley," Miss Delecki snaps, her eyes piercing into Paisley's in a way that's almost scary. Paisley stops like an obedient puppy called to heel and her sidekick Bronwyn giggles like an idiot.

For the rest of the class I attempt to remember how to speak while simultaneously taking deep breaths to try to lower my heart rate. Feelings flood me. I'm so angry I'm shaking. I want to cry furious tears and throw something at the wall and watch it break. I hate how much shame I'm carrying. I hate how broken I feel. I hate how much I hate myself. I'd give anything to be as confident as Rye or June. Literally anything.

9

Fin

When the bell rings – at last – I practically break the door off its hinge with the force of my departure. I'm pissed. Really pissed. Mostly at Paisley, but also at my situation. As if high school – make that my first day at a new high school – weren't hard enough without dealing with all this.

I leave D-block and make a right through the field that doubles as a running track, basketball court and soccer pitch. The sky is a perfect blue and the wind whips at my cheeks as I make another right down A-block and arrive at the cafeteria. I'm hit with the smell of over-processed mac 'n' cheese, noodles and salad. I'm not hungry in the slightest after the hour I've just endured so I opt for a muesli bar and an iced coffee.

I make a beeline for an empty table in the corner of the room but realise midway that I've forgotten a metal straw for my iced coffee. It's a *must* when you're dealing with ice cubes in a drink. Don't fight me on this, I'll win. I turn and head back to the cutlery table and see out of the corner of my eye a giant balloon with the words "Sorry For Your Loss" written on the front. I look down and see Rye and Poppy sitting together. They're waving and ushering me over.

"Um … Hey," I say, unable to stop staring at the balloon.

"I know. I'm sorry. We wanted to get a 'Welcome' balloon, but this was the only one left in the store," Rye says.

After Paisley's horror show, this is the sweetest thing imaginable. Even if the balloon is wrong on every level. People are walking by and staring. I giggle.

"Thanks," I say, smiling at both of them.

"How has your first day been?" Poppy asks.

"Mmm. Yeah. It's been something." I don't know how to begin. They both look at me expecting me to say more.

"I had maths with Paisley and Bronwyn," I say, taking a bite out of my muesli bar, which tastes like a block of compressed dust. "And they kind of outed me in the middle of class."

Poppy drops her fork. "Are you fucking kidding me?" She looks furious. Like, next level rage. Rye looks angry too but seems to have a lid on it.

"Poppy, don't bother with those scumbags," Rye says, a piece of advice which she completely ignores. She's glaring around the cafeteria now, like a savage dog that's about to slip its chain.

At that moment, Paisley and Bronwyn enter the room and Poppy stands. They both smirk at her with a look that says, *What you gonna do?* Rye grabs hold of her arm and I look up at her, my cheeks burning.

"It's fine. Honest. Please … Just sit," I say. My voice sounds faraway like it belongs to someone else.

To my amazement, Poppy sits and Paisley and Bronwyn find a table with the guys who were at the wharf yesterday. They truly look like a bunch of vampires. Not the sexy kind.

More like the walkers of the earth, pale as milk, iron-deficient kind.

"I can't stand them," Poppy says, glaring at them across the room.

Rye looks over at me. "You okay?" he asks.

I nod, but my heart's beating so fast I feel like it's going to burst out of my chest.

"Thanks again for the ... For this," I say, gesturing to the slowly deflating sympathy balloon above our heads.

"No problem," Poppy quips. Then, adopting a serious look: "We are very, *very* sorry for your loss."

I laugh. I like how easy this feels. If there's one thing I was worried about more than anything it was finding new friends. Thankfully the universe had my back on that at least.

June arrives and gives me a hug before sitting next to me.

"Um, where are our hugs?" Poppy says, motioning between herself and Rye, who is smiling; I can't help noticing he has dimples for days.

"Mwah, mwah," June blows two kisses in their direction which Rye catches and Poppy swats away like a fly.

"Not gonna cut it, June-bug."

June sighs, rolls her eyes and then leans over to give Poppy a hug which she happily accepts.

"Thank you kindly," Poppy says with what I think could be a loved-up grin. I wonder if they're together but before I can take that thought further, I'm distracted by June's next words.

"You all still coming to the QSA meeting after fifth period?" she asks as she takes a spoonful of yoghurt. "Got to keep on top of this campaign!"

We nod in unison, but inside my stomach cramps and I feel like bolting. What am I signing up for? Do parents automatically get notified if their kid attends one of these meetings? Will they get word of it from one of the other parents? Or will it come out in the wash anyway because of how painfully small the town we're now living in is? I feel like the cafeteria floor is shaking but realise I'm just bouncing my knee like a jack hammer. I need to remind myself: I'm doing nothing wrong. Nothing.

"How's Eric?" June asks Rye, finishing her yoghurt and pointing her spoon at him. "Sore head after last night?"

"Yeah, good." Rye ignores her comment about Eric's drinking. I get the sense he's still embarrassed by his boyfriend. "He's taking me somewhere special tonight, I think. It's our two-month anniversary."

"Two months already?" Poppy says. "Wow. It feels like it's flown by." I get the impression she means that sarcastically.

"Yep. I think we're heading to that place with the curly fries? Not the regular curly fries, the ones with –"

"– with cheese inside?" June replies. "They're uh-mazing."

She grins happily at him; Poppy shifts in her seat uncomfortably.

I look up and catch Rye's eye but he's smiling and his mind is obviously elsewhere, most likely thinking of Eric.

"Does Eric go here, too?" I ask.

"No, he's at the college up on Grandview Close. Eddison Private? He's a bit older than us and his dad is some kind of hotshot CEO so they have a ton of money," Rye says.

"Does he still have to wear that dumb bowler hat?" Poppy asks, squirting some ketchup on her pancake.

"They're not dumb. I think they're kinda cool. Also, what the hell are you putting on your pancake?" Rye replies.

"Don't knock it till you try it, my man," Poppy says. "And not cool. Strange. Bowler hats are strange. Very cult-like."

Rye rolls his eyes.

"Has he taken you to any college parties yet?" June asks, seeming to be genuinely interested.

"Not yet, but he's said he'll take me after he tells people about us. We're taking it slow, so –"

"*He* is taking it slow. You've told all of us. He hasn't told anyone," Poppy says.

"Okay, what?"

"Come on, Rye. It's not like he isn't out."

"So what, though? You think he's hiding me or something?"

Rye looks upset, but Poppy isn't disguising her annoyance. I get the feeling this conversation has happened before.

"Guys, can we not? It's Fin's first day. Maybe we could wait till tomorrow before we start throwing the verbal grenades at each other." June smiles at me. I smile sheepishly back at everyone.

The bell rings and I check my timetable for my last class of the day. Gym. My favourite – insert massive eye roll here.

*

After the clusterfuck that was my last class, it's good to know that Poppy and Rye are both in my class. I'll have backup if I need it.

We head to the gym lockers and get changed into our gear and meet back on the oval. Considering it looked like it might rain this morning, the weather has turned up and the sun is shining. There's a chill in the air, but the sky is mostly blue and I can smell the salt and fish from the harbour. Nice.

"Today you will all be doing the circuit track on loop for the entire class because I have, what you kids would call, a ballin' hangover." Mr Prager is maybe mid-forties with ridiculous beefed-up muscles and a moustache that belongs in a seventies porno.

"Nobody would say that," someone shouts from behind us.

"Whatever. I got lit this past weekend and I need as little interaction as possible."

Lit. Did our gym teacher just say lit?

"Is he always like this?" I whisper to Poppy.

"He got divorced for the second time last year. Hasn't completely recovered."

Mr Prager blows a whistle and then heads over to take refuge in the shade of a nearby tree. I'm assuming this means we need to start the running. The circuit is basically a giant track that we run around with the occasional bench to spring over, boxes for "explosive" jumping, skipping ropes and some of those heavy battle ropes you're supposed to whip. Mr Prager looks like he's already asleep under the tree.

"You coming?" Poppy says to Rye, who has found himself a spot in the shade too.

"Can't. Mum said Saturn is in retrograde and that if I do any exercise today, I'll break my leg."

Poppy smiles. I giggle. We start jogging.

"Rye's mum is amazing," Poppy says. "She's a cleaner. And a psychic."

"A psychic?"

"I guess that's the word. Tarot card reader? Mystic? She's into crystals and sage and stuff like that."

"Cool."

"Very. Karen also has one of the best record collections I have ever seen."

We get to the first station on our circuit and do push-ups, and by "do push-ups" I mean kneel on the ground and pretend.

"I'm talking all the greats. Fleetwood Mac, Cher, Cyndi Lauper, Led Zeppelin, Bob Marley, Streisand, Midler, etc. Their house is like a gay utopia of music. What are you into?"

"All of the above," I say.

"Nice. Rye isn't much of a fan of the show tune stuff. But his mum loves her Broadway musicals and when Rye came out she spent the night playing 'I Am What I Am' from *La Cage Aux Folles* and creating a rainbow crystal shrine to meditate around. He was stoked that it wasn't a big deal to her, but maybe not so keen on being thrown a pride parade on day one. Rye's not one for a spectacle."

"What about his dad?" I ask, attempting an actual push-up just to see if I can. Surprisingly I manage to do twelve before buckling. Not bad.

"Long gone. Left when he was a kid."

Poppy smashes out some push-ups, an easy fifteen in a row. I attempt another couple and then we start jogging again.

"What were your parents like when you came out?" Poppy asks.

I look across at her. My chest feels tight and it's not from the jogging.

"They um …" I start.

At that moment, as if by divine intervention, or my stratospheric clumsiness, I trip and face plant into the grass. I'm talking full blown, ass-in-the-air-level of plunging into the dirt.

"Ow –" I say, lifting my head slowly.

"Shit. Are you hurt?" Poppy looks genuinely concerned until

she realises I'm okay, then bursts into a laugh and collapses in a heap next to me.

I giggle too. Then my nose starts bleeding. Between gulps of air to catch her breath, Poppy leads me to the nurse's station and I'm given an ice pack and a bunch of tissues.

Rye must have seen my Saturn in Retrograde idiocy from afar, asking, "My GOD, Fin. Are you okay?" when he arrives not long after.

I give a thumbs-up.

"The QSA meeting starts as soon as the bell goes. You think you'll be in a fit state for it?" Poppy asks, still unable to contain her giggles every time she looks at me.

I give a thumbs-up again. "Mmhmm."

*

About a dozen students are standing around waiting outside a music room in C-block. We arrive just as June does and we follow her in; I'm trying not to drag my feet. But you can tell she was born to lead. She's glowing as she stands at the front and does a roll-call in which people introduce themselves and identify. I'm thinking this is perhaps for my benefit as a new QSA member.

"Alan, gay."

"Chrissy, bi."

"Gus, ally."

"Poppy, pan."

I look around as everyone says who they are and I feel this rush like butterflies in my stomach, but different to butterflies because it's not constant. It's sporadic. It glows and it dims. Glows and then dims.

It feels like fireflies.

"Ali, lesbian."

"Rye, gay."

"Fin ..." I take a breath. "Gay."

I can feel Rye's eyes on me, and when I turn to him, he's smiling at me. More fireflies.

"And me, June, trans," June says, beaming at everyone. "Thanks for coming, you bunch of legends." She smiles and gestures at me. "First things first, we need to bring our newest member up to speed. As the rest of you know, since the start of senior year, the mothers of our favourite comrades – Paisley and Bronwyn – have been having a conniption about trans students using the bathroom they identify with."

Everyone groans.

"Uh-huh." June raises her hands at our frustration. "They want to stage a protest at the school. We're taking serious action to squish their bigotry once and for all."

Everyone's groans turn to nods of approval, and there's a *woop!* from Poppy at the back of the room.

From there, June highlights her ideas for the counter-protest before we go around the room and each one of us gets a chance to talk about anything we're struggling with: school, home, after-school jobs, emotions or whatever. We then announce to the room some stuff that's going great.

I feel a bit overwhelmed and I pass when it's my turn; the thought of sharing more than my name and sexuality seems like shooting for the moon for my first meeting. Thankfully, it's no big deal. I keep sensing Rye looking over at me, but I'm too nervous to meet his eye.

After everyone has had a turn, June hands around some leaflets about sexual health, online support forums and youth counsellors. It seems like these are for my benefit too, as everyone else declines like they've seen them a hundred times already.

*

Before long, the meeting's over and we head out together into the afternoon sunlight. It's that time of year where the sun feels like a cuddle and the air is crisp and perfect. But the mood is spoiled for me when I realise it's getting late and I know Dad will be suspicious that I'm not home yet.

"I'm gonna head to Kettle Lake for a bit," Rye says. He smiles and heads off.

"You need a lift?" Poppy asks as we near her ancient grass-green Toyota Corolla.

"I'm good, thanks," I say. I've decided to walk the fifteen minutes home because I need to figure out an adequate story about the day's events that will pass as "correct and entirely normal straight guy" behaviour at home.

But before I head off …

"What's at Kettle Lake anyway?" I ask Poppy, attempting to sound nonchalant.

"Rye goes there to watch the fireflies. He's sweet like that."

My heart rattles around in my chest like some insane parrot in a cage.

I stand rooted to the spot for a minute, my whole body vibrating.

Fireflies.

10

Rye

I love this time of year so much. The leaves are dry and crackly, the air is salty and smoky from beach bonfires nearby, and the sky permanently looks like a watercolour painting.

It's a good season for my large collection of shirts – one that I am extremely proud of too. Today I'm wearing an oversized one that is burnt red in colour with a mustard stripe across one arm. It's weird and vintagey and I'm a bit obsessed.

I leave Poppy, June and Fin in the car park at school and head straight for the track through the forest. Mum has Carl over tonight for dinner which is fine because, whatever, I guess she has to date, but middle-aged lovebirds, not my jam. I figured I'd give them some alone time before I get home and make things awkward.

I arrive at the entrance to Gully Forest and my phone vibrates in my back pocket.

Poppy: Have fun tonight with E. If it goes to shit and you wanna hang, hit me up.

I roll my eyes and don't even bother to reply. Like, I get it. Eric can be a bit hit and miss and maybe he's not always the greatest, but who is? I wish Poppy would back off a little. She hasn't liked him from the beginning and I get so tired of being in the middle of them. Secondly, it's our anniversary and he has been telling me to prepare for an amazing date night. I know he can be flaky, but he'll come through.

I find the makeshift track I've created from years of coming here and make my way through the undergrowth. The light pools in fragments around my feet as it makes its way through the gaps in the canopy of branches and leaves overhead and the last of the afternoon light warms my skin.

Gully's Forest is magic and I love everything about it. Ever since I can remember, anxiety has been part of my life, but when I'm here it seems to all go away and I finally feel myself settle. At least for a little while.

I arrive at my home away from home, but instead of heading to my usual decked-out cave that I've created, I instead head to my rock – yes, I know that technically it's not *my* rock, but nobody else knows about it, so shhh – and put my backpack next to me. I breathe in and out a few times and sit still and watch the tiny stream in front of me. Old branches and leaves are carried down over the rocks and the water splashes up at me every now and then, bringing me back to the moment. I take a few more breaths and then close my eyes and lie on my back. I don't know of anywhere so peaceful. This is my happy place.

My phone buzzes again and I decide to ignore it. It can wait. I'm focusing on the now. Now is all that ma– it buzzes again, twice this time. I breathe in deeply and retrieve it from my back pocket.

Eric: Running a bit late. Pick U up around 8 instead of 7.
    Hope that's k?
Me: Sure, see you then x

I take another few breaths and remind myself to focus on my chest moving up and down, feeling my breath travelling along the length of my spine. I let my mind drift and it throws random things at me: calculus homework, what to wear tomorrow, what to wear tonight, Poppy, June and Fin, raspberry liquorice (my favourite), Fin again – this time no Poppy or June, what I should make Thelma for her bulldog birthday dinner next week, cinnamon scrolls, iced coffee.

I sit up and rub my eyes. The sun is almost gone, the sky a deep pink after its slow descent, when I catch my first glimpse. As it twinkles to life just across the stream, I see the first firefly. Less than ten seconds later another one glows to life and then disappears. It's almost completely dark now and the reeds, logs and undergrowth of the forest are alight and twinkling and I feel myself completely and utterly relax. Every last muscle in my body releases.

After half an hour or so, I grab my backpack, brush the bits of twig and dirt off my clothes and head through the clearing and back to the track towards home.

When I arrive at our street, Thelma is sitting in the front yard waiting for me. Well, technically she is sound asleep and snoring, but I prefer to think that Thelma is moping and longing for me while I'm at school all day.

"Hey, my beautiful girl," I say, throwing my backpack down and army crawling on the grass towards her. She looks up, stretches and does the same towards me, her jowls sagging and her beautiful big brown eyes looking at me like I'm the only person on the planet. Dogs are the best. And Thelma is the bestest.

Thelma follows me inside and, as I enter the kitchen, the smell of cinnamon chai lattes instantly assaults my nostrils. Cher's "Believe" is blaring from the Bluetooth speaker I bought Mum from the Downtown Discount store last week.

"Hey," I say, turning it down and wafting the burnt chai smell from my face.

"Hiiiiii –" Mum says, turning it way back up and grabbing my hands to pull me in for a dance.

"I can furrrrrl some thurrrrng insaaaaade maserrrrrlf."

Mum singing sounds kinda similar to Cher, but her attempt at the over-the-shoulder hair flick is a miss. I can't help but smile. Mum's energy is magic.

"How was school?" she asks.

"Good," I say. "Where's Carl?"

"Left about fifteen minutes ago. Work." Mum rolls her eyes. "His chakras are all out of whack because of that job he has."

Carl is the manager of a gym in town and is beyond smitten with Mum. She likes him back and I guess he's not awful. He's always friendly to me and even offered me a complimentary gym membership to help him with his social media accounts. I helped him for free because the thought of going to Steel Bros for anything other than checking out the guys who train there is about as appealing as shutting my privates in a car door. I know, I know. Graphic. Plus, I got to ogle all the professional photos of male fitness models that Carl hired to rep his Steel Bros merch.

I grab a slice of bread from the cupboard and tear it into little pieces.

"Thelma, come!" I yell and in bounds my little pudding.

"You want some risotto?" Mum asks, stirring a pot next to the cinnamon milk on the stove.

"I'm good, thanks, Mum. Eric is taking me out," I say, giving Thelma a piece of bread and rubbing her ears.

"Okay. No probs," Mum says, and I immediately sense that she wants to say something more, but she's holding herself back.

"What is it?" I ask.

"Hmm?" She's good at keeping her feelings under control, but not that good. Ever since Eric turned up mad drunk at three a.m. a week after we "officially" started being a couple and banged on our front door asking for "sexy time" (no, I'm not kidding. I was mortified), Mum has been a little uneasy around him. Which I guess is somewhat fair.

"What's up?" I ask again, my eyebrows raised.

"It's … Look, promise you won't get mad? Otherwise I won't say a word."

I take a deep breath. I have a feeling this is another version of a conversation we've had before.

"I just think he –"

I brace myself, but she stops. I can see she is thinking of a productive way to express what she is desperate to say.

"– should come over more. I'd … I'd like to get to know him."

That was definitely not what she had planned, but I nod slowly. I guess she's trying to show that she is willing to give Eric a chance.

"Sure," I say. "It's a deal." I grab another slice of bread and head to my room, Thelma plodding along behind after me.

I hang my backpack on the back of my door, get undressed down to my underwear and a tee, then head to my prized possession: my vinyl record player. I got it for Christmas two years ago from Mum, who found it at a flea market in town and, surprisingly, it works perfectly. I've slowly been building up my vinyl collection ever since Mum first introduced me to Cyndi Lauper when I was four. So far, I have Dire Straits – *Love Over Gold*, Fleetwood Mac – *Greatest Hits*, Led Zeppelin – *Led Zeppelin II*, Marvin Gaye – *What's Going On*, David Bowie – *Ziggy Stardust*, Bob Marley – *Legend*, The Strokes – *Is This It*, and Cher – *Believe*. Mum calls me an "old soul" because of my music taste.

I put on some Fleetwood Mac, sprawl out on my bed and stare up at the glow-in-the-dark stars and planets on the ceiling that I've left there from when I was little. Thelma comes and cuddles up next to me and I rub her belly.

"You Make Loving Fun" finishes and "As Long As You Follow" scratches to life as I start sifting through my wardrobe for something to wear tonight. Before long I'm singing along with Stevie and Christine; the fairy lights I've strung up around my window make me feel like I'm on a stage at Glastonbury music festival in front of a sea of adoring fans.

I eventually settle on black skinny jeans, an oversize flannelette shirt, my white Converse and a bunch of urban jewellery I picked up at the Gimme Zen festival last year with Mum.

I'm definitely feeling my look and I get that funny feeling in my stomach. I've worked out it's a mix between anticipation, giddiness and straight up horniness. Well, horniness or not, Eric and I haven't gone past second base and I'm in no rush to either – much to Eric's annoyance.

I spray coconut spray in my hair and rub my neck and wrists with some cologne from a sample packet I pulled out of a magazine, then give myself a once over in the mirror.

Nice. Hot, in fact.

11

Rye

I'm flyin' high with Marvin's lush vocals as Thelma waddles around the room with me in an easy kind of dance.

"You're the best, bub," I tell her, bending down to scratch her chin.

She looks up at me expectantly, as if in agreement.

My phone buzzes. It's Eric.

"Hey," I say, putting him on speaker.

There's a pause and I think I hear a stifled laugh, but I can't be sure. Then, "Hey, how are you?"

I catch a slur in his words. "I'm good. I – Are you on your way? Or …?"

"Oh, that. I, um. Well, I was wondering if we could rain check?"

I sit on my bed and take him off speaker. "Uh. Yeah, no that's … Yeah. Of course. Is everything okay?" All of a sudden, that giddy feeling in my stomach switches itself off and I feel stupid for even thinking tonight would be anything. It's only a dumb two-month anniversary anyway. It's not like we're married or mean anything special to each other. I'm surprised he wants to date me at all to be honest.

This time, I definitely hear a giggle in the background.

"Is …Are you with someone?" I ask.

"It's Kell," he says, although the giggle didn't sound like his sister at all. Not remotely Kelly-ish, unless he is referring to Kelly Slater, pro-surfer and mega babe, who I highly doubt has the time to be hanging out with Eric right now.

"Um. Okay. Guess I'll talk to you later then," I say, trying not to sound as defeated as I feel.

"Yep. For sure. Cool," Eric says, then cuts the call.

I throw my phone down next to my bed which makes Thelma jump and fart simultaneously.

"Didn't mean to freak you out, hun," I say, leaning down to kiss her on the head.

Nearly as bad as being stood up is the fact that I now need to somehow avoid telling Mum that Eric has ditched me. I'm really not in the mood for an "I told you so" conversation right now, but I'm all out of excuses for him.

This is my own fault. This is what I get for coming on too strong and expecting Eric to feel the same. I'm too full on. I know I am. All or nothing Rye, as usual. Wanting the big romantic happy-ever-after when all Eric's interested in some *sexy time*. I realise I push people away because I'm a hot mess of neediness like that. I guess I just want to make sure that Eric is definitely the guy I want to lose my virginity to. I really don't want to be forgotten about the moment I finally build up the courage to go all the way.

I get changed into some sweatpants and a singlet, stretch out on my bed and scroll through Instagram. Of course, I eventually land on Eric's profile. There he is. Gym selfie, flexing gym selfie, a photo of an egg-white drink that makes me want to throw up a bit in my mouth, another gym selfie, a "Hustle For That Muscle" quote. I cringe. Eric is good-looking, sure, but a little bit in love with himself. Okay, massively. Our second date was to his gym so he could show me "how it's done". Sweet, but a little misguided.

I close Instagram and open up a new message to him. I start typing and then deleting over and over because I have no clue what I'm even trying to say.

"Rye!" Mum calls from down the hall. "What time are you leaving?"

Ugh.

"I'm …" I put my face in my hands and take a really deep breath. "I'm not going anymore. He … It's … We're going to go another time because the restaurant was overbooked or something and, you know, it's …"

Mum pokes her head around the door with a look that says, *It's all good.*

"You okay, hun?" she asks me quietly.

I feel a lump form in my throat. Mum sits at the end of my bed and Thelma waddles over to greet her with a sniff.

"You wanna talk about it?" Mum asks.

"Not really."

"You sure?"

I nod.

We sit in silence for a minute, while Mum rubs Thelma's tummy. That dog is needier than me, and that's saying something.

"I just finished making brownies. You wanna lick the bowl then play Guess Who?" Mum says, her eyes lighting up.

"If it's those weird avocado brownies you made last time, then not really."

"Nope. Store bought, in a box. Full of artificial colours, flavours and unnaturally, teeth-destroyingly sweet." She winks.

I grin.

We head to the kitchen and I go to town on the bowl of sugary goodness while Mum makes us cups of hot chocolate. I can hear the wind pick up outside. I grab a blanket from the cupboard next to the fireplace and wrap Thelma up in it, which makes her look like a Russian babushka doll. Mum hands me my hot chocolate and then sets up Guess Who. And nope. Not Heads Up on our phones. Guess Who. The original. Well, the new version considering the *original* original was literally just white characters and nobody wants to see that.

"You can start," I say.

"Are you male?" Mum asks.

"Nope."

"Are you white?"

"Nope."

"Do you wear glasses?"

"Yes."

I take a sip of my hot chocolate. It's amazing. Mum always puts in two layers of mini marshmallows, one at the bottom before the pour and then another layer on top. They all eventually glob together into one giant radioactive marshmallow and it's like sex in a cup. (Not that I'd know, but yeah. Second base in a cup I guess?)

"Do you have long hair?"

"Yes."

Mum flicks down a few more of her characters.

"Are you Ava?"

I smile. "You're good, Mum. That was a record time I think."

Mum tips her character board upside down and they all flip back to standing upright. "They don't call me 'Karen, Queen of Guess Who', for nothing," she says.

"Who calls you that?"

"You do."

"Umm. No, I would never say that," I say, breaking into a grin.

"Ah ha! A smile. There he is." Mum taps my nose with her finger. Her smile fades a little. "You okay, honey?" she sings like a lyric from *RENT*.

I hesitate. "Actually no," I admit. I've decided I'm not going to pretend I'm cool with how things are tonight. "Eric decided to tell me fifteen minutes before I thought we were going out that he can't make it and I wasted a sample pack of Bleu de Chanel from a beauty magazine for nothing."

Mum stares at me while I talk, and really listens. Like every word I say is extremely important and she doesn't want to miss a thing.

"Well, I for one think you smell fabulous. And I also think you are brave for talking to me about it. We both know I'm not his biggest fan."

"It's just … Lochport is hard enough to grow up in as it is, but I figured when I finally met someone it wouldn't feel like so much effort."

Mum smiles at me with this sad smile that I can't figure out.

"Hun, 'effort' should not be in your relationship vocabulary when you're sixteen. Twenty-six, maybe. But not sixteen. Especially two months in."

She has a point. Maybe it's not that I'm needy. Maybe I just hanker after that great big love story you see in old movies. And why shouldn't I?

"Look, I think it's a good idea if you just forget about it for the rest of the night. Start afresh tomorrow. Maybe even go over to his place and just nut it out with him."

I sit stunned and feel the moisture leave my eyes as I stare with my mouth open.

"I mean …" Mum scrambles for words like someone catching confetti in the wind. "Oh my GOD, Rye. I meant, like, talk it through. Isn't that what people say? I … Oh my GOD. I really … It was a turn of phrase. Sort of … Ugh."

I can't help it. I burst into fits of laughter and, before we know it, we are both rolling around on the floor, clutching our stomachs and cry-laughing. Thelma crawls her way out of the blanket and stands near us, wondering what all the fuss is about.

"Want another round of this?" Mum says, wiping a tear from her eye. "Or Battleships?"

"Nah, it's all good. I'll make myself a snack and then head to bed."

Mum stretches her arms above her head as she stands up.

"Do we have any peaNUT butter, Mum?" I ask, looking in the pantry cupboard. I turn and see her drop her head and start giggling to herself again.

"Second shelf," she says. "Night, Rye-bread."

"Night, Mum."

I make myself some PB&J on toast and then head to my room. Thelma follows and gets herself comfy on her plush cushion at the foot of my bed and I scroll through Twitter like a zombie for a while until I see a Sea Shepherd post about whales and their fins and my mind weirdly responds and wakes up like I've been hit on the head. Fin. I wonder how he's liking Lochport so far. I wonder if he's ever had a boyfriend. I wonder if he's ever "done the deed". I wonder if he even says weird stuff like that.

I open a message box, type in his name and write:

Hey :)

12

Fin

"Fin, don't make me ask again." Dad looks at me with tired eyes and I feel like he just wants to cry and throw the breadbasket across the table at me.

"For the tenth time, I'm not lying to you," I say, exhausted from the interrogation and desperate to be anywhere but here.

"Charles, come on. Enough," Mum says, pushing chunks of sweet potato around her plate. "Fin's not six any more. He has his own life."

I feel bad for making her have to deal with this. She puts in really long hours from home doing the marketing for a start-up tech company and she hasn't stopped for months. The last thing she needs is more drama.

My phone buzzes in my pocket and I ignore it.

"No, it's not enough. I want our son to be honest for a change." The implication hurts. It's not like I've lied about anything – including my sexuality – to my parents, until now.

"I told you, I was late getting home because I stayed back to ask my teacher about some homework." I'm lying through my teeth to avoid revealing my attendance at the QSA meeting, which ended up dragging on later than I expected. Everyone was really welcoming, but I would've felt super awkward leaving early. Even so, anything would be better than this.

Dad sits and stares at me, barely blinking. Mum doesn't say a word. The air weighs down on us, thick and heavy.

"Thanks for dinner," I say, standing to take my plate to the sink.

Dad bashes the table with his fist and everyone flinches. "SIT!" he bellows.

I lower my eyes and do as I'm asked. I don't understand what he wants, but I'm not willing to challenge any of this.

I sit there in silence until Dad's finally finished his food. He looks up at me and waves his hands at the plates. "Clear up," he barks, then stands, grabs his keys and storms out. Mum offers to help, but I tell her not to worry and, seething, do it myself. I hate how miserable his drama makes us both feel, but seriously, I just wish she'd sometimes stand up to him.

Once I've tidied everything away and wiped the table clean, I head up to my room and lie on my bed. A blustery wind is battering the tree opposite the window seat.

I fish my phone out of my pocket and unlock it. Next thing, I feel my heart go into overdrive, like one of those surround sound speaker systems they use at concerts.

Rye: Hey :)

One simple word and an even simpler emoji. I smile as I open the text box and begin typing. I'm guessing he's just got home from his anniversary date.

Me: Hi :)

Rye: How's your night?

Me: Meh … Yours? How was your date?

Rye: Meh is accurate.

I smile. I'm not happy that his date sucked but … Okay, maybe I am slightly happy about it. I start typing again when another message comes through.

Rye: How are you liking Lochport?

Me: About a 4 out of 10.

Rye: Ooooh, only 4?

Me: Maybe 4.5 during classes without Paisley or Bronwyn.

Rye: Fair call.

I'm desperate for him to keep talking, so my next message is a bit lame.

Me: Have you always lived here?

Rye: Yep. Born and raised.

Me: Nice.

I'm racking my brain for something else to ask when his next message appears.

Rye: Have you got a boyfriend back home?

Me: Nope. Solo. Single. All alone.

Rye: ;)

A wink emoji!? My stomach does a backflip.

Me: One day.

Rye: Yeah. :)

I'm about to give up with my increasingly pitiful attempts at conversation when the typing bubble appears in the message window.

Rye: Hey, can I call you? Easier than texting.

I feel giddy as I run my hand through my hair and then check my breath like an idiot who has forgotten how a phone works.

Me: For sure.

Thirty seconds later my phone is buzzing. I let it ring a few times so as not to seem like a desperate fool and then answer.

"Hey."

"Hey."

"Sorry, I'm weird and old school. Easier to talk on the phone that's all."

"No, totally cool. I like old school."

"Nice."

I feel like he's smiling on the other end of the line.

"So, um. Where'd you go for your date?" I ask.

"We uh … It – Well, it didn't end up happening."

"Oh."

"Yeah, but it's … I mean, it's all good."

"Totally."

"Yeah."

His voice sounds a bit reserved, like he wants to say something but isn't sure how.

"So, what's there to do around –" I start, when he cuts in.

"My mum isn't a fan of Eric."

I pause, unsure what to say back. "Oh. That's. Um. That's a shame," I try.

"Yeah. It's … I think she's worried he doesn't care about me much, ya know? Overprotective parent stuff."

"Mmm," I say. I have absolutely no idea what it would be like to confide in my parents about a guy I'm seeing.

"I guess it didn't help that he blew me off tonight, but still … I dunno. What are your folks like?"

I tense up. "They're … I guess we're not that close."

"Fair enough. That doesn't sound all bad. My mum practically

74

threw me a pride parade when I came out." He laughs. "But I love her for it."

I smile. I wonder what it would be like to not be terrified of being open about who you are. "That's pretty amazing," I say.

"Yeah. She's currently catching up on *RuPaul's Drag Race* and screaming 'Shangela was robbed' every thirty seconds."

I laugh. "She sounds epic," I say, smiling some more.

A crack of thunder outside makes the lights flicker and I hear Rye's dog bark a few times.

"Thelma, come here, it's okay."

I can hear Thelma panting through the phone and the sound of Rye kissing her head.

"Cute," I say out loud without realising, then slap my hand to my mouth like it's not connected to me.

Rye doesn't say anything.

"Not … I didn't mean *you're* cute. I meant, the dog. Not that you're *not* cute. I didn't mean that either. I meant … like, it was a cute thing to – I'm … Fuck. I'm going to just shut up now because it's –"

"Fin, it's cool," Rye says, and I can tell he's grinning.

I take a deep breath. "Sorry," I say.

"Don't be."

I hear footsteps on the landing below my room. The ladder doesn't creak so I know I'm good for now, but I feel my ears click into supersonic mode and everything sounds amplified.

"I need to apologise," Rye says sheepishly.

"What for?"

"For Eric the other day."

"You don't need to apologise for him."

"No, I do. He never will, so I definitely should."

"It's … Honestly, it's not your apology to make. It's cool," I say, though I feel bad that he thinks he even has to. I don't get why guys as awesome as Rye would ever go for guys as awful as Eric. He's buff, sure, but still it baffles me.

"Well, just for the record, I think it was awesome how comfortable you were with saying you're gay during that cringe-fest at the diner."

I laugh. "Are you serious? I was terrified."

"In that case then, you're a great actor."

"I'm not. I think I just went into shock."

Rye giggles.

"I'm more impressed at how you don't give a toss what anyone thinks of you," I say. "I wish I had a sprinkle of that."

"Oh no. Nope. It's all an illusion. Deep down I'm a hot mess."

"I highly doubt it. Well, not the hot part," I say. I'm feeling a surge of adrenaline that is a mixture of nerves and a pinch of anger. I hate that Eric assumes he can get away with being a dick and Rye is such a decent person that he feels he needs to make amends on Eric's behalf. It's gross.

Rye is quiet again.

"Sorry. I was just being dumb," I say.

"No, it's not. I was just … Never mind."

"No, go on," I say, holding my breath a little.

"You're sweet, Fin."

My cheeks blaze and I'm tipped back to my extremely shy self.

"Thanks," Rye says. "Thanks for keeping me company."

"Anytime," I say.

We both hang up and I stare blankly at my screen for a while.

I turn over and plug my phone in next to my bed and when I turn back around Dad is staring at me through the loft hatch.

"Who was that?" he asks.

He has no discernible expression on his face and I can't help but be unnerved by the monotone way he's speaking.

"Poppy," I say, fully aware that my best attempt at sounding nonchalant is failing miserably.

He clearly doesn't buy it. We stare at each other for what feels like an hour.

"Why do you do this, Fin?"

I start to object, but he holds his hand up to silence me and shakes his head.

"If we find out you are back to your old ways, we will have no choice but to find someone who can help you with this destructive and unhealthy phase you're going through. This is not a life you want, Fin," he says, looking strangely furious and concerned all at once.

"What is that supposed to mean?" I ask, my heart thumping through my T-shirt.

"You know exactly what it means," Dad says, making his way back down the ladder.

I lie staring at the ceiling for a while. I'm trying not to let my thoughts overwhelm me when my phone buzzes and the blue light from the screen illuminates the room.

Rye: Goodnight Fin x

The *x* might as well be bold, italicised, underlined and drawn in actual exploding fireworks because it's all I'm looking at. Goodnight *kiss*. Even though we'd only just said goodnight less than ten minutes ago he wanted to message me again. My stomach is buzzing like a lunatic and I text back.

Me: Night Rye x

13

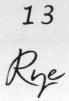

It's a relief to make it to the end of the week. It's Saturday morning and I leave Thelma snoring on her bed in my room and head to the kitchen. Mum is making cinnamon porridge and berries. It smells delicious and I practically inhale my bowl and immediately go for a second helping.

"How you feeling, hun?" Mum asks as she pours us both some coffee.

"Meh," I say.

"It's Saturday, which means that is not allowed."

"Meh is always allowed. Like coffee."

"Coffee and meh should never be used in the same sentence," Mum says, adding a spoon of sugar to mine and some almond milk to hers. "How's Eric?" She hasn't asked me about him for a couple of days – obviously giving me space – and her tone is carefully casual.

I shrug.

"I thought I heard you talking to the other night?"

"Mum, were you eavesdropping?"

"Me? Dropping of eaves? How very dare you."

"Well, no. It was ... someone else."

Mum's eyes light up like she's just hit the jackpot on the slots.

"Nope. No, Mum. Don't go there," I say, standing to leave. Mum grabs my arm and wheels me back to my seat.

"Spill."

I take a deep breath. "Fin. New friend at school. Just moved here from Pittford."

"And you and him are ... close? I take it?"

"Um ... No. I've known him for, like, five days. We're friends and I was bored so I gave him a friendly call and we had a *friendly* chat," I say.

Mum gives me this sarcastic look that says, *Oh right I totally believe you*, and then she lets me tidy up the kitchen.

The sun seems to be trying to make an appearance outside and, apart from a few grey clouds and a chilly wind, it looks like a pretty nice day. I check my phone and realise I have three missed calls from Eric. I call him back and head to the front porch where Thelma is curled in a chunky ball at the top of the steps.

"Hey."

"Hey, I've been calling you."

"Sorry, I was just with Mum," I say, taking a seat at the top of the steps and letting Thelma rest her head on my lap. I don't have the energy to point out that he hasn't called me or replied to my messages for days. I know it's pathetic, but I'm so happy to hear from him.

"Look, Rye, I'm sorry about our anniversary night."

"It's okay. We can do something some other –"

"No, it's not okay. I'm a dick for bailing out on you last minute like that. The whole two-month-anniversary thing was my idea to begin with –"

"Thanks," I say.

We're quiet for a moment. I don't really know what to say, I'm all out of energy.

"My friend Dan is having a party tonight. Will you go with me?"

He sounds sweet and genuine and I want more than anything for him to show me how much I mean to him.

"Um … Yeah," I start, taking a moment to be sure. "No, yeah, that sounds fun."

"Great," he says. "You're the best, Rye."

"Nah, not even close," I say, but it doesn't take much for my heart to flutter erratically when it comes to Eric.

"I'll pick you up at six, okay?"

"Okay," I say, smiling as I end the call.

I turn and head back inside. I don't even realise I'm smiling until Mum gives me a funny look.

"That your friend Fin?"

"What?" I ask, baffled. "Oh … I – No, it was Eric. He, um … He's taking me out tonight to make up for the anniversary non-dinner," I say, speaking quickly to get the conversation over and done with.

Mum just nods before turning back to the kitchen counter and putting the kettle on.

*

By mid-morning the clouds are nearly all gone, so I grab my fishing rod, saddle Thelma up in her leash and head for the wharf.

My pride and joy, the *S.S. Buoyancé*, is my tiny tin boat with oars. One of Mum's friends she gives tarot readings to was going to sell it for scrap metal last Christmas, but Mum offered to buy it off of him in exchange for free readings for three months. It is by far the greatest gift I have ever received and one I'll never stop being grateful for.

Thelma wiggles and gets comfy on the bed I've made her underneath the bow and I push off from the wharf and start rowing.

The mist on the surface of the water reminds me of those old black and white horror movies and when I cast my line out I half imagine that I'm about to pull in the creature from the black lagoon.

I sit and watch my line bob up and down in the water and Thelma starts snoring. I swear that dog could sleep and dribble her way through the apocalypse.

I'm trying as hard as I can not to overthink everything with Eric and simply be grateful that he's making it up to me tonight, but the harder I try the more my mind buzzes. I guess I just feel like I'm chasing someone who doesn't particularly want to be chased. I'm a massive sucker for a love story and I can't help but feel like I'm more of a booty call than a happy-ever-after for Eric. I dunno. Maybe tonight he'll change my mind. Then again, maybe Thelma will learn to play bass and we will start a band. Both scenarios seem highly unlikely.

The line goes tight and I reel it in. A clump of seaweed dangles from the end of the rod and I untangle it.

"Maybe I'm just being way too sensitive," I suggest to Thelma, who rolls over onto her back and lets the soft sun that's starting to appear warm her belly.

As usual I catch absolutely zero fish and after an hour or so I head back in. It's the intention that counts – that's what Mum says.

Thelma wakes up from her nap and waddles off the boat and up the wharf towards home. When we walk through the front door Mum is sitting on Carl's lap and they're giggling like school kids.

"Gross," I say, making a beeline for my bedroom and kicking off my sneakers.

I get myself comfy on my bed and scroll through Tumblr on my laptop for a bit when a Skype call from June interrupts my reblogging of a screenshot of a young Rock Hudson in *Pillow Talk*.

"Hey," I say.

"Hey, whatcha doing?"

"Just went fishing and now avoiding Mum and Carl who are fondling in the dining room by getting stuck down a Tumblr hole."

"Fun. Hey, so I have something I need to ask you." June looks nervous, which is weird for her.

"Shoot."

"Okay ..." She just sits there.

"Are you ... going to say something?"

"I'm working on it," she says.

I wait.

"So ... remember before Halloween when Poppy got all weird when you asked if her and me would ever get back together?"

I nod. It was probably the most awkward fifteen seconds of my life. I only suggested it because I was feeling all upbeat and giggly at some party we were at (yes, some vodka was involved), and besides, I've always thought their on-again off-again relationship works out that way because they're both too stubborn to ever admit they're in the wrong. Poppy is openly pan and has confided multiple times to me that she truly believes June is the love of her life, but this past breakup has lasted six months and when I mentioned them getting back together Poppy just sort of sat there looking at me like I'd thrown my drink over her. She finally smiled and quickly changed the subject to something irrelevant and weird like how they get the chocolate to stay soft on the inside and hard on the outside of those Lindt chocolate balls.

"Well, after her and Fin left my place on Halloween, I thought we were all good, so I sent her a message asking if she wanted to see a movie this weekend just the two of us – totally as friends – and she never replied. Then today she barely said a word to me. And yes, she's seen the message."

"I'm sorry, June," I say. I feel awful. Me and my big, dumb, stupid mouth.

"Oh my god, NO. This wasn't some kind of attack at you. It's weird because she's not being, like, weird enough for me to question anything. Surface level, she seems all good … I was just … I dunno, I was wondering if she'd mentioned anything to you?"

She looks at me like I'm holding the Powerball numbers in my hand.

"No, but I can talk to her if you want?"

"You would?" June asks.

"Of course."

She smiles.

"We all know how tricky Poppy can be, but she's got a great heart," I say, distracted by attempting to pluck one of my nose hairs out – I know, gross, sorry.

"How's Eric?"

"He's good," I say with my best cheesy grin.

June sees right through it. "Rye," she says and just gives me this look that makes me know there's no judgement. That I can talk to her if I want.

I swear, June is one of the best human beings I've ever known. Period. Her parents adopted her from India when she was a few weeks old and she knew who she was from as early as second grade. By fourth grade she'd chosen her name. From then on, we were to call her June, because it was her favourite month of the year. I can only imagine what it must be like to be trans *and* a person of colour in a world that is so full of people like Paisley and Bronwyn, a world so deliberately cruel and ignorant; yet June proves that regardless of the bin fire that society can be, she's still an absolute badass legend. Her parents are amazing, they're so on side with her, which obviously helps, but I've always been so floored at how strong she is. She genuinely takes no prisoners at all. Girl boss personified.

"Okay, so the other night Eric bailed on me for our anniversary thing."

June rolls her eyes like she knew that was coming.

"But I guess it's only two months. I was making a big deal out of nothing and –"

"No, Rye. You don't get to do that. It wouldn't matter if it were two days. You guys had plans and he ditched you last minute. That's not cool."

"Yeah, but I *am* like crazy clingy and –"

"Wait, hold up a second. Why is liking someone a bad thing? When did the honeymoon period become irrelevant? This is supposed to be the fun bit."

There's no answer when she makes solid points like that.

"I guess he's taking me out tonight, so he's trying to fix it." I shrug.

June smiles. "Well, just know that I'll kick his ass if he hurts you, Rye-bread," she says, still smiling, though I'm pretty sure she's being deadly serious.

"What would I do without you, June-bug?" I roll over and cuddle up with Thelma.

Saturdays are for fishing, food and naps. Naps most importantly. I am the Mayor of Nap Town. The King of Nap Nation. I love naps so much and the weather today is perfect for one. I let Thelma snuggle up next to me and put a blanket half on my legs and half not and then we doze off together.

When I wake up Thelma is drooling over my arm and snoring like she hasn't slept in weeks. I wipe my eyes and check my phone: 5:03 p.m. Eric is picking me up in less than an hour, so I get showered, put some salt spray in my hair to give it that "I'm not bothered how I look, but secretly please like it" vibe and then throw on my super skinny jeans, a plain white tee and my denim jacket. I wipe the stale remnants of the sample Chanel on my neck and wrists. I feel pretty cool.

"Rye, you look like a movie star," Mum says as I grab the water pitcher from the fridge. Carl is gone so we can have a proper conversation without me worrying about interrupting the love birds in their love nest. "But one of those indie movie stars who wins all the awards." She gives me a hug and I can't help but reciprocate.

"Thanks," I say and take a swig of water. "How's Carl?"

"He's good. He thinks you hate him."

I roll my eyes. Here we go.

"Why would I hate Carl? I don't really know the guy."

"That could have something to do with it."

"I would try to get to know him, but he doesn't detach himself from your side long enough to have a conversation." Mum starts to say something, but I go on. "And I'm not going to chat about the weather with him while you're sitting on his lap. Sorry," I say, putting my hands up.

"Okay. Fair," Mum says. "Less PDA. Understandable."

"Deal."

"So, where's the party tonight?" Mum asks.

"Over on Sweetzer. The big one."

"There is no big *one* on Sweetzer. They're all mansions. The garage of number hundred and two is bigger than this entire house."

"Yeah, but they don't have us living in there so I bet it's a miserable hovel," I say, smiling and giving her a cheesy high-five. "See you later."

"Back no later than midnight," Mum calls out after me.

"But what if I wanted to have an orgy? In a hot tub? It would be silly to come home at midnight and miss out on a hot tub orgy … I'd never be able to get to sleep," I yell.

"Not funny. Not one bit," Mum calls back, but I can tell she's giggling to herself.

I check my phone. Eric hasn't messaged to cancel so that's a good sign so far. As I'm about to put my phone away it buzzes and a message appears.

Poppy: A birdie told me you have plans – have fun tonight :)

14

Rye

The sky is deep purple, the sun barely clinging to the horizon. I inhale a big gulp of briny air and stuff my hands in my pockets and sit on the porch steps.

I'm glad Poppy texted; it feels like she's being genuine and I appreciate it. Nothing worse than trying to juggle your friends and who you're dating. I send her a GIF of Kristen Wiig in *Bridesmaids* saying "I'm ready to partayyyy".

And then there's the honk of a car horn from down the street.

Eric pulls up and almost mounts the kerb in his dad's Mercedes. The car looks like a transformer and I have the feeling it's worth more than our house and all its contents put together.

I wave sheepishly and he cocks his head for me to get in. I make my way over and open the door. I'm hit by that new car smell and everything looks like it's been polished.

"Hey."

"Hey," Eric says as he leans over and kisses me hard on the mouth.

I smile awkwardly.

"Ready?" he asks, and I give him a thumbs-up then feel dumb for doing it.

We drive for fifteen minutes barely talking as the speakers blast his techno music; I've never heard of any of it. He's wearing an extremely tight polo shirt, jeans and smells of some expensive cologne he probably has bottles of stashed away at home. Eric's family is loaded, his dad the CEO of Albright Bank and his mum is some mining dynasty heiress. Weirdly enough, I don't find it impressive at all. I liked Eric at first because he was so passionately into me. I'd never known what it was like to be adored and he wanted to constantly be with me. Perhaps he thought he was rescuing me from my un-glam life. When I didn't want to go all the way he backed off entirely and now I don't really know where we are or what our future together looks like. If there is a future, even.

We arrive outside 102 Sweetzer and the place looks like a bloody palace. Three storeys and a lake out front. Yes, an ACTUAL lake. There are even swans on it. Who the hell has a swan lake in their front yard?

We get out the car and walk up the ridiculously long path up to the house. I go to take Eric's hand, but he acts like he has an itch and avoids it completely.

Inside there is nothing but gleaming marble, crystal chandeliers and long velvet curtains. I feel like I've stepped into some period drama and suddenly feel incredibly underdressed. All the guys are wearing polo shirts that show off pecs and biceps and abs and all the girls look like the white cast from *The Help*. It's really unnerving and I kind of want to leave.

One of Eric's beefcake buddies greets us holding a red cup that I saw him fill with Belvedere vodka and soda moments before.

"E.T.!" says the beefcake, giving Eric a bro-hug and taking a sip of his drink.

"Hey, Dan," Eric says. "This is my friend, Rye."

Friend?

Dan puts his fist out which I bump lamely and then leads us to the dazzling kitchen to get a drink.

Eric pours us vodka sodas and chugs his immediately before refilling and chugging it down again.

"You okay?" I whisper. He gives me a confused look like I'd asked him to explain Pythagoras's theorem.

"Why wouldn't I be?"

"Oh, no ... I just meant. Like, you seem a bit on edge and... and you called me your friend." I smile to try and seem casual about it.

"It's a *party*," he says like I'm the biggest idiot in the world. "And you are my friend, one who I'd like to undress and have my way with." He says the last bit under his breath in my ear and yes, it turns me on, but simultaneously pisses me off.

We head into another room and take a seat at a couch in the middle with a bunch of other preppy-looking guys and girls. It seriously looks like a photo shoot in here. Eric sits next to me and puts his hand behind my back so nobody can see. The more he drinks the more his hand strokes my back and I can't help but feel giddy.

"I hope you're having fun?" he asks.

"Just glad to be hanging with you," I say.

He smiles and for the briefest moment everything feels really good. I remember what made me so excited when we first started dating. His piercing eyes, massive arms and a sexy edge to his smile that knocked me off my feet.

Sitting near us are a bunch of beautiful people who look like they've stepped out of an Abercrombie & Fitch catalogue. A girl with blood-red hair and electric apple-green nails sits down next to Eric. His hand quickly leaves my back and the two of them become engrossed in an animated conversation that I can't quite hear. I sit and stir my drink with a straw and half-heartedly tap my foot to the music – some weird boppy garbage that you'd need to be electrocuted to dance to – when Dan comes and sits on the coffee table in front of us holding two drinks.

"Here you go E-man," Dan says, blanking me.

Eric practically shouts "cheers!" and continues talking to the girl.

I take out my phone and check the time: 8:38 p.m. I'm about to check Instagram when an enormous crash from the kitchen makes everyone jump.

We all head in to find a tipped-over chocolate fondue fountain on the floor. There's a giant lake of chocolate spreading thickly. No swans. In the middle of it is a guy in nothing but his underwear.

"What the FUCK?" Dan shouts. Everyone goes quiet. "Where was MY invite?"

There's a huge cheer and suddenly everyone is sliding around the marble floor in the melted chocolate.

It's a mess and I'm not interested. This is some weird privileged shit and I'd rather stick my hand in a blender than be a part of it.

Eric looks over at me and shrugs like it's something that happens often enough in his social circles and I just stand there feeling odder and odder.

"Come on," Eric says in my ear before winking and beckoning for me to follow him.

The mess in the kitchen is still going strong as we make our way out into a hallway. Eric leads us into a bathroom, making sure nobody is watching before he closes the door behind us.

"I got us a present."

"What –" I say, but before I can say anything else, he's kissing me hard and his hands are all over me. I'm not going to say I don't enjoy it; I do. It's more that it feels artificial when he's so hammered. I want the real Eric. The one who doesn't need fourteen Belvedere vodkas to come near me in a public place.

He puts his thumb on my chin and gives me a peck on the nose and then fishes in his back pocket for something.

When I look down, he's holding two little green pills in his palm.

"What the hell are those?" I ask and I'm suddenly pissed. Really pissed. I get that people take recreational drugs and whatever. But I cannot believe he's offering me this after I told him about my dad and –

"Ecstasy. That girl I was talking to back there hooked me up and I thought we could –"

"Eric, seriously? What the fuck?" My body's trembling and I want to leave. The room feels really small.

"Babe, calm down you're –"

"NO, you calm down. You have no idea. No idea what that shit can lead to. I told you about my –"

"I do not need this, Rye. I've been trying all night to make things right."

"Make things right?" I can feel myself losing it, but at this point I don't care. "Eric, you introduced me as your *friend*, have barely said three words to me all night and have smashed back about six drinks in the space of half an hour."

"So when I was stroking your back in there, what? That meant nothing?"

"Sure, Eric. I felt great when you removed your hand at the first sign of anyone noticing and when you could score yourself some drugs instead."

"So what?" He shrugs, indifferent. "Rye, you're being a brat."

"*I'm* being a brat? Are you kidding me right now? Do *any* of your friends know about me? Do any of your friends know about *you*?"

"Fuck, Rye, who cares about any of that?" He pulls back from me. "What do you even want from me?"

We both glower at each other.

I'm not angry that he isn't out to his friends yet. I'm angry that I have to play along with a charade I really didn't sign up for.

"I … Nothing. I'm gonna go."

"Rye, come on. Give me another chance."

I stare up at him and for the first time all night he seems sincere. The drunken glaze in his eyes seems to have gone and it's like the real Eric is looking back at me for a second.

I nod my silent agreement and we leave the bathroom together and head for the kitchen where the commotion has died down slightly.

I head to the bench and pour myself a soda water. I'm not remotely interested in drinking anymore. I'd much rather leave with Eric and go and hang out just the two of us, but I doubt that's going to happen. My scene is more hot chocolate on the couch watching a movie than a chocolate-fondue sliding scrum on a rich person's kitchen floor.

When I turn around Eric is talking animatedly to Dan and I head over and stand awkwardly near them both.

"Having fun?" Dan says, looking me up and down.

"Yeah. Love the house. Very cool."

"Nah, this is nothing. Our holiday house in Lake Miracle is dope as hell."

I can't begin to imagine what it must be like to think that the house we are in right now is "nothing".

I turn to catch Eric's eye and notice that he's gone all weird. He's chewing the inside of his lip and his eyes dart around the room like he's trying to find something he's lost.

"You okay?" I ask. He's in his own world, looking around like a lunatic meerkat.

Dan glances at Eric and something clicks in his eyes and he's suddenly smiling.

The song changes and a track with heavy bass blasts through the speakers dotted around the house.

The red-haired girl with the green nails shows up out of nowhere, her face and dress covered in chocolate from rolling around like an idiot, and she grabs Eric's hand and leads him to the dance floor.

Dan looks at me and bounces his eyebrows up and down a few times.

"Looks like someone's getting lucky tonight," Dan says before clinking my cup with his and downing it in one go.

My stomach clenches and I have this overwhelming sensation of wanting to cry, right here in the middle of this ridiculous kitchen.

Dan wanders off and I head outside to where a bunch of people are smoking and talking.

A guy wearing a giant trench coat and a mustard yellow scarf is holding forth about his internship at some art gallery. By the sound of it, it's going "amazingly" and he will be "absolutely hired" by the time he's done. A girl standing nearby rolls her eyes at me in recognition of the spectacle Mr Mustard Scarf is making of himself. She smiles before offering me a cigarette.

"I'm fine, thanks," I say. Then as she turns to leave: "Um, actually, yeah I will. Thanks."

I don't smoke at all, but I'm feeling like crap and I couldn't care less right now.

I light mine off of the end of hers and we stand huddled together.

"I'm Lily," she says.

She's very pretty. Her green eyes and porcelain white skin look almost unnatural, like she's had fifteen thousand chemical peels.

"Who are you here with?" she asks, taking a drag of her cigarette.

"My b– My friend Eric." I nod inside to where he is dancing with the redhead, spinning her around like a maniac.

Lily smiles. "Great party, huh?"

"Yeah," I say, taking a shallow drag and exhaling quickly.

"I haven't seen you at many of these get-togethers. Are you new here?"

"Nope. No, I'm just poor," I say and Lily bursts out laughing.

I smile, unsure of whether she thinks I was joking or whether the truth was really that funny.

Lily starts to say something, but the music inside stops and I hear a bunch of hollering from the dance floor.

Eric is dancing to music only he can hear and shaking his fists above his head like a gladiator at a rave. A few of his cronies are cheering him on, but mostly people are looking on confused.

"I'm gonna head inside," I say. "It was nice to meet you, Lily."

"Likewise," Lily says.

The smell of vodka and Red Bull lingers in the air. Someone has put another track on and now Eric is going at it harder than ever.

"Hey babe," I say in his ear. "You okay?"

"Yep yep yep yep."

"I was thinking maybe we could head home soon? Just us two? I'd –"

"But the party, man. The party is just getting gooooood. We're just getting *going*, you know?"

He can't seem to keep any part of his body still and there's something about his eyes that's a lot more than vodka. Also, did he just call me "man"?

"Sure, but maybe we could go chill for a bit before I have to go home."

No answer. He simply dances erratically some more, his eyes darting around and refusing to engage with me.

Then it hits me. "Eric… did you… did you take that pill?"

He stops his unpredictable head twisting thing and turns to stare at me. "Nooooo."

I don't believe him. His pupils are dilated. His face is glazed with sweat and he looks like he's just had a shot of adrenaline to the heart.

Then he leans in close to me.

"I took both." He grins like the Joker, like he's single-handedly solved the most complex maths equation known to mankind.

I feel my throat dry up. "Are you serious?"

He throws me one last grin, swivels around and bounces back to take his spot on the dance floor.

My vision blurs and my heart speeds up. I don't feel as if I'm a part of my body anymore. I know I'm having a panic attack because my entire body is trembling and I feel like I'm going to pass out. The music is too much and the people are pressing too close to me and the air seems thinner and my throat is closing up.

Nothing makes sense.

I make my way through the house to the front door and fumble with the handle. I'm in complete overwhelming panic. Finally, I open it and head out and I don't know what to do so I walk. I walk to the ridiculous lake in their front yard where the swans are gliding about and I breathe like my lungs are collapsing. My mind is a blur and however much I try to rationalise things, it only makes them all the more confusing.

Flashes of life with my dad bounce around my brain.

Unpredictable. Frightening. Toxic.

Glasses shattering against walls. Storms of tears and angry yelling.

I take a few more shallow breaths and then feel my feet go numb and my knees buckle and then nothing but black.

15

Rye

I'm lying face down in the grass, cold air blowing over me. I feel sick and tired and terrified all at once. I sit up and spit some dirt from my mouth, wipe my forehead and instantly want to throw up. I crawl to a bush and heave up the Belvedere vodka then lie on my back and try to breathe.

I don't bother to go and find Eric. His family is so different from mine, but still I told him about what happened with my dad. And then, after all that, after every conversation where I explained how terrified I was as a kid growing up, he does this. I guess he wasn't listening, not really.

My hands are over my eyes, blocking everything out, when my phone buzzes. It's Mum. I swear that woman actually is psychic.

Mum: How's the party going?

I rub my head. Send back a thumbs-up emoji and an 'x'.

I then dial Poppy's number. She answers after the first ring.

"Rye-bread!" Her voice is full of energy.

I breathe and realise I'm not saying anything.

"Hun, you okay?"

"Yeah." *Breathe.* "I … um." *Breathe.*

"You having a picnic?"

"Uh huh." *Breathe.*

We call my panic attacks picnics because we were on a picnic the first time Poppy saw me have one and she thought I was having a heart attack and called an ambulance. Looking back, it was dramatic and kind of hilarious, but it felt nice to know she cared and the term has stuck.

"Head between your knees and put me on speaker."

I do as I'm told and feel my arms and legs trembling.

"Breathe in with me … two, three, four," Poppy says.

I breathe when she tells me to and exhale when she tells me to. Within ten minutes I'm quiet but feel as battered and exhausted as if I've just done ten rounds with King Kong.

"You okay, mister?" Poppy asks and I can hear her keys jingle in the background. "Where are you? I'm on my way."

*

Before I know it, I'm safely in Poppy's car and we're working our way through a slurpee each. She really is a legend.

"You wanna talk about what happened, or?" Poppy is being completely genuine and I know that if I say no, she will let it go. Yet I hear myself retelling the events of the past couple of hours and I'm beyond relieved to lift this anchor off my chest.

Poppy sits and nods at all the right moments and when I'm done she takes my hand and rests her head on my shoulder.

"What are we gonna do with you, Rye-bread?"

We stay like that for a while. Eventually Poppy sits up, sends a text and then starts her car. Ten minutes later we pull into the Pancake Parlour. From the giant clock above the entrance, I realise it's nearly eleven o'clock.

"Nah, I'm not feeling pancakes right now," I say.

"Good, neither am I. Waffles, on the other hand, are calling my name."

We get out and head inside and Poppy leads us to a table at the back where, oddly enough, June and Fin are sitting.

"Scoot over," Poppy says to Fin and then gestures for me to sit, which I do.

"This is an inter-friend-sion," Poppy says.

June and Fin look at one another like this is news to them.

"It is?" June says.

"Yes." Poppy signals the waiter and orders us a round of raspberry cola and waffles.

Fin looks uncomfortable, like he didn't realise this was what he was stepping into when he came out for a diner experience on a Friday night. I stare at the table and try to breathe. The last thing I need after a panic attack is a random arbitration conference at the Pancake Parlour.

I want to cry. No, I want my dog and my boat and I want to go to Kettle Lake to watch the fireflies. Anywhere but here right now. This is not what I need.

"Poppy, I'm leaving."

She grabs my arm as I go to stand. "Nope, no you're not."

I sit down obediently and our food arrives, but I don't even bother trying to eat anything. I'm not hungry and still feel slightly sick from blacking out.

But Poppy has switched to her military mode and her calm and compassionate side seems to have evaporated into the ceiling. She's about business and she means it.

"Rye, Eric is garbage. The sooner you realise that, the easier you can move on, find someone decent – hell, don't find anyone at all, be single, do whatever you want – but this is ridiculous." Poppy slowly emphasises each syllable of "ri-dic-u-lous" so the point is driven home.

I sit there and take it. I have no defence against what she's saying. Even though I know she has a point, it stings. I still can't admit it. Not yet.

"Poppy, just … Let's give Rye some time. You know, to think things over?" June says, looking at her directly and not blinking.

Poppy seems to have not heard. Either that or she's blatantly ignoring her. She disregards the food and drink in front of her and doesn't even take a breath before she's back in the saddle and tearing me up.

"I mean, Jesus, Rye. What will it take before you drop this douche bag? Look at how he treats you. And now, tonight? After everything with your dad and –"

June and Fin look at one another across the table and my heartbeat hammers against my chest. I don't want to go over this again.

"Like, the first time, whatever, you know? But this is what? The fourth?"

"I get it."

"The fifth?"

"I get it."

"The tenth? I mean what is it going to –"

"I SAID I GET IT, POPPY," I shout, choking on the last word. My face is burning and tears fill my eyes.

Poppy stares at me silently.

I fish a ten-dollar note out of my pocket, throw it on the table and leave. June calls my name and I hear Poppy call out too, but I'm already gone.

It's freezing, but for a while I don't feel it. My face is still burning and I'm trembling with anxiety. I keep walking until I see Thelma staring at me through my bedroom window as I approach home.

My heartbeat starts to slow and my mind becomes untangled.

"Honey, you still have half an hour left until curfew," Mum says as I enter the kitchen.

I think about telling her everything. I think about listing every single rubbishy thing that Eric has ever done, about how Poppy can be such a pain, but instead I just burst into tears.

Mum wraps me up in a hug and lets me cry. I sob the kind of sobs where you lose air in your lungs and there's nothing but a whistle.

When I finally stop, she puts her hands on my arms and looks at me.

"You are perfect, Rye-bread. And you deserve all the love in the world. Don't you dare ever think otherwise."

That's it. No lectures. No advice. Yet her words hit me in my core.

*

It's around midnight by the time I get myself a glass of water and head to my bedroom where Thelma wiggles with excitement when she sees me. My eyes feel puffy and there's snot at the back of my throat but the very sight of her cheers me up. I give her a kiss on the head and rub behind her ears before kicking off my shoes and lying down.

I take my phone out and immediately see four missed calls from Eric, three texts from Poppy, two new Instagram followers and a voicemail.

I unlock my phone and as I'm about to listen to my voicemail, a call shakes my phone to life. I hesitate for a beat and then accept.

"Ryeeeee, where are you? We should – hmmm?" It's Eric, but with someone else in the background. "– I'll be there in a sec, just – yeah I know." There's a muffled sound like he's changing hands. "Anyway, Ryeeeee, look, let's go to mine."

I sit up, pissed. "Why would we do that?"

"You know why," he says in this sleazy voice that is the furthest thing from a turn on.

"Yeah, I do," I tell him. "So you can, what? Have sex? You want me to have my first time while you're hammered? Seriously?"

"Someone's in a terrific mood," Eric scoffs, sarcastically.

"And you wonder why? Wasn't tonight supposed to make up for the last shitty thing you did?"

Silence. And when I check the screen he's no longer there. Either he hung up or the line cut out. Whatever. I don't have the energy to call him back.

I'm about to throw my phone across the room when it buzzes again. I smack the screen with my finger angrily, expecting to see a message from Eric, but it's not him.

Fin: Just wanted to make sure you're okay? xx

I take a long deep breath and wonder why these simple words make me feel so happy. I don't know Fin at all really. He could be a serial killer. Or part of an international drug cartel. Okay, highly unlikely, yes, but I still don't really know him. And yet here I am, beaming at my phone and smiling in the same goofy way Thelma stares at peanut butter.

16

Fin

I don't know why in the fresh hell I felt the need to text Rye but I did, and now I'm sitting here terrified while the little bubble with the dots moves on the bottom corner of my phone screen.

He looked so hurt and bewildered at the Pancake Parlour and I wanted him to know that someone who doesn't know all the details about his situation is here if he needs to talk.

Rye: Thanks Fin.

I cringe my eyes so tight I see stars. I'm such an idiot. Of course he doesn't want to talk. Especially not to me. His boyfriend might be a douche, but he's a ridiculously buff and wealthy douche. No way can I match up to that.

I'm about to get up and pace around my room when the little dots appear in the corner again.

Rye: You know any bad dating stories to cheer me up...?
Just putting it out there.

I smile.

Me: Haven't dated much. Last time I tried, it provoked my dad to move us all the way here.

I feel weird telling him that bizarre family fact, but at the same time it's therapeutic. I haven't spoken to anyone here about it and I feel it weighing me down every single day.

Rye: Are you serious?

Me: 100%.

Rye: Wow.

Neither of us type anything for a while. I sit feeling awkward, like I've revealed too much. Then my phone vibrates with an incoming call.

"Hey."

"Hey, so, texting didn't feel so appropriate to talk about this kind of stuff."

Rye's voice sounds softer than usual, like he's tired. Maybe he's just being gentle with me.

"So, you moved here why? Your family thought they'd leave Gay Fin behind in Pittford?"

I giggle. "Dad's family are mega religious," I tell him. "Well, actually, no. It's not so much the religion. They're not like any other Christians I've met. My friend back home, Emily, she was brought up in the church and would *never* think anything of anyone else's sexuality or whatever."

I pause, and Rye's silence encourages me to go on.

"But Dad's family – they're … something else. He's so traditional, you know? His whole life, he's followed convention – captain of the football team, respectable job, married a 'nice girl'. My brother seems to be on the same path, no problem, but me … Dad's completely out of his depth."

I get up from the bed and quietly open the latch in the floor to make sure nobody has their ear to it, listening in. All clear. I shut it again and put a pillow over it to stifle our chat.

"And your mum? Is she ... ? Does she have a problem with Gay Fin?"

"I think she likes him more than Dad –" I hesitate and then continue. "To be honest, I don't even know if my dad is genuinely freaked out about my sexuality or whether he's just doing what he thinks he should do. Like, trying to keep up appearances for what he thinks is expected, what he thinks is normal, you know?"

"Trying to do right by his *Children of the Corn* family?" Rye says and I sense him smiling down the phone.

I giggle again. "Quick question," I say, getting under my covers and kicking a leg out underneath the blanket. "How did we end up talking about me when I wanted to make sure *you* were okay?"

"My crappy kiss-and-not-make-up date isn't much of a comparison now, is it?" Rye says and I smile, glad he brought up his date.

"What happened?" I ask. Then: "I mean, don't feel like you have to tell me. I didn't mean it like that ... I just ... If you want to talk, I'm here."

"Thanks," Rye says.

We both don't speak for a moment and I consider changing the subject.

"It was ... I really thought he liked me ..." Rye's voice sounds shaky and I'm worried that I'm not cut out to be of any help to him. "When we first got together, he was nothing but amazing. I was terrified of having a boyfriend and yet he was so persistent. He messaged me non-stop, liked every Instagram I ever posted and was constantly asking me to hang out."

"What changed?" I ask, trying to be of some value to the conversation.

"Maybe boredom? Maybe ..."

"What?"

"I'm … we've never … you know."

I feel my face burn red. "You … You think he's bored because you won't …?"

I hear him sigh. "I think so."

"And – you don't want to?"

"I mean, yeah. I do. A lot … But not because I feel like I have to." He pauses. "How did we end up here? I'm sorry. You don't need to hear all this."

"No, no way. I'm happy to help. Well, I'm not helping really, but, I'm glad to at least –"

"You are."

I smile to myself and squeeze my eyes tight.

"You're awesome, Fin."

I'm about to tell him how amazing he is. How great and wonderful and perfect he is and how anyone would be crazy to treat him with anything but love, when he starts talking again.

"You know, I think I'm being too hard on him. I … He's a couple of years older than us and I guess I just have a lot to learn about relationships. I'm being way too sensitive."

"No," I start. "I really don't think –"

"I'm going to call him. Sort it out. Well, try to. Thanks, Fin. I owe you one."

I feel like I've had the wind kicked out of me. That's so not the outcome I thought we were heading for. I want to yell at him and tell him to not be so naive. Instead I say, "Anytime," but then realise he's hung up already.

17
Fin

June's waiting by my locker with a massive smile on her face. The perfect Monday morning welcome committee.

"Hey," I say, entering the combination on my lock and throwing my lunch inside.

Poppy appears behind me and hooks her arm in mine. June follows suit and hooks my other arm and we walk down the hall like some wannabe cabaret act with no moves.

"Where are we going?" I ask, realising I haven't checked my timetable this morning.

"Religion," they say in unison.

We get to B-block and head to the back of the class where we sit in a row with me in the middle. Poppy is chewing her hair and June is biting her nails. I can sense an invisible tension between the two of them and I don't know why, but I'm suddenly hyper aware of my breath and how fast my heart is beating. This is my first religion class since Pittford and back there it was all fire and brimstone and burning for all eternity in hell. Each class would finish and I would be hit by a few solid days of depression, followed by a few days of pep-talking myself up for the next class the following week. So, today, I brace myself as the door opens.

Miss Reynolds is about six foot tall with long red hair and fair skin. She reminds me of a folk singer with her flower headband and floaty clothes.

"Morning," she says, brightly, scanning the room and smiling sweetly.

I've seen this before. This holier-than-thou attitude like life is nothing but blue skies and campfire singing and Disney movies. I don't buy it, but I settle in for the hour and face the inevitable.

My introduction is made with a brief "Hi" from her, which I appreciate. So far, so good. June and Poppy don't seem half as worried as me, but then again they've not experienced a religion class in Pittford.

We begin with a poem from Miss Reynolds about love and compassion and we then settle in for a group discussion. Today's subject is about what religion means to each of us. Miss Reynolds starts.

"Religion, for me, is about the very basic principle of treating others the way I would like to be treated. It's always been about trying my best to find good in others and, likewise, to find the good within me."

I feel myself smiling. She actually sounds completely genuine. There's no bubbly cheesiness behind her words. None of that happy-clappy stuff you sometimes get with people handing out leaflets at train stations. The words seem to come straight from her heart – and she looks as if she lives her life by them, too.

Next is a guy with curly brown hair and a backward baseball cap who mumbles something about loving thy neighbour and then another girl says a few more sentences about love.

Next to take a turn is Paisley. I already have a burning desire to lob my textbook at the back of her smug head and her next words do nothing to change that.

"I believe in following the scripture," she pipes up. "Our after-school study group spent last week discussing the sins our society now feels it's okay to indulge in –" she throws this back to me, June and Poppy before continuing, "– and I feel that if we ignore the Bible's very simple teachings, we neglect it all."

Miss Reynolds nods her acknowledgement, but her face has taken on a wary look.

"Okay," she says, but just as another guy's about to speak, her eyes shoot back to Paisley.

"Actually, sorry, Brian, let's just take one step back. Can you give the class an example, Paisley?"

Paisley looks stunned, clearly not used to being challenged. I'm guessing the ability to elaborate is beyond her brain capacity.

"Well." She sits up straight and inhales sharply. "For example, homosexuality."

Her cronies snicker and some of the other students sitting near her smirk as she turns and blatantly looks at me, Poppy and June. I feel my lungs fill with ice – I've heard all this before – but Poppy and June simply lengthen out their spines and, taller, glare back at Paisley.

"What about homosexuality?" Miss Reynolds asks.

"The Bible tells us it's a sin. But here we are, in Australia, and everyone's celebrating men *loving* men and women *loving* women. There's students in this very class who parade about as out-and-proud homosexuals. The whole thing's an abomination." She thumps her fist on the desk before ranting on. "Don't even get me started on the rules about who can use the toilets here –"

"Never mind the toilets, Paisley. Let's stick to the subject." Miss Reynolds sighs. "The Bible is always open to interpretation. Plus, it's a book that reflects the time it was written in. And those were very different times. Take your sweater, for example."

"What?" Paisley looks at her, confused.

"Your sweater, Paisley, looks like it's made of two different fabrics. Leviticus 19:19 tell us that we must not 'wear a garment upon you of two kinds of material mixed together'. So, does this mean you are also ignoring the teachings of the scriptures?"

"What are you *on* about?" Bronwyn jumps in, looking at Miss Reynolds like she's a complete idiot. The two jocks at the next table grin.

"Ah, Bronwyn. You offer us another example – your haircut."

Bronwyn's eyes dart from left to right. "I'm sorry, *what*?"

"Leviticus 19:27 reads, 'You shall not round off the side-growth of your head …' Which means, taken literally, your current haircut is also not acceptable …"

I look at June, who is grinning openly, and Poppy who's bolt upright with a look of undisguised awe on her face.

"So, you see, not everything that's written in the Bible is as black and white as it might seem. How might you choose which rules still stand and which do not?"

Miss Reynolds is practically doing a mic drop right in front of us. Paisley's already pale face has now changed to an alarming shade of grey.

"I don't pick and choose," she stammers. "It's what the Bible clearly states and –" Paisley runs out of words.

At which point one of the jocks raises his hand with a smirk. "What about masturbation, miss? Pretty sure the Bible says we'll have to cut off our –"

The other jock coughs and the class erupts.

"Hands. Less of the dirty minds, kids." Miss Reynolds wraps up her epic burns by placing her hands on her hips. "Can we go on? Brian, you were saying?"

The class murmurs in reluctant agreement as Brian takes his turn. Paisley and Bronwyn both simply glower and grumble under their breath.

Peace 'n' Love: one – Hatred: nil.

*

After class, I walk down the hall in B-block in a complete blur. I've never seen an adult demolish a kid like that before with cold hard facts. Miss Reynolds is seriously *baaaad-ass*. I start fantasising about letting her loose on my parents, but I know it wouldn't make much of a difference.

We turn the corner and head down another corridor and, through the giant arched window at the end of the hall, I see it has started to drizzle. A few brown leaves stick to the window like soggy pancakes and the tree beyond rattles the glass with its long branches.

"Boo," comes a voice from behind us. It's Rye, his cheeks flushed and his brown eyes as shiny as marbles.

"Hey," June says wrapping him in a hug.

Poppy holds back, clearly unsure how to behave after the events of Saturday night.

"Hey, Fin," Rye says.

I smile. June and Poppy both give Rye a raised eyebrow.

"How you feeling?" Poppy asks.

"Meh." Rye shrugs. "Can we talk later?"

"No problem."

"Fin, you ever been to Kettle Lake?" Rye asks, switching his attention from Poppy to me and changing the conversation abruptly.

"Nope," I say.

"I'll take you sometime. It's really something."

I can feel Poppy and June's eyes burning into us, but I try to keep my face as blush-free as possible. I have no idea what is going on. I'm getting a thousand different signals from Rye right now and I have no idea how to interpret a single one of them.

"Sounds good," I murmur and then a message alert makes us all take a dive into our pockets to see whose phone it is.

Rye puts his hand up and we all put our phones away, except for Poppy who takes a pic on Snapchat with the dog filter and laughs to herself like it's the first time she's ever seen it.

"It's Eric," Rye says, still looking down at his phone. I see Poppy attempt an eye roll to herself, which is a miserable fail because I notice it immediately. June shuffles from one foot to the other. "He wants me to go round to his tomorrow. Do you think I should?"

I can't be certain, but he seems to be almost pleading for us to give him advice. Like he needs confirmation that he's doing the right thing. Then again, maybe that's wishful thinking on my part.

"Sounds ... good," Poppy says, taking another pic on Snapchat, obviously trying not to say how she really feels.

"I would love to talk about this more, Rye-bread, but I have practice for the QSA's first choir performance tonight for next week's school assembly. We're doing the ending of *Sister Act*: the 'I Will Follow Him' song. I'm playing Whoopi and the rest of our nuns will be totally bedazzled. It's going to be dope." June looks really excited. "If any of you want to join, there's still some parts to fill –"

"No offence, but I'd rather eat a steaming turd burger than participate in that," Poppy says. I can't help but laugh. June can't either.

Rye looks distracted but says, "Thanks, June, but I'm good." He's about to add something else when the bell goes and we each scatter for our next classes.

June has geography, Poppy has science. Rye looks over my shoulder at my timetable and points at my next class. "History. D-block. I'm in maths right near there. Wanna walk with me?" he says, flashing me his killer smile.

I follow Rye down the hall towards the double doors that lead to the other blocks. The wind has really picked up and now it's pouring down with rain.

"Crap," Rye says, looking over at me with a half-grin.

"Do you have an ... an um–"

"Ummmbrella? Nope." Rye is now giggling as a crack of thunder sounds somewhere in the distance.

"How fast can you run?" I ask, bending down to tie my shoelace which is soaked through to the plastic cord.

"Pretty fast, actually. I'm kind of a big deal around here."

I do a double take. "Are you serious?"

Rye nods, like his sprinting prowess is something I should have known.

"But ... didn't you ... I thought you skipped P.E. yesterday because of some ..."

"Fin, I'm messing with you."

I laugh, my infamous honk laugh making its appearance once again. "Pretty fast *and* pretty funny," I say sarcastically.

"I know. I know."

We both smile at each other for what feels like a moment too long.

"Hey, I'll make you a bet," Rye says, breaking our gaze. "If I make it to D-block across the quad first, you have to tell me something you've never told anyone. If you win, I have to tell you the same."

I squint at him, wondering if he's serious. There's not a hint of a joke in his big almond eyes.

"Deal," I say, putting my hand out for him to shake.

With that he takes my hand, and as I wait for him to shake it, he lifts it up like I'm the Queen of England and pecks it with a kiss before bolting across the field.

I'm half stunned to the spot by what just happened when I realise I should be running. I tear off across the sloppy mud, the wind slapping my cheeks and the rain drenching my hair and clothes.

I'm gaining ground on him.

"Not bad for a Pittford boy," Rye shouts behind him, the dirt from his sneakers erupting from the ground like mini volcanoes.

"Not bad for a guy who shouldn't be running because of Saturn's retrograde!" I shout back.

I hear him burst out laughing as I close the distance between us.

We're neck and neck and both of us are smiling at each other. I have giant fireflies in my tummy, circling and spinning and doing backflips as I look at him. I desperately want to win. I want to know as much about him as I can.

We're thirty paces from D-block and I can feel a hardcore stitch coming on. We both slap the side of the building and collapse with our backs to the wall, heaving our breath like our lungs weigh a ton.

"I won," we say in unison, then catch each other's eyes and grin.

"No way," I say, shaking the rain from my fringe and out of my eyes. We are under a canopy but it's still hammering at the roof and pooling in puddles just outside our little sanctuary.

"Tie?" Rye says, his eyes pleading and giving me a feeling that makes me want to simultaneously faint and lean over to kiss him. (If that were possible … It *should so* be possible for this very moment.)

We sit breathing for a while. I glance sideways at his smooth skin and defined chest, the few tiny hairs sprouting from the V in his T-shirt. I guess him and Eric hang out at the gym together. I look back at my own body and feel mega self-conscious about what Rye would think of it.

"You wanna go first or should I?" he asks, getting his water bottle from his bag and taking a swig.

"I'll go," I say. "I once went to prison for grand theft auto."

Rye looks at me with his mouth open and his eyes round like the full moon.

I hold his gaze for as long as I can and then crack up laughing. He takes a moment and then is laughing too.

"You're so *weird*," Rye says between laughs. "In the best way."

I blush but I don't think he notices because he's still laughing.

"But seriously, what's your secret?" he asks once he has calmed down.

"To be honest? I kind of told you it last night …" I say.

"Moving here, you mean?" Rye asks, suddenly serious.

"Uh-huh. I didn't think I'd ever really talk about it. I figured

I'd keep it hidden and try to lie low until I was old enough to leave home and find a place of my own. High school's nearly over. College next, so depending on where I end up, I'll hopefully either get a scholarship and head to a dorm or I'll go and work and rent a room or something."

Rye looks at me with something deeper than sadness. It's not pity either. Maybe it's empathy pure and simple, but it looks like he wants to hug me. I sit on my hands to stop them from trembling.

"Fin, is it really that bad ... ? At home, I mean ..."

"I ... I mean I love my parents and ..." My throat becomes tight and I realise I sound a bit like Kermit the Frog. I cough to pull myself together. "I know they love me ... I know that. They just don't understand. They ..." I rub my face. "You know one of the things my dad said to me when he first found out?"

Rye shakes his head and his soft, sad smile encourages me to go on.

"He said, 'Life is hard enough, I don't want it to be any harder than it needs to be for you.'"

We both sit quietly for a second.

"Maybe he doesn't realise that the thing that's making life really hard for you right now, is him?" Rye says.

I can only nod in reply and, when I'm sure Rye isn't looking, I brush a tear from the corner of my eye. I don't want him to think I'm a complete mess of a human.

Rye goes to stand.

"Wait. Your turn," I say, standing to face him. "It was a tie remember?"

"I know," he says, looking deep into my eyes. "Not here, though. Are you free tonight?"

My heart skips a beat. "Yeah."

"Meet me at Kettle Lake at seven, deal?"

He puts his hand out for me to shake. And, because I'm feeling bolder than usual, I peck the top of it like he's the Queen of England now.

*

After school I practically run the entire way home. I haven't felt this buzzed since that one time when I drank four Red Bulls and ate a double pack of Pop Rocks and nearly collapsed. It's no longer raining but the humidity clings to my skin like a wet blanket.

When I get home there's a car I don't recognise in our drive. The house smells of expensive perfume and I hear a high-pitched squeal from the living room as I walk through the hall.

"Fin Whittle, as I live and breathe, how *tall* have you got?"

I groan as I instantly recognise the voice of Mum's friend, Alison Lane. They met back in grade school and have been in solid competition with each other ever since. When Alison got a minivan for her four kids, Mum suddenly got a new compact van for me and Elliot – totally unnecessary as Elliot was already driving and I caught the bus to school. When Alison got her hair done in a Katie Holmes bob, Mum did the same but instead somehow looked like she'd had her hair cut with a ceiling fan. Alison now conveniently lives in the next town over (yay for us) and helped with the move when we left Pittford.

I take a deep breath. "Hey, Mrs Lane," I say as she pulls me in for a hug and a kiss on each cheek. Great. Now I've got lipstick on my face.

"Your mum and I were just talking about Lorna from Pittford Parish."

"Lorna? Elliot's ex?"

"Exactly – apparently, she's gone *les-bi-an*." She enunciates the three syllables of lesbian like it's the most difficult word in the world.

Mum appears behind her. "Ali, your tea is getting cold."

This makes zero sense considering Alison has been talking to me for less than two minutes, but I'm glad for the rescue.

"Oh hey, I was just telling Fin here about *Lorna*," she stage whispers, conspiratorially. I must have cringed because next thing she's snapping at me, "Fin, dear, do stop it before the wind changes."

Mum looks fearful like she's expecting dancing unicorns in rainbow-striped socks to prance down the hall at the very mention of the word *les-bi-an*.

"Nice to see you, Mrs Lane," I say before heading up the stairs to my room.

I'm at the base of the ladder when I feel a hand on my shoulder and turn to find Mum.

"Fin, I …" she starts, then stops. "I'm sorry."

I blink, swallow and try to figure out what would be more beneficial: responding, or climbing the ladder and throwing myself back down it.

"For what?" I ask.

"For letting her … For letting Alison go on like that," Mum says, scrunching up her forehead as if only just realising how intensely awkward it all was. "I just … Forget it."

"No, what?" I ask.

"I … I just don't know how to do this … Any of this."

I'm stumped, out of words. I genuinely have no idea how to respond. Part of me wants to yell at her. She's my *mum* and it's not my job to make life easier for her. I don't get why I have to navigate for my parents while working everything out for myself, too.

But instead I just nod and head up to my room.

I shuffle some boxes around, certain I'll unpack more soon, and sift through my clothes box until I find my skinny jeans, a grey T-shirt and a burgundy sloppy sweater. I then get changed, lace my Converse up, throw on a grey slouch beanie and some fingerless gloves and head back down the ladder.

When I get outside Dad is just arriving home. His tie is loose and half of his shirt is untucked and scrunched up at the side.

I wave and he smiles. I'm relieved; he's in a good mood.

"Where are you off to?" he asks, brushing some dust off of his trouser leg.

"Just into town," I say.

"Meeting Poppy?"

"Nope, just thought it'd be good to take a walk before dinner."

"All right, then." He looks over my shoulder and groans. "Please tell me Alison is not in there."

I smile. Dad and I always used to laugh at how ridiculously conservative she is. (Yes, highly ironic now considering Dad carted us to a new town because he found out I like dudes.)

"She's in a mood. Have fun."

18

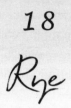

Of all the days for Mum to look after Barney – a Saint Bernard that belongs to one of her tarot clients – today was not the day. The giant fluffy mess reminds me of Cujo (if Cujo didn't kill people), and I love all eighty-two kilos of him, but the last thing I needed when I walked out of my room, feeling good in my checked Sherpa jacket, black jeans and Timberland boots, was to be given a slobbery kiss from Barney.

"Fuck," I yell, holding his ginormous head back and scratching his ears.

"Language," Mum says, appearing from a closet by the dining room as if by magic.

"Sorry but – hey can you – just… it's… maybe don't… BARNEY."

His big dopey eyes look up at me and he flumps down on his belly.

"Oooh, you've done it now B-man," Mum says, grabbing some white vinegar and baking soda from the kitchen shelf and dabbing it on my T-shirt while Thelma runs over and sits by my feet, looking down at Barney like the teacher's pet that she is.

"Thanks," I say to Mum who is already luring Barney away from me with a YumYummy dog cookie she buys in bulk from the farmer's market. Thelma looks on with jealousy burning in her eyes, a feeling I try to ease by giving her a legendary ear scratch.

"Where are you off to this fine evening?" Mum says.

"Poppy," I say, avoiding eye contact.

"Poppy?" Mum says, shutting the door as Barney attempts to bound back inside.

"Yep." I'm still attempting to avoid meeting her gaze for longer than a moment. I don't want to talk to her about Fin just yet.

"*Interesting*," Mum says, barely blinking.

I give her a look that says, *What are you talking about?*

"It's just I saw Isla when I went to McElroy's tonight to pick up some chips and she said Poppy was –"

"Eric," I say. "I'm going to see Eric." Another lie, I know. But I don't really feel like talking about Fin right now, especially as we're just hanging out as friends.

Mum doesn't say anything for what feels like an hour.

"Right," she says at last, nodding slowly.

"Yep."

"Are you and Eric … you know, okay?"

"Sure."

"Sure?"

"Sure," I say, grabbing my phone from the bench, giving Thelma one final chin rub and a kiss on the nose and heading out the front door.

From the top of our street I can see the sunset start to dip below the horizon and cast an orange glow that looks like the sky is on fire. From up here I can see McElroy's Fish & Chippie and a couple of old fishermen casting off from the wharf.

I take a left down Briar Avenue and follow it past the mechanic's. The owner, Roy, walks like a duck and spits when he talks like he's fresh from the Wild West. I give him a wave and nearly jump into the bushes when a loud honk erupts from behind me. I'm convinced I'm about to be bonnet-rolled by a truck.

"Doctor Jones" by Aqua is blasting on the stereo as I turn to look and see Poppy, laughing her head off.

"You're so *jumpy*," she says, throwing her head back to laugh silently like that old Muttley cartoon dog.

"Yes, Pops, it's called anxiety, remember?" I say, opening the door and getting in. She owes me a ride to Kettle Lake for nearly making me literally shit my pants in the middle of the street.

"God, you're funny, Rye-bread."

I roll my eyes and open the window; the air caressing my face is the best feeling I've had all day.

"Can you drop me near the lake?" I ask.

"Okey smokey," she says, taking a cigarette from the glove compartment and lighting it.

"Ew," I say, taking it out of her hand and butting it out in the pull-out ashtray.

"Hey!"

"No, don't even. It's 2020, and that habit is disgusting."

"Sheesh. Who made you the anti-smoking police?"

"I just would love to inhale the fresh air without that filth blowing all over my face."

Poppy lets out a snort. "Speaking of blowing all over your face … You off to meet Eric?"

She's a disgrace, but I love her. "No, actually. I'm meeting Fin."

Poppy's eyes light up but before she can get too carried away, I change the conversation.

"I'm definitely heading to Eric's tomorrow, by the way. The guy deserves a second chance."

The spark seems to dim in her eyes but she keeps talking. "*Head*-ing to Eric's?"

"My god, you're gross," I say. It's not that I don't find it kinda funny talking about that stuff, but I can't find the fun in it when she talks about Eric. I feel so much pressure around him and it takes all the excitement away.

"And you're a repressed prude," Poppy says, grabbing another cigarette from the glove compartment and lighting it before I can snatch it away.

I feign an asthma attack and she slaps me on the arm. I give in. Poppy always wins.

"Why are they called 'glove compartments'?" Poppy asks as she snaps it shut. "There's nothing but the car manual in there."

"It used to be for gloves I guess. You know, *driving* gloves." I pause. "But then, don't you think cars should come with gloves if that's the case?"

"You're truly weird," Poppy says.

"No, I'm not. It's that putrid smoke messing with my thought process."

"Or Fin."

I turn and glare at her.

"Oh, come on Rye. Don't act like you haven't thought about him. About those big eyes. That big –"

"Jesus, Poppy. What is *wrong* with you tonight?"

"– smile, Rye. His big *smile*. But thanks for sharing where your mind is at." She does this over-exaggerated wink and I crack a smile. Poppy needs to be on TV. Or in an asylum. Or in an asylum on TV.

∗

Poppy drops me off at the old dirt path that leads up towards Kettle Lake and suddenly I'm nervous. I don't know why. It's not like Fin and I have ever said more than a few words to each other. He's only been here a week or so. We don't call each other and dissect new Netflix series like me and Poppy or have Skype sing-along sessions like me and June.

Yet here I am, walking in the direction of a place I've been coming to my entire life, like it's perched atop a sheer cliff.

The sun is practically gone, but you wouldn't know it. Everything is glowing orange and the trees feel alive. I know my mum's hippie ways have rubbed off on me, but I'm actually really stoked. I take off my shoes so I can walk barefoot. Nothing beats being outside in this. The sound of the lake in the distance gets my heart going and, sure enough, as I round the corner I see Fin.

He's facing the water and doesn't hear me. I stand and watch him for a minute. He looks self-conscious, running his hands through his hair a few times and bouncing up and down on his heels.

"Nice, huh?" I say, leaning over his shoulder.

He jumps.

"Hey! I mean, yeah!" His face turns red almost instantly. "Do you come here often?" he says, and I can't help but laugh. He's really cute when he's nervous, even though I'm not sure why he's nervous. Or why I am for that matter.

"Nice line," I say and he looks at me puzzled. "Are you trying to pick me up?"

"Pick you – oh *god*. Sorry. I wasn't trying to be like, funny, or anything. I was –"

"It's cool, Fin."

"Cool." He nods about thirty times in a row.

"Cool."

I walk around the edge of the water and I hear Fin kick off his shoes and follow behind me.

Our feet are in sync as they crunch on the pebbles and I let the cool water tickle my toes as we near my spot.

When I first started coming to Kettle Lake, Mum suggested I make it my own somehow. She explained that, when my anxiety was bad, I could come here and feel like I was in another peaceful home. An old driftwood tree hangs low near the water creating a cave-like spot that over time I've attempted to furnish. Inside sits a rustic old blanket that Aunt Sandy gave Mum years ago, a bunch of small lanterns strung up in the tree, a makeshift kennel I crafted using some bits of washed up driftwood for when I bring Thelma, and a wooden box in which I keep a couple of empty jars that I sometimes use to catch fireflies before letting them go again.

I crawl in and pat the blanket next to me, then instantly regret it because I'm scared he will think I'm coming on to him. Fin hesitates before rolling up his neat sleeves and crawling in after me. He dusts the sand from his feet and trousers and looks around like a meerkat.

"This is AMAZING," he says, touching Thelma's driftwood house like it's made of gold.

"Nah, it's just my little cove."

"I wish I had somewhere like this," Fin says, taking in the string lights.

"Well, you can use this whenever you like," I say, my cheeks burning the moment the words leave my mouth. I have no idea why I'm so weird around this guy. He's not really my type. Not that I even really know my type. Eric has a decent body I guess, which is kind of awesome, but it's more the smile and eyes that get me. Fin has nice eyes. His smile is pretty rad too. His lips are plush as well and ... Okay. Enough. This is insane.

"So, how long have you actually been coming here?" Fin asks.

"Since I was about five. The decor was Mum's idea."

"Nice. What do your parents do?"

He's being sweet and I can feel his nervousness pulsing through his skin.

"Mum's got a lot of feathers in her bow ... Cleaner, tarot reader, crystal healer, naturopath and massage therapist to name a few. Dad's not around."

"Okay, firstly, that's amazing about your mum. Second, sorry about your dad."

"No, I mean. He's not dead. Well, not that I know of."

Fin nods.

"He left ... When I was a kid."

He nods again.

"Alcohol, drugs, anything he could get his hands on ... It's ... He went to rehab for a bit. Got out, stayed clean but then ... I guess ..."

Fin's eyes are wide.

"I'm sorry, this is heavy talk. We don't have to –"

"Oh god, no. Are you serious? We can talk about it ... If you want ... But not if – like only if it's ... If you want."

He's crazy keen to do the right thing and it makes me smile. I don't know quite why, but he's outrageously adorable.

I take a breath. "Dad and Mum used to fight a lot and when he came out of rehab and relapsed things were different. Darker. Like he had tried and failed and then totally given up. He walked out one night and we haven't heard from him again since."

Fin is staring at me, really staring, like he's listening with all his heart. He blinks. "I'm so sorry."

I shrug, pulling up some grass around my ankles. Fin does the same near his. We sit for a bit and listen to the sound of the crickets and cicadas clicking and humming.

"What about you?" I ask. "What else don't I know about Fin?"

He smiles and something happens inside my tummy. Some weird buzzing that I haven't had before.

"What do you want to know?"

Everything I think, but instead say, "What's your favourite food?"

"Hmm. Pizza."

"Wait, out of everything on the planet, Pizza is your favourite food?"

"Uh-huh." Fin's deadly serious. "Wait no, Pop Tarts."

I blink and hold back a laugh. "So, if you were stranded on a desert island and had literally nothing but Pop Tarts, you'd be happy?"

"I'd be ecstatic," Fin says, cracking that perfect smile again. "What about you?"

"Probably ... mango. Wait, no, kiwi fruit. I love kiwi fruit."

Fin rolls his eyes sarcastically. "Oh okay, mister 'my body is a temple' health-nut."

I give him a nudge and laugh, then instantly feel self-conscious.

He keeps glancing over at me as we both stare out at the lake. It's almost dark and so I light some of the little lanterns and we sit in silence for a while.

Something is happening and I don't really understand what. Fin makes me nervous in the best possible way. He looks over at me again and smiles and even in this semi-darkness I can see him blushing.

As the last flicker of sunlight disappears I have that same feeling again, that bumbling in my tummy that feels like lightning mixed with helicopter propellers, like I'm running downhill, like … I look up as my mind searches for the word. A flicker catches the corner of my eye. Then another and another. The lake is glowing, the reeds look like they've been hit by fairy dust and the night erupts and comes alive. It's absolutely beautiful. They're everywhere.

Fireflies.

19

Fin

What the hell is happening right now? Is Rye flirting with me or am I losing my mind? Did I just say *Pop Tarts* when he asked me what I'd eat if I was stranded on a desert island? What in the fresh hell is wrong with me? Am I five?

I cannot believe I am sitting here with this guy, in this unreal makeshift Neverland cave thing that he has created, talking about nothing and everything and watching fireflies – yes, *actual fireflies* – burst to life around us. I feel like I'm in a fairy tale. All I need now is a little red crab to start singing and I'd be in my element.

Rye looks up at me and I'm almost certain he can see me blushing, even though it's practically pitch black now besides the lanterns and fireflies and – see what I mean? Lanterns and fireflies? What?!

"They're beautiful," I say, gesturing to the thousands of blinking lights that dip and dance through the reeds and brush.

Rye nods, with a faint hint of a smile. "It's – did you ever see that movie *Swiss Family Robinson*?" he asks.

"Nope," I say.

"Me neither," he says and I burst out laughing.

He cracks a smile too. "I mean, not the whole way through. I just remember my dad watching it a couple of weeks before he left. I must've been about five. They lived in this insane treehouse and lived off the land. It looked so peaceful. Maybe it was the family thing I was looking for – they all seemed so happy. So together."

"Families are weird," I say which makes him smile.

"Yeah." Then: "When Dad left I came here and tried to make my own hideaway like the movie. I mean, it's not a treehouse, but I always feel better after coming here. I get ... My anxiety messes with me sometimes."

"As in, like, panic attacks or ...?" I ask, tentatively.

"Sometimes. Mostly it's just this morbid, terrified feeling inside that doesn't shake. It can be specific, like getting sick or crashing my boat or losing Thelma. And then it can just come out of nowhere and I feel terrified of nothing and everything all at once."

Nobody has ever spoken so openly with me before. Not about stuff like this.

"Did it start when your dad left?" I ask. Then, quickly: "Sorry – you come here to relax. This is probably the last thing you want to discuss with a random new guy at school who –"

"No, it's fine," he says and gently touches my arm which sends my heart into the atmosphere. "Dad leaving was definitely something. The drugs and alcohol was what scared me, though. Seeing someone you love and depend on lose all control and not remember what they've done or said the next day is terrifying. I mean I was five, so I don't remember it all, but what I do –"

I let the words settle around us as he stares off across the lake.

"That sounds pretty rough, but I think you've turned out pretty awesome," I say softly, because I don't care if he thinks I'm pathetic. I really don't. Rye *is* awesome. He deserves to know.

He looks over and smiles, holding my gaze.

"I think you're pretty great too," he says, his words quieter than before.

He stares kind of intensely at my mouth, at my bottom lip before quickly looking away and I feel my body hum.

Rye gazes out at the lake and ruffles his hair, his curls landing wherever they want. He takes his phone out of his pocket and opens up his music library. I try to get a glimpse but I know he's not a big fan of Broadway musical numbers, so I'm assuming he's into hipster bands or something. What I don't expect is Fleetwood Mac's "Landslide" to start playing. I love this song.

"This okay?" he asks, looking up at me like I'm some world-renowned DJ and like *I'd* be judging *him* on his music.

"I love Fleetwood Mac," I say.

"You do?"

"Oh my god, are you kidding? They're legendary."

He smiles.

I smile back.

We sit and listen; the crickets and bullfrogs trying to harmonise with Stevie Knicks.

"My friend Emily back in Pittford gave me the thirty-fifth anniversary vinyl of *Rumours* for my birthday last year," I say, desperate to break the silence.

Rye's looks over at me so fast I worry he will get whiplash. "*What?!*"

"Yeah, but I don't have a record player." I laugh. Emily's the most thoughtful friend I've ever had, but she would always forget stuff – like me not having a record player for her vinyl gift or making a stack of PBJ sandwiches for a picnic one afternoon, which we had to cancel and instead listen to music in her car when I reminded her, for the sixteenth time, that I'm allergic to nuts.

"*I have one!*" Rye says, practically shouting. "Oh my god, this is meant to be." His cheeks flush, adorably. "I mean –"

I laugh. He's fidgeting and averting his eyes. He's too sweet. I'm talking next level adorable right now and – he has a boyfriend. *He has a boyfriend.* Enough. I need to stop looking into everything. Nothing could ever possibly happen between us. It's not just the boyfriend thing. Yeah, this won't end well.

"Landslide" finishes and "Dreams" by the Cranberries starts playing.

"Nice," I say as I go to pull up some grass and feel Rye do the same. Our hands brush each other and linger for longer than half a second. The tips of his fingers are semi-holding my knuckles and we both kind of freeze. It happens in the space of a few seconds but feels like an eternity of a million emotions as I look up at him and he looks back. I feel lightheaded and full of energy as we both half-smile before awkwardly moving our hands apart. What I wouldn't give for another few seconds of lightly touching his hands.

The cicadas all go silent in harmony and the only sounds now are Rye's music and the water lapping up along the pebbles.

I notice the sound of his breath. The few hairs sprouting up around his defined chest. He smells like herbal deodorant and lavender and his jaw looks clenched, like he is trying to avoid saying something.

"Have you –" he says when his phone lights up and the song cuts off, interrupted by two loud beeps. I can't help but read the message that appears on the screen.

Eric: Wanna chat?

Whatever Rye was about to say evaporates into the reeds as he unlocks his phone and begins typing. I don't look, not because I think it inappropriate, but because I really don't want to know what he's saying to his boyfriend.

"I um ... I should go ..." Rye says, looking down at his shoes.

"Yeah ... Of course. Sounds good."

Sounds good? What did I say that for?

Rye stands and offers me his hand. I take it and he pulls me up. We brush the bark and sand from our clothes and when we turn back, we are both standing extremely close to each other. Rye is taller than me but not by a whole lot. We're basically touching chests.

"Thanks," I say, feeling my breath catch.

We stand for a moment longer and then make our way out towards the water's edge.

"I'll see you at school?" Rye says.

I nod, forcing myself to smile.

Then, trying not to let what feels horribly like jealousy creep into my voice: "Have fun ..."

... chatting to Eric.

20

Rye

The next evening, as I head over to Eric's, I'm still thinking about what happened between Fin and me at Kettle Lake. I feel weird. Not entirely in a bad way either. Weird like when you eat a bag of pop rocks and even though they are *so amazingly good*, you also know you probably shouldn't have eaten all of them, ya know?

As I left, I turned back to see Fin looking over at me. Clearly I am as uncool as I thought I was because he smiled and I smiled and then I immediately felt my cheeks burn.

Ugh, what is going on?

I check my phone and see a text from Eric. Two emojis: the eggplant and the purple devil one. I roll my eyes. Eric is the kind of guy who expects you to be sexually ready whenever he feels like it, yet when he doesn't feel like hanging out, he'll avoid you like the plague – which currently feels like 99.9% of the time. Great stuff.

I arrive onto Bayview Road and start walking towards his place. I don't think it's probably the best thing that I'm not exactly looking forward to seeing my boyfriend, but then again, he's my first "proper" boyfriend. Who the hell knows what any of this is supposed to feel like?

The sky is alight with a million stars and I take a second to stare up at them. I inhale and let the mist from the ocean bring me back to the now. I can feel my insides trembling and I know I'm anxious. My head is swimming and my shoulders are tight and even though nothing is happening that I should be profoundly anxious about, I can't help it. My body seems to seek it out.

I turn a corner and am not far from Eric's when my phone buzzes and another text appears on the screen.

Poppy: I'm done with June.

Not again. I really don't have time for this right now, but it kind of helps me feel less guilty about not being overly excited to see Eric and so I turn and head across the road.

I take a seat on the grass against a whitewashed picket fence. Eric's told me that the mansion behind me belongs to a Mr Knight, who owns half of Lochport. I hope the sight of me bothers him, the miserable old bastard.

I unlock my phone and another message comes through like a dodgeball.

Poppy: She's impossible and I'm done.

I attempt to write a text but instead just dial her number and call. I don't have the finger strength to keep up with her when she's erratic like this.

"Ugh," she says when she answers.

"You okay?" I ask.

"Far from it. So far from it."

"What happened?"

"Oh, just June being June."

"Use your words, Pops."

"Don't patronise me. It started because I told her I couldn't make the QSA meeting next week and she got pissed because apparently I 'don't put in enough effort' with the alliance."

I inhale slowly, waiting for her to go on.

"I mean, what? Because I have other things to do besides go to a meeting and talk about fixing a world that will always be broken?"

"Woah, Poppy. Let's just ... Can we take a breath for a second? This is way too deep for a fight over a QSA meeting."

I can hear her sniff and I wonder if she's been crying.

"It's more than that though. She's always going on about how privileged I am and how my being a pan white girl while she's a trans person of colour is something that makes us so different. Apparently, I will never know what it's like and that's why we always break up and –"

"But, I mean ..." I say, tentatively. "She kind of has got a point there."

"What?" Poppy says, a hint of ice in her voice.

"Well, I mean, she's right. You don't know what it's like being trans and a person of colour. I'm not saying you don't have your own struggles and stuff, not by any stretch of the ima–"

"So, what are you saying then?" Poppy barges in, bluntly.

I do *not* need this right now. "Poppy. I love you. Please, don't go there with this. I am trying to see things from both sides here."

"And I love you for that, Rye. I really do. But sometimes I would love it if you were on my side. You know, just wholly on my side for a change."

I shake my head. "Did you ask her to get back together again?"

Poppy is quiet for a while and I realise this is what started the argument to begin with. Poppy is always the first to break things off with June but also the first to run back and beg to start over.

"Maybe you should stay being single for a while, Pops?" I say, trying to send good vibes down the phone.

"Maybe," she says, and I think I've won her back over. Thank fuck.

"What are you up to?" she asks.

"About to go to Eric's."

"Speaking of fun relationships," she says with a hint of aggression.

"Okay, I'm gonna go," I say, throwing back her sassiness with an extra dollop of it for good measure.

When I knock on Eric's front door, I hear him slowly make his way to answer it.

"Babe," he says, his eyes glossy like marbles.

"Hi," I say, doing everything I can not to turn around and leave. I can tell immediately that he's high and I feel my blood boil. The bonus so far is that he isn't *completely* off his tree. He's just mellow and acting all mushy. To be honest, it's kind of a nice change from the usual shrug-off I get whenever I see him.

"You're so cute," he says, tapping my nose with a "bop" and taking my hand.

I follow him into the house. His parents clearly aren't home because there are pizza boxes scattered around and three crushed beer cans dumped in the fruit bowl. It looks like the sort of bizarre contemporary sculpture that some highbrow art critic would like.

"Big night?" I ask, taking my shoes off and wandering over to the couch.

"Not really. Just watched some Netflix, ate some pizza, thought about my boyfriend." He looks over at me with this puppy dog face and I can't help but smile. Sometimes, he's kind of adorable.

"And the weed?" I ask, holding my anger at bay but still trying to show him that I'm unimpressed.

He rolls his eyes. "Babe, c'mon. I had one teeny-tiny joint with the guys after the gym and then ate some Pringles. I'm not injecting heroin into my eyeballs."

I shake my head but he doesn't seem to notice.

I run my hands through my hair as Eric yawns and stretches. I can see the V of his abs where his shirt rides up, a trail of fine blond hair leading below his underwear. I feel tingly all of a sudden when he looks over at me and smiles.

"Did I ever tell you that you have the most amazing eyes?" he says, slowly making his way over to me.

I'm trying to make a point of being mad at him, but my horny hormones are telling me different. Plus, his tight sweatpants show off his sculpted legs and the singlet he's wearing does wonders for his chest and arms.

"No, you don't usually say much like that," I say, my voice surprisingly soft.

Before I know what's happening, he's kissing me and I'm kissing him back, hard. His sleepy eyes have come alive and his body presses up against mine with a strength that almost makes me gasp.

His hands lower towards my jeans, but I shift to the side as we keep kissing. I don't know why but I don't want to go further than this. This feels so good and I'm loving the way his body feels against mine, but as his hips press into mine I'm suddenly aware of how intense he's being.

It's kind of frightening.

"Hey," I say, soothingly, trying to talk to him and at the same time take a breath to stop him from eating my face. "Let's just chill for a bit."

We're lying on the couch now and he takes my legs, wrapping them around his waist as I force a fake laugh.

"C'mon. Let's just watch some TV and –"

"I've had enough of TV," he says, reaching for my pants again. "I want you."

"It's … can you – Eric. Stop," I say, but he isn't stopping. He's got this fierce, blank look in his eyes and his hands are too strong for me. I can feel my heart beating quicker and panic settling in like a strong current.

"C'mon, Rye. Just go with it. I've been patient. Let's just –"

I deliberately slow my breathing as he becomes more insistent, more aggressive.

"No, stop," I say more loudly, but Eric in no way eases off. "Eric, really, no –" His weight is on me and I'm full of stress and fear, my whole body's jittery with it. Anxiety is turning my mind dark and my heart feels like it's about to burst through my ribcage.

Eric is pulling his sweatpants down. "Rye, come *on* –"

It's like he hasn't heard a word I've said.

Enough is enough. I need to do something.

"GET OFF!" I shout so loud I feel my chest vibrate.

I brace myself, then push him hard off of me and stand, my breathing fast and haphazard as I try to figure out what the hell to do next.

"Rye, just – c'mon, don't be like this."

"What the hell is the matter with you?" I shout. I feel nothing but contempt at the sight of him, but my voice is strong and without a hint of the vulnerability I'm actually feeling.

He does this sulky shrug and eye-roll thing that sets all my anger on fire. I can't believe just a few minutes ago I found him actually adorable or hot, even. That feeling of contempt is strong. And – yes – there's more than a bit of fear, too.

"You think that was okay?" I demand. "You think when I'm telling you no, it's okay to ignore me?"

He interlaces his hands behind his head and barely looks up.

"Fuck you, Eric," I say, turning to leave.

As I get to the door, I hear his pathetic reply: "Yeah, if only."

I slam the front door behind me and head into the night.

*

I walk through the streets, turning corner after corner, and don't even realise I'm crying until I taste the salt on my lips. I feel sick at how awful that was. How scary it felt to say no and have him disregard me. What is *wrong* with me? Why do I keep putting up with him? Does he actually think that, just because he's fit, he's got a licence to treat me like this?

I arrive at Kettle Lake and crawl into my hideout. As my heart rate slows, I feel an overwhelming desperation to sob and sob and sob. I just don't get it. I don't get why it's so bad to want something more than making out and all the other stuff. Why is it weird to want someone to sweep me off my feet as I sweep them off theirs and tell me I mean something to them? To have that happy-ever-after that everyone else seems to enjoy? Or even just a normal hang-out without any of this awful, toxic pressure.

I lie back and let the leaves crunch around me.

My phone vibrates and I know it's not Eric. He's way too stubborn to bother chasing after me.

Poppy: I managed to have another fight with June . . .

I shake my head. That's twice in one day. Poppy and June really are hopeless.

Me: That makes two of us.

Poppy: You're fighting with June too?

Me: No, Eric.

Poppy: Go figure.

Then again, maybe Eric and I are hopeless too.

Me: You wanna do something?

Poppy: You at your spot?

I send a thumbs-up emoji.

Soon enough Poppy is sitting with me while I ugly cry into the crook of my arm. Not even the presence of the fireflies makes me feel any better. The worst part is that I know that I can only give him so many chances. Maybe it's not working out with Eric for a reason. And I'm starting to realise that that reason has nothing to do with me.

"What you thinking about?" Poppy asks, looking over at me and giving me a nudge.

"Life," I say, rubbing my eyes and sniffing up some phlegm from the back of my throat.

"So deep, Rye. And gross. Do you want a tissue or . . .?" She hands me a Kleenex from the inside pocket of her denim jacket. "Rye, I think this needs to stop."

I let the words fall around me. She's right. I can't argue with her anymore. So I just sit.

"What's the go with you and June?" I say after a while.

"That's something else that needs to stop," Poppy says. She seems to say it to herself more than me.

"Poppy, June really loves you," I say.

"Rye, just …" She trails off and stares across the lake, where the reflection of the fireflies on the water makes them seem to double in number.

"You know what I think?" Poppy asks, clearly onto a rapid change of subject.

"What?" I ask.

"It's only eight o'clock. I think we need to scoop Fin up and then go stuff our faces with pancakes."

I can't help but smile. Regardless of the situation, Poppy's answer to everything is pancakes. It could be the apocalypse and her first course of action would be to stop at the Parlour and smash a twelve-stack. I love her for it.

We head to her car and start driving towards Fin's place.

"It's on Angeleno Avenue. The one with the big red – there it is!" Poppy says as we pull over to the kerb and take in the *Gone With the Wind*-style house that stands before us.

"This is definitely a murder house or something," she says, staring up at the giant columns that surround the entryway.

"For *sure*," I say as we exit the car and head towards the red front door. "There is no way anyone going to Lochport High could afford to live someplace like this unless someone was killed in the basement."

Poppy knocks three times and then hits the doorbell which seems to echo all the way to the back yard, which I'm guessing is enormous too.

"I'll get it," we hear Fin say from inside.

When he opens the door, he stares at us like we've just thrown a brick through the window. A brick with a love note attached, but a brick, nonetheless. It's a look of happiness mixed with intense panic.

"R-Rye. Hey … Poppy – It's …"

His eyes dart between us and the blood drains from his face. Maybe that murder story is true after all.

"Hey," I say, unsure what's going on. "You okay?"

At that moment a woman with a dark bob haircut – I'm assuming his mother – comes up behind him.

There's a second where Fin looks like he might collapse at our feet.

"Hello, there," the woman says brightly, yet at the same time regarding us both like we could potentially be handing out flyers for a satanic gathering.

I say hello as I try to put on my best "meet the parents" face, but I still feel a bit ridiculous.

"Hi, Mrs Whittle," Poppy says, beaming her best over-the-top smile and leaning in to shake her hand. "I'm Poppy. This is my friend Rye." She gestures to me like I'm the first prize at a raffle. "We were just nearby and thought we'd see if Fin would like to get pancakes with us."

The corner of Fin's lip trembles upward into a half-smile and beads of sweat form across his forehead.

"You're Poppy?" she asks, intrigued, as she glances between Fin and Poppy and then looks, slightly puzzled, at me. It's like I'm interrupting something. This whole thing feels off.

"I am. I'm sure Fin has spoken non-stop about my charm and good looks," she says with a grin.

Mrs Whittle smiles a little awkwardly and turns to Fin. "Very charming," she says, still confused as if she's pondering something. "Would your … friends like to come in?"

Fin looks completely panicked as her words sort of hang in the air.

"I … Mum, it's okay. I'm …" Fin's face turns purple and he stares at us unblinkingly. "I'll see you guys at school," he says, then closes the door.

Poppy and I stare each other for a solid thirty seconds and don't say a word. The only thoughts in both of our minds is clear:

What the hell was that about?

21

Fin

I feel like my heart is going to punch a hole right through my ribcage like that scene in *Alien*. Why would they just show up at my front door? No warning. No message? Then it hits me: because they're my friends. That's what friends do. They know one another's families. They know one another's history and they are open and honest. I suddenly feel like a horrible person for dragging them into the clusterfuck that is my life right now. I also feel ridiculous for making such a big deal out of this. Mum didn't even seem to notice that I'm obsessed with Rye, or that Poppy absolutely isn't my girlfriend.

I follow Mum back into the kitchen and she runs her hands through her hair, making sure her bob is a perfect helmet of respectability. She pats her clothes and then with a quick shake of the head she is back at the chopping board dicing onions like nothing happened. Not that anything even *did* happen. My two friends from school turned up to see if I wanted pancakes – that's it. My two friends, one of whom I'm painfully attracted to and the other one of whom I virtually told my parents is my girlfriend.

What. A. Mess.

But even so, I help cut up some vegetables and mix some gravy and within an hour Dad is home and we are around the dinner table. I'm barely halfway through my first bite of meatloaf when the front doorbell sounds again. I could very well go into cardiac arrest at any moment. My cheeks prickle and turn numb.

We sit and stare at one another and eventually Dad gets up, striding over to the door with a look of mild concern etched across his face. I'm right on his heels, thinking on my feet about what I'm going to say for round two of "Meet the Parents" when the door opens and a stranger is standing there on the step. His hair looks shaggy and unwashed and his face is stubbly like he hasn't shaved properly in weeks. Funnily enough he has this fresh look about him, regardless of the congealed sweat and dirt that sticks to his forehead, he seems really *alive*.

"Sally, I think you need to sign for this," Dad shouts back into the dining room. He smiles and puts a finger to his lips so both of us keep quiet and go along with it. His sudden playfulness is disconcerting – I haven't seen him joke around for what feels like ages.

Behind us Mum is fussing around with chairs and cutlery and muttering to herself.

"I mean, it's nine o'clock in the evening, do they have *no* consideration for any – ELLIOT!"

Mum grabs him and pulls him in for a bear hug. Dad and I jump in shortly after. I'm not sure how long exactly it's been – I think half a year at least – since we last saw him and he's still the same old Elliot yet something is different about him. He's been hit by something strange (lightning isn't out of the question from the state of his hair), something unusually life-affirming by the looks of it. He seems to have filled out, grown up, become an adult.

We head into the dining room and Mum rustles up Elliot a plate. Before long, life feels like it has morphed back to some sort of normality. We could as well be living in Pittford five years ago. It's as if nothing has happened. There's no speak of *why* we are here or what caused the major uproot. Or what has transformed my brother into an adult. Elliot just asks the basic questions: How's work? How's school? How's the new town?

It's a little unnerving.

It's nearly ten o'clock by the time Elliot is on to his story about tarantulas the size of dinner plates and I realise I'm falling asleep with my eyes open.

But I'm still listening as he tells us about the Borneo rainforest and how he volunteered at a sanctuary for orphaned orangutans and became friends with a particularly sweet one named Buttercup. His phone is passed around the table so we can admire the photos. Some of him with a wheelbarrow full of big-eyed fluffy orangutans; others of him dancing under cascading waterfalls. Some sipping tea in glass cups outside a little hut as the sun goes down. It's pretty impressive, but I'm still struggling with the consciousness thing until I hear him change the subject.

"How's Lorna?" he asks Mum and I flinch at the thought of what's coming.

"Oh hun, you *don't* want to know," Mum says, knocking her food around her plate with her fork as if Lorna being an openly gay woman is one of the most embarrassing, unspeakable things that could ever happen.

"Yeah I do," Elliot says, eyes wide and unblinking in a way that is completely innocent and Elliot-like. He's never been any good at reading the room.

"Son, it's…" Dad makes a *pfft* motion with his hand, as if sweeping the conversation out of the way. "So, how was Brazil?" he says, changing the subject.

I put my head down as I feel my cheeks begin to burn. This is too mortifying.

Elliot laughs. "You two are being so weird. How's *Lorna*?" he asks, looking at me and frowning for half a second before beaming his silly smile to Mum and Dad.

"She's a lesbian," I say. My voice comes out from somewhere quiet within me and I feel my throat catch those few words and want to swallow them back like a shot of vodka.

Elliot pauses for a second and then looks up at us and smiles.

"Oh, cool … Great," he says, before taking a mouthful of broccoli. "See? That wasn't hard, was it? Thank you, Fin."

Did he just call his ex-girlfriend being a lesbian "great"?

I feel like I'm about to pass out. Elliot has never been like this before. He's so … chilled with himself and at ease with this unusual-for-us conversation. I know he's being genuine too, because there's not a hint of sarcasm or malice in his voice.

"And Brazil was rad," he says to Dad, popping the intensely awkward bubble that has surrounded all of us.

Mum and Dad shift in their seats. I feel like my mouthful of meatloaf is about to take a projectile course across the table.

"I wouldn't necessarily call it 'great', Elliot," Dad says, as pompously as if the air sucked from the room has now puffed up his chest.

Elliot smiles his innocent smile again, but I suddenly see through it. He's challenging Dad and I don't quite know why.

"What would you call it then, Dad?" he asks, his face unfaltering.

Mum charges through the awkwardness like a Marvel comic hero crashing through a building that's on fire. "That's enough for one night, I think."

Dad and Elliot stare at one another for a beat before Elliot stands and helps tidy away the dishes like the excellent son he is.

An excellent brother, too? Maybe, just maybe, Elliot will be equally as chilled when he finds out exactly why we had to move to Lochport.

Feeling dizzy, I give my brother a hug, tell him I'm glad he's home, wish everyone goodnight and head to my room. Somehow, I don't feel so alone.

I sense myself drift off before my head even hits the pillow, glad that sleep has always been my escape when life gets hectic.

*

As I walk into school the following morning the sun beams down on the back of my neck. I keep my head down and my eyes on my Converse. I don't really know if I want to see Poppy and Rye. I am praying to the universe to give me a day to just go to school, eat and come home. I cannot deal with this constant feeling of strangeness that weighs down so heavily on my chest.

I get to my locker and my prayers are immediately rejected when Poppy walks over, cautiously, like she's approaching a caged lion.

"You okay?" she asks quietly.

I nod. "I'm so sorry about last night ... about ..." I say, but I have no idea where else to go with my sentence. I can't seem to figure out what happened either.

"Don't be," Poppy says, holding up her hand to stop me from taking a one-way train to panic town.

"Where's Rye?" I ask, scanning the corridors to see if he's nearby.

"He's devastated," Poppy says as she twists a curl of hair around her finger. "About Eric, I mean. They had another fight. But I keep telling him and he doesn't do anything..." She sighs and leans back against the locker.

I'm about to say how it's probably a lot more difficult when you're actually in his situation but don't get the words out because June appears seemingly out of thin air and is standing in front of Poppy, her eyes glazed and her nose snotty. Not her usual look at all.

"Can we talk?"

"June, not now, I –"

"Poppy. Please."

I turn and face my locker, feeling extremely awkward. Seems not just Rye and Eric had an argument last night. When I turn back around Poppy and June have left and, thankfully, I'm able to take a breath. Just in time for Rye to show up and punch the wind right out of me again with those eyes of his.

"Hey."

"Hey," I say, wiping my forehead with the back of my hand.

He looks awful. His eyes are sunken and dark rings give him a panda look.

"How ar– stupid question," I say, shaking my head.

He smiles. "How are *you* would be the easier question right now," he says, brushing a curl from out of his eyes.

"I'm ... yeah. Firstly, I'm so sorry about last night."

"Yeah what was that?" Rye asks, looking at me curiously, like his friendly visit had revealed I moonlight as a stripper at Legs Eleven.

"It's ... I actually don't even know where to begin. But I'm sorry." Rye waves his hand and his eyes scan my face and then my chest. I have this feeling he's checking me out, but soon enough his eyes are back on mine and an innocent smile is plastered across his face.

"My brother Elliot just got home so ... I mean that's good." I don't know why this is important information or why Rye would be remotely interested, but there you go. I'd give him the pin to my ATM card if he asked. This guy does something to me that I've never felt before. I want to tell him everything and I want to know everything about him.

"That's awesome," he says. "Are you close?"

"Yeah. I mean we were or ... no, we are. He's –"

"Fin, are you okay?"

The past twenty-four hours have sent me all over the place emotionally and I don't really have a clue what's going on. The only good thing I can think of is that Elliot seems to be someone I can count on right now. I need that.

"So, you and Eric?" I say, my desperate attempt at changing the subject seems to work as Rye sighs. He looks exhausted.

"Yeah, we're done," he says and, as bad as I feel for him, I'm also kind of stoked. He deserves to be treated the way he treats everyone else, kindly, and he couldn't have picked a worse fit than Eric.

"I'm so sorry – he was a bit of an ass-hat –" I stumble to a halt at the look he gives me. I realise I've messed up.

"I really liked him, Fin," he says quietly, but I can hear a note of hurt and irritation in his voice. "I thought he liked me too – and I wish people would stop making me feel stupid for believing that. Poppy's bad enough but now you –"

Rye looks devastated and now *I* feel like the ass-hat.

"I'm sorry, please don't listen to me. It was a dumb ..." I try again. "Look, can ... can I do anything?"

Rye looks at me for a second, and I hold my breath.

"Nah, I'm good. Really," he says, and his eyes linger on mine. My tummy rolls like the mixers in our food tech class. "I have Thelma and my mum and my fireflies. And I'm sorry for snapping – it's a lot, you know?"

Not for the first time, I wonder what went on between him and Eric.

"Well, here if you need me," I say, trying to play it cool. No point thinking I stand a chance when Eric is so clearly like a magnet to him. I take the last of my books from my locker and spin the dial to lock it shut.

I'm walking away when I hear him call:

"Do you fancy Penny's Diner tonight? You, me, June and Pops?" There's a sweet hopefulness in his voice that wasn't there a moment before.

"That sounds fun," I say. "You sure June and Poppy are okay, though?"

"Ugh, I swear those two are getting worse every month. They'll be fine. They just need to realise how much they love each other and stop this messed-up immature behaviour. It's really boring."

Rye seems visibly annoyed at them. Maybe the talk of relationships wasn't the best course of conversation from yours truly.

"I'll text Poppy now and see if they're in. Meet there at seven?

Does that work for you?" He's smiling again and I feel like his eyes are pulling me in, magnetic.

"I'll be there," I say.

*

I'm sitting at Penny's Diner with a double chocolate thick shake and a plate of onion rings in front of me. As usual I'm early, and I'm talking like *hours* early. Ever since Rye told me about his anxiety and how he goes to Kettle Lake to watch the fireflies to calm himself down I've been thinking of ways I could do something special for him without coming across like a needy loser who has never met another human being before. I think I've done pretty well, but then again, he may hate what I've brought him. He may think I'm borderline pathetic and never speak to me again. However, I don't really care at this point. I don't have a huge amount to lose I guess, except my dignity which, meh, who needs that.

Penny's Diner really is dope. It's like going back in time to the fifties but without the blindingly ignorant humans. The retro jukeboxes on every table allow everyone to pick a song in the queue for the speaker system and the pinball machines are all inspired by eighties movies like *The Goonies* and *Beetlejuice*.

I chow down my onion rings which hit-the-SPOT and then take my time on the thick shake. It's one of those really thick, thick shakes that taste like you're just sucking up creamy, sugary fat through the straw. I love it.

I check Instagram and see Poppy's story – her and June singing along to "Dancing Queen" as they skip – yes, literally, skip – down the street together. I guess they're okay now. I hope they are. They seem to genuinely care about each other. If they weren't constantly at each other's throats it would be as sweet and gorgeous as this shake. But at least they are brave enough to deal with the crap life throws at them, however messy it gets.

I close Instagram and when I look back up from my phone Rye is standing there smiling at me. He looks so damn cute. He's wearing a white tee and jeans that are rolled up at the bottom. His Converse are scuffed but they suit him. He shakes his curls from his eyes and suddenly I feel like I'm melting into my seat.

"Hey," he says, a beautiful grin on his face.

"Hey. How are you?"

I scoot over and he slides in next to me.

"I'm actually really good," he says.

"Good. That's – yeah. I'm glad," I say, the back of my neck prickly and warm. I had this all planned out in my head. To the extent that I even rehearsed how it would go down, but now I just feel like a weirdo who's seen too many cheesy movies.

"You okay?" he asks, smiling slightly.

"Yep. Yep, all good. I just …" I shake my head, desperately trying to get myself together.

"You just … what?" Rye asks, his eyes on mine.

"Just. I'm so sorry for what I said earlier. It's not my place to badmouth Eric … Here," I say, fishing out from my bag the big stupid gesture I've been planning since hearing about his breakup with Eric.

"Fin … I …"

Oh my god, is Rye going to burst into tears? His eyes have this glossy sheen to them and his cheeks are flushed.

"It's for when you're anxious and you can't get to the lake … Kind of like an SOS firefly kit," I say sheepishly.

He turns the mason jar around in his hand, the glow-in-the-dark paint I'd splattered within coming to life as shadows pass over it.

"This is … One of the sweetest things anyone's ever done for me … I …" He looks at me and I have this overwhelming urge to kiss him. I lean closer but stop. The atom bomb that dropped the last time I acted on impulse back in Pittford reverberates in my mind and instead I just give him a funny kind of one-shouldered shrug.

Rye leans in and hugs me; not in a "we're friends, thank you so much" way. More of a "this really is special" kind of way – if that makes any sense whatsoever.

"Sorry to break up the partayyy," comes a voice that sounds anything but sorry.

I turn and see Poppy and June, hand in hand and leaning across the table looking at us hugging. We pull apart far too fast and I take a sip of my thick shake.

"Hey, Pops," Rye says. "You look ace, June," he continues. "Those plaits are fire."

We all squish together into the booth.

"Look at us, double-dating," Poppy says which makes my face flush and Rye go tense.

"It's not … We're not …" I say, trying to give Rye the knowledge that I'm not expecting anything. He looks over at me and half smiles then nudges me warmly with the side of his body, just enough for me to feel and nobody else to see.

"So, how are you doing, Rye-bread?" Poppy asks, ignoring the sudden awkward curve ball she's thrown into the room.

"I'm good. It's obviously a lot, but I'm doing better than I thought."

June nods kindly. "You're really special, Rye. Don't forget that, okay?" she says.

"I second that," Poppy chimes in.

"So you both are … good? Now?" Rye asks the pair of them, deftly throwing the awkward Molotov cocktail back in Poppy's direction like a ninja.

June squirms slightly, but Poppy looks as if Rye asked her whether she showered this morning.

"A-okay. Perfecto. Couldn't be better," Poppy says, waving to the waiter as she swiftly avoids any further talk about anyone's relationship status.

We order a few more drinks, another portion of onion rings and a plate of pancakes to share for dessert. June is super friendly with our waiter, Jerry. According to her, he's one of the sweetest guys not only in Lochport, but in the entire universe. When he can, he gives her milkshakes on the house, which obviously adds bonus points to his legendary status.

Within less than half an hour we are all eating delicious mouthfuls of the pancake stack as we sing along to some classic Cyndi Lauper that Rye requested from the jukebox.

"Kevin McAllister is a douche bag. I have every right to my opinion," Poppy says, licking the maple syrup from her fingers. The fact that we are debating the problems we have with *Home Alone 2: Lost in New York* sums up exactly what level of insanity we find ourselves in this evening.

"He was, like, ten years old," Rye says, suppressing a laugh.

"Ten years old and conveniently able to use his dad's credit cards to check in to the Plaza and gallivant around New York City? Please. Give me a break."

I laugh.

"And don't even get me started on his treatment of that poor homeless bird lady."

Rye gives her a look that says *what is wrong with you*, but Poppy is on a roll.

"Seriously, Rye. He makes friends with a homeless lady who is *covered* in birds, she saves his fucking life from two robbers who want him dead and then the asshole gives her two plastic *turtle doves* as a thank you?!"

I can't help it – I'm crying with laughter.

"Meanwhile, this little sociopath is living it up at the Plaza and instead of offering her a warm bath, some new clothes or a sandwich, he gives her some weird tree ornament." Rye scoffs, clearly being persuaded. "WHERE'S SHE GONNA HANG THAT, RYE? SHE LIVES OUTSIDE WITH BIRDS AND THE TRASH!"

We're all hunched over belly laughing at this point and I can barely see through the tears in my eyes.

"He definitely grew up to be the Jigsaw killer from the *Saw* movies. No kid can deck out a torture house like Kevin McCallister and grow up to be a bank manager or something. He's out for blood. Crazy weird, man." Poppy grossly dips an onion ring into her thick shake, takes a bite and smiles, relaxing her shoulders, clearly winning the argument as none of us say anything, we're all catching our breath and grabbing our sides to nurse laughter stitches.

"Poppy, you're a mess. I can't be –" Rye stops mid-sentence and loses his glow suddenly.

I follow his eyeline to the front of the restaurant and realise what has made the blood leave his face.

Eric is sliding into a booth by the pinball machines and he's not alone.

"Is that Chad fucking Haig?" June says loudly over the clatter of cutlery. She's dropped the F-bomb, which even I know is rare for June.

Rye shakes his head and I'm sure his eyes are welling up "Um – who's Chad?" I ask.

"That little creep," Poppy says, half standing.

"Chad is this guy Eric was caught messaging a while ago. Some pretty raunchy stuff too, but he swears it was just a joke," June says quietly to me as Rye looks on mortified.

"I ... I'm sorry I have to go," Rye says, standing and throwing his backpack over his shoulder.

"No way. Sit," Poppy says. Clearly livid, she storms over to Eric, who doesn't even try to hide how much he's loving the drama and attention.

June and I follow her, half expecting to have to intervene. She looks like she wants to throw a punch. Rye joins us slowly, his expression both devastated and sort of resigned.

"What are you playing at, you douche?" Poppy says, standing over Eric and glaring at him like he's the most revolting person she's ever seen.

"Um. Excuse me?" Eric says, laughing to Chad who sits smugly beside him.

"Uh. B-bu-buuh. Are you having trouble computing? This all a bit too much for you?"

"Poppy, how about you go sit down and have another milk-shake? You're being hysterical as usual."

"Oh I am, am I?" Poppy gestures over at Chad. "Seriously, Eric. You traded in a Porsche for a Toyota Camry."

"Hey, fuck you," Chad says as I hold a laugh back with my hand.

"No, fuck you. You're the asshole who was sexting Eric when you knew he was with Rye. What kind of douche canoe does that?"

"Actually, Poppy," Eric says, turning a vicious grin towards Rye. "I was the one who started it with Chad. I mean, little house on the prairie over here never wanted to put out. What am I supposed to do? Wait around for him?"

We all go silent in mass shock. I cannot believe he just said that. I can't believe someone would admit to being such a jerk.

"I ... loved you," Rye says under his breath, almost to himself.

Something inside me erupts – whether it's perfectly legitimate outrage or just pure jealousy that this dude is so special to Rye – and I'm furious.

"Man, you're a real pile of garbage," I say, not recognising my own voice.

I stand rooted to the spot as Eric gapes stupidly and I feel everyone's eyes on me. He goes to say something, but more words spill out of me with the force of a flash flood.

"I mean, seriously. Look at you. You're a big man-baby who threw a tantrum because his boyfriend wanted to take his time before sleeping with you. And then you jumped into bed with the first dumbass you could find."

"Do you people not realise I'm sitting *right here*?" Chad says.

"No, we do," June says, holding her hand up to him in the *Stop right now thank you very much* Spice Girl pose.

"Rye is one of the coolest people I've ever met," I say, my voice embarrassingly high-pitched. "And you're a jackass for treating him like this."

Eric stands and I'm expecting him to either throw something at me, or pick me up and just throw me.

"I'm out of here," Rye says, pushing past all of us and out the front doors. None of us has the capacity to fire anything more at Eric and Chad so instead we leave, Poppy raising her middle finger at them both as we follow Rye out silently.

"Rye, come back," Poppy says, her hand entwined with June's as we catch up to him.

"Not now, Poppy," Rye says, his feet slapping the pavement as he shoves his hands into his pockets.

"I'm sorry for getting involved," I say.

Rye stops and turns.

"What you did was ..." I wait for it. Bracing myself for the slap of disappointment in his voice. "Beautiful and really kind ..."

Oh. My shoulders sag in relief.

"I just really have to go." And he turns on his heel and walks away.

22

Rye

I'm barely onto Oakview Crescent when I start crying. Before I know it, I'm hunched over and bawling. It's the kind of crying when your body feels like it's being carved out like a pumpkin from the inside.

Then I'm shouting at the roadside grass and tearing it up in chunks. I feel like an idiot. A complete and total failure of a human being for letting Eric pull the wool over my eyes for so long. Am I really that dense, that desperate?

When I get to the patio outside our house, Thelma waddles over and I bury my face in her soft fur. I can tell Mum has given her a bath because she smells of lavender and her ears feel like velvet.

"Hey babe," I say, kissing her on the nose. I grab her water bowl and head to the tap on the side of the house. The grass is green and lush and the air smells of brine, corn and faraway bonfires.

"Here you go," I say, placing her bowl down and then sitting next to her, not bothering to head inside. My face feels swollen from all the crying and there's phlegm stuck in the back of my throat that I try to hock up and spit out.

"What are we gonna do, huh?" I ask, Thelma's big head leaning on my thigh as she lets out a doggy sigh.

I hear the screen door creak open and turn to see Mum's fluffy bunny slippers, the ones she bought for a dollar at a car boot sale last winter.

"You're home early," she says, leaning down and brushing the hair from my eyes. "You okay, hun?"

I look up at her and don't need to say anything. She kneels down and gives me this smile that is comforting without pitying me. She just wraps me in a hug and kisses me on the forehead.

"Love you, Rye-bread."

"Love you, Mum."

∗

An hour later I'm still wide awake, staring up at the ceiling while Thelma snores loudly at the foot of my bed. I unlock my phone and scroll through Facebook, then Twitter and then Pinterest, followed by a nice pivot over to Tumblr, Snapchat, TikTok and Wattpad before getting comfy on Instagram. This cycle repeats a few times until I'm back on the Gram and scrolling through Eric's old photos. I can't help it. I know it's pathetic and predictably stalker-ish to sit and scroll through my ex's Insta feed, but it's like my thumbs are possessed and I can't control them.

I click on a photo of Eric that he posted this morning. He's in his car outside a Dunkin' Donuts with an iced coffee and a pink glazed cronut and I'm suddenly holding my chest and trying to squint back tears. That was our thing. Yet here he is acting like it's just another day. I guess to him it is.

I tap out of the photo and keep scrolling, my whole body numb as I enter layer after layer of this torture vortex I've gotten myself into.

I'm about to tap on a photo of a mini-golf club that I remember him posting after our first date when a text illuminates my phone and snaps me out of my Insta-funk and back into the present moment.

Fin: Hey, I just wanted to see if you were okay? I'm sorry for saying anything to Eric. That was dumb.

I close Instagram and wipe a crusty tear from my cheek. Thelma wiggles in her sleep and makes a half-bark sound and does a little half-run in the air. She's clearly dreaming.

Me: I honestly can't tell you how much it meant that you stood up for me . . .

I hit send and instantly feel weird.

People rarely stand up to Eric. He's one of those guys who loves to shift blame, to get his own way no matter what. I could never win a fight with him. I could never be the good guy. He had to be right, always, so the fact that somebody else, some adorable nice guy, who seems to look at me a lot, would stand up to him makes me feel all kinds of weird – but mostly weird in a good way.

The three dots of the "typing" bubble appear and another wave of something rushes through me. Why do I suddenly care about what Fin has to say? Maybe it's just nice to feel like someone gives a damn about me. That I actually mean something to someone. Not that I know that I do. Maybe I don't. Maybe Fin is simply a really nice human being.

Fin: You don't deserve to be treated like that, Rye.

He used my first name. He's serious.

Me: Thanks . . . You're sweet.

Fin: No, I'm serious. You deserve someone to tell you how great you are. Every day.

I feel my face burn. Why is he being so sweet? What could he possibly want to be sweet to me for?

I crawl to the end of the bed and give Thelma a belly rub.

Fin: I'm sorry if I'm overstepping the mark. I just think you're great.

I start typing then stop myself. Then stupidly send a thumbs-up emoji like I'm ten years old and cringe at myself so hard it hurts.

I roll over. The breeze through the window feels soft on my skin and I kick a leg out of the blanket to be half in, half out – the only way to lie in bed – and let my eyes close.

I'm halfway to the land of nod when I hear Thelma scratching my backpack on the floor. I know what she's after. I bought her some organic dog treats the other day and forgot they were in the side pocket. I crawl out of bed, unzip my bag and give her one of the treats – which she eats like she hasn't just had dinner an hour ago followed by whatever Mum and Carl have been giving her. Greedy doesn't come close.

It's when I unzip the main compartment to find my phone charger that I spot it. The mason jar with the glow-in-the-dark paint. From Fin.

My heart jumps around like I've just been startled awake from a nap.

I stare down at the jar in my hand.

I plug my phone on charge, put the firefly jar next to my bed and open up my messages.

Me: I think you're great too. Like ... really, really great.
Send.

23

Fin

Waking up this morning feels different. I feel different. I suspect it has a lot to do with Rye saying last night that he thought I was great. Not just "great" either. *Really really great* – which is basically a proposal. He clearly wants to be my husband. Okay, I'm not serious. Then again, if he was, I would a hundred per cent be down for eloping, marrying, running away together; the whole kit and caboodle. Okay. Enough. I sound insane.

I brush my teeth then throw on an old basketball singlet with the words "Toon Squad" on the front and Jordan on the back. It used to be Elliot's – *Space Jam* is actually his favourite movie.

When I get to the kitchen, Elliot and Dad look like they're deep in conversation about something. I walk in and feel both their eyes burn into me. It's so obvious that they were talking about me. I'm assuming Dad is telling Elliot about what an embarrassment the last few weeks have been.

"Fin!" Elliot says, the steel in his eyes replaced with dimples and a big smile.

"Morning," I say, heading to the cupboard and getting myself a bowl of cereal.

"How was last night?" Dad asks.

"Great. What did you guys do?" I ask back.

"Me and Elliot chucked a football around the yard, then he showed us a bunch more photos of his trip, we gave him an update on your progress, we had some foo–"

"Sorry, what?" I say. My legs feel like someone's just filled them with concrete.

"We had some food at the bistro in town and –"

"No, you said my *progress*?" I ask, my voice louder than I intend it. I breathe slowly, trying to calm my heart rate. "What are you talking about?"

"We wanted to get Elliot up to speed about what's been happening. It's nothing to get upset over, Fin," Dad says calmly, taking a bite out of his toast and a sip of his tea.

"You still haven't answered my question, though," I ask, my blood pulsing under my skin.

"You are progressing fine. I was telling Elliot how, since the previous incident, you have been on the straight and narrow – ha! How very appropriate."

I flinch. I can't wrap my head around any of this.

"I explained that we had an episode – a little road bump – back in Pittford. You've since met a girl, but I'd still like you to consider a workshop –"

"Workshop?" I scrunch my face up.

"Yes, son." Dad shifts in his seat. "A workshop I've read about. It's for young men who need some grounding and guidance. It's to help get you back on track, nothing more than that."

"What are you *talking* about?" I ask, my mouth void of all saliva.

"I said *some* grounding and guidance," Dad says, exasperated, as if I'm making a big deal out of nothing.

I look to Elliot who is staring at Dad in complete incomprehension.

"Wait, Dad. You can't be serious," Elliot says.

I wipe my upper lip which is drenched in sweat. "Dad, can we please not do this right now?" I ask. I don't know what is going on, but I can feel my chest contracting and I'm struggling to breathe.

"There's nothing to freak out about, Fin. Like we discussed, you're doing great. Your new girlfriend proves that –"

"Dad, stop," I say.

He looks at me sharply but continues as if I hadn't spoken. "The workshop looks ideal, perfect for you. It's a grounding course for young men. It is a way to provide a foundation for a happy life. To provide core life skills to understand the principles of being a responsible man –"

"We get it, Dad," Elliot says, taking a bite out of his toast.

I shift uncomfortably from one foot to the other. I can't quite believe what I'm hearing.

"Look, let me give you an example," Dad goes on conversationally – as if he's trying to sell the workshop to himself, as much as to us. "There's a boy at your school who thinks he's a girl named June. Now, he could've –"

"Dad, STOP." I take a breath. "You have absolutely no idea what you're talking about. Zero. So please. Stop."

The words bounce around the walls, slapping each of us across the face as they ricochet off the cupboards.

Elliot gives me a hint of a smile – he's on my side at least – but Dad just stares, his face blank.

The silence that follows my little protest seems to drag on for hours.

"Be that as it may," Dad says at last, his voice rigid with authority. "It starts first thing tomorrow morning. School will understand. Your mother will take you."

End of discussion, if you can call it that.

*

When I arrive at school my phone buzzes.

Elliot: Love you bro.

Three simple words and I want to ugly-cry like I always do at the end of *Titanic*. I send back a simple *Love you too x* and head inside A-block.

I get to my locker, take out a muesli bar and head over to first period: history.

Poppy is waiting for me when I get there with arms wide open awaiting a hug. This is new to me. Poppy is usually far less affectionate, especially in the morning.

"And how are you on this fine day?" she asks.

"Swell," I lie. "You?"

"Oh, Fin. The grass is green, the sky is blue. Rye is no longer dating the human equivalent of an overflowing sewage tank. June and I are fab-u-*lous*. Life is dandy, my man."

I force a smile. "How's Rye doing?" I ask.

"He will be absolutely fine," Poppy says, tapping my nose. "I've decided that we are all going to the Coney Fair tonight. Rye needs a distraction, and what's more distracting than a snaggle-toothed fairground guy who looks like he might want to wear our skin as a coat?"

I giggle. "Sure, I'm in," I say. Mum and Dad will be thrilled that I'm going to a fair with Poppy. I'll leave out the Rye bit.

Poppy and I start walking to our class and I wonder if Rye is even coming when he puffs up to us, wiping his forehead with the back of his hand and rubbing his eyes. It looks like he's been crying. Perhaps he's been watching *Titanic* too.

Poppy gives him a kiss on the cheek. "Hey you," she says.

"Hey," he says, with something between a wince and a smile.

In return I give him my best smile (a bit of teeth, dimples engaged) and re-read his text in my head: *I think you're great too. Like... really, really great.*

"How are you?" I ask, my voice sounding all raspy.

"Good," he says, then looks at me and smiles. Like, *really* smiles. My heart kicks the hell out of my ribcage.

Poppy glances between us and I see her trying to hide a smirk.

We find our way to the back of the class and sit in a row next to each other. Poppy sits in the middle which drives me insane because I have this uncanny feeling she's enjoying seeing me attempt to get a peek at Rye without being obvious.

Ms Chester wanders in and sits at her desk. I'm not going to lie, she looks like she's had a catastrophic start to the day. Her eyes are bloodshot and her hair is all over the place. She's prone to the occasional midweek meltdown – so Poppy says.

"Class, today we're going to be watching a documentary on the rise of the Roman Empire, narrated by the extremely talented Benedict Cumberbatch," Ms Chester says, rubbing her eyes.

"It's Stephen Fry," someone near us yells out as the programme starts playing.

"Ah, well. Life sometimes gives you a Fry when you ask for a Cumberbatch. Get used to it." She shrugs and takes a swig from her water bottle on her desk – although I'm wondering whether it's actually filled with water judging by the squint she makes.

The documentary drones on and Poppy passes me a note. With a whisper she says, "From him," and gestures across at Rye.

I nearly let out a squeal but thankfully manage to contain myself.

My hands feel numb as I open up the note to see a few words in Rye's inky handwriting.

Thanks again for everything. Means a lot.

I want to climb over Poppy and plant a big fat kiss on his perfect lips, but instead grab a pencil from my bag and start scribbling.

Don't thank me. I'm sorry I can't do more.

I look over to Poppy who seems thoroughly entertained. She takes my note and hands it to Rye, all the while keeping her eyes glued to the TV as Stephen Fry's mesmerising voice narrates the documentary.

Ms Chester seems to be hypnotised by his dreamy English tones too; either that or she's taking a nap with her eyes open.

I try to seem nonchalant while taking a quick glance over at Rye who is opening up the note. I see a smile flicker on his lips.

I should've asked something. I should've tried to keep the conversation going. I'm so bad at this.

Rye puts the note in his pocket and stares at the TV. I guess that's it for the note swapping.

I try to concentrate on what's going on on the screen but I

can't, for the life of me, focus on anything but Rye's profile in my peripheral vision.

I see him shift over on his chair and I think he's retrieving something from his pocket but I'm too awkward to look. I'm terrified of coming across as some desperate loser who waits for –

Bzzzzz.

My phone vibrates and I nearly punch a hole in my pocket trying to pull it out.

Rye's name lights up in my palm. I look up and he's smiling at me. My stomach completely backflips.

Rye: I thought it'd be easier to text. Poppy is giving me the creeps. :-P

Me: I think she knows we're messaging each other.

Rye: I am seriously considering sending you an extremely dirty message to see her reaction.

I can't help but cross my legs and feel all tingly at the thought of any kind of message like that from Rye.

Me: Are you doing okay ...? You know, with everything?

Rye: I am now.

More stomach backflips. I glance over at Poppy who is giving us both a look that says: *Really?* before rolling her eyes.

This could've all been avoided had she correctly taken the social cues and let us sit next to each other when we first got to class. Something tells me she's more than enjoying this.

She takes out her phone and within thirty seconds we are all in a three-way group chat. I love how easily we are getting away with this. Ms Chester appears close to comatose and seems not to notice (or care) that we are completely ignoring Stephen Fry.

Poppy: You two are joining June and me at the Christmas Coney Fair tonight (yes, it's only November but Christmas is happening, okay). It can be a double date.

Rye suddenly looks uncomfortable. The word *date* clearly threw a spanner in the works.

Poppy rolls her eyes again.

Poppy: Fine fine fine. Double-non-date. Happy?

Rye chuckles.

I smile sheepishly. Is it wrong of me that I would've loved it if it had been a date?

Rye: Same as last year? Meet out front of the Ghost Train?

"*Six thirty?*" Rye mouths to us, looking up from his phone. We all nod as the bell goes and Ms Chester wakes up from her dream world.

The rest of the day goes by in a daze. I think about Rye more often than not and when I'm not thinking about Rye, I'm thinking of the workshop that's now looming on the horizon. Anyone who organises something like that is going to be a creep at best. I really don't like the idea of someone like that lecturing me on "normal" life skills. But, in the end, I force these thoughts out of my mind and instead focus on maths, science, geography and then lunch with June and Poppy while Rye heads home to feed Thelma. Technically we're not supposed to leave school grounds at lunch, but Rye lives about a five-minute walk away so I guess the teachers just give him a pass. June told me that Thelma sometimes waddles up to the school gate and waits for him out front for the end-of-school bell and chums him home – I know. He's so cute, it actually hurts.

*

Coney Fair is on the very edge of town and has some of the most rickety old rides on the face of the earth.

FIN

It's your typical carnival. The Zooper-Dooper, Ferris Wheel, Ghost Train, Love Tunnel, plus a million creepy stalls where you can win an oversized stuffed soft toy koala.

I stand next to the Ghost Train and check my phone. No messages. I have this sinking feeling that they are going to bail on me. That I'm going to be abandoned in the middle of this fair with nobody. As usual I catastrophise and freak out long before I assess any facts or my life has a chance to actually go wrong.

A guy about my age is leaning up against the Ghost Train scrolling through his phone.

"You got a wrist band?" he asks, looking me up and down.

"I ... No, not yet," I say, noticing that he's wearing a name badge that reads "Warren".

"You need a wrist band to ride the Ghost Train, buddy."

Ugh. I hate when people call me "buddy".

"Warren," I say, "I'm waiting for some friends. I'll buy my wrist band in a sec."

He gives me another short look up and down, rolls his eyes and goes back to leaning against the ride.

I look around before checking my phone again. 6:12 p.m.

At which point, it rings and Elliot's face appears on the screen.

"Hey."

"What's up?"

"Fin, I need to talk to you."

"Um ... Now's probably not the best time," I say, kicking my shoe into the dust.

"No, I know. I know. I'm not going to come and ambush you or anything. I just want to know what the hell changed while I was away."

I scratch my nose. "Mum's the same. Dad's just …Dad." I take a breath in. "I dunno."

"Fin, Mum told me what happened in Pittford."

I feel like I could throw up. I don't bother saying anything. I stand and wait for him to grill me.

"I'm so sorry, Fin," he says. His voice is quieter than it has been. Quieter than I've heard it in a really long time.

My mouth feels dry and tears well up. "El, it's … You don't need to be so –"

"No, actually I do," he says, as I try to hold it together, attracting a funny look from Warren for my efforts.

"I always knew Dad could kick off about stuff like this. He's so strict and traditional when he wants to be, but honestly I never imagined …I never thought he'd be like this when you told him."

"I guess I just –" I start. Then "Wait, what do you mean, *when*? Did you already know?" His words are falling into place more quickly than my brain can process them.

The line goes quiet.

"Fin, I've kinda known since you were a kid."

What?

Have I always been this secret problem they've all been prepped to deal with? Waiting for an announcement so something could be done about it? So they could address the issue that is me? Is that what my whole life has been up until this point?

"I can't believe you," I say. I don't even know why I'm so angry at him but I am and it's an anger that's red hot and boiling.

"I had an inkling, Fin, but I wanted you to feel safe enough to be able to tell us one day. I never expected Dad to do any of this. When Mum told me, I lost it. I've always wanted to be there for you when –"

"Stop. Okay? You don't get to be the older brother hero right now. You went travelling and left me here to deal with all this. I mean, fuck. They MOVED us to a new town – and all I'd done was tell them the truth!"

There's a headache pressing behind my eyes and I'm shaking, but I keep going.

"What were you hoping would happen, Elliot? When has Dad EVER shown any kind of sign that he would be okay with anything like this?"

"Dad's just scared and doesn't understand. He's spent his whole life trying to fit some idea of what's 'normal' and he doesn't know –"

"You're dead right there!" I yell. "Do you have *any idea* how hard it is for me? You heard Dad this morning. That bullshit 'Making a Responsible Man' workshop? What the hell?"

Elliot breathes slowly on the end of the line. "Fin, I've been talking to Mum. She sees how irrational Dad's being, but I think she feels she needs to support him. All his reactions are grounded in some old-school take on the world, when what he's really afraid of is what this will mean for you and for us – as a *family*." He pauses. "But, you know, it's bullshit. Fuck all that."

I choke out a laugh. Elliot almost never swears.

"Look, I hate that I wasn't there when this all kicked off, okay? I never meant for that to happen. I never in a million years expected Mum and Dad to behave like they have."

His words sink in and I feel my heart calm. I wipe my upper lip with the back of my hand and catch the few tears that have escaped my eyes.

"I have to go," I say, exhaling a long breath.

"Okay," Elliot says. "I'm here now, Fin. Okay? That should count for something."

"It does. Love you, bro." And I hear the echo of my words in his, too.

We hang up.

Warren stares over at me with a mix of pity and confusion. I give him my best *yeah? what?* shrug, then turn towards the candy-floss stall.

I see Rye, Poppy and June heading past the Ferris Wheel and towards me.

I sniff and wipe my eyes with my sleeve once more for good measure.

"Hey, man!" Poppy calls.

I hug her and June, and then Rye and I do this awkward handshake which also turns into a hug that leaves us both blushing. June and Poppy obviously find the whole thing hilarious.

"Are you two done being weird?" Poppy says.

June gives her a nudge. "I like your shirt, Fin," she says.

"Thanks." I smooth down the material and smile as Rye looks over at me.

"What should we go on first?" June asks, taking some chewing gum out of her bag and giving us all a piece each.

"Ghost Train. Let's get that the hell out of the way," Rye says and for a second I catch a genuinely terrified look in his eyes.

"Nooooo. I need at least two laps on the Ferris Wheel before I can convince myself that the Ghost Train is a good idea," Poppy says as we all troop towards the counter and buy our unlimited rides wristbands.

We get to the front of the line straight away because there's only about fifteen other people who are at the fair so early.

At the Ferris Wheel, we shuffle in and sit in the pod as it starts its first slow and steady loop. Rye sits next to me and I'm immediately aware of how close he is. Our legs are touching and if you didn't know us, you'd think we were a thing.

Are we a thing?

Poppy and June snuggle up together opposite us and my heart melts. They radiate love when they're happy like this. I look over at Rye and he gives me a smile which I save, print and file away in my mind.

After a few Ferris Wheel loops, we get off and smash out the Rotary (a spinning monstrosity that glues you to the wall as it spins while the floor disappears, sticking you to the side like flies to crap), the Dodgems, followed by a few goes on the Win-A-Prize Basketball Game, which I lose at more than once.

We make our way towards the Ghost Train and I see Rye's shoulders clench up. It's made to look like a creepy old house and the "train" part of it is a straight-up lie because you actually just walk through the various rooms.

We get to the entrance and our "tour guide" greets us. She's wearing a long Dracula cape and plastic fangs as fake blood drips from her mouth.

"Velcome to zee house of 'orrors," she says.

"Is she trying to be French? Or Dracula?" I whisper to Rye who nudges me and giggles.

We are instructed to all form a single file and hold the person in front by the waist. We do as we are told and Rye stands in front. He looks back and gives me a grin and, as I place my hands gently on his hips, a warm tingle spreads through me.

"Follow meeee," our guide says. "AND BEVARE OF ZE ZOMBIES!"

"Seriously, is that meant to be French?" I whisper again in Rye's ear.

He scoffs and looks back at me and our faces are closer than they've ever been before. He smiles again but, even in the dark, I see his cheeks blush and my heartbeat goes into overdrive at our sudden intimacy.

We make our way through room after room filled with zombies that jump through windows, vampires that burst through closets and axe murderers who appear out of nowhere. I have to admit, it's actually kind of intense.

We're all pretty stoked to get out of there by the final room. But Poppy and June seem to have been more interested in watching Rye and me so close together.

"I think we're going to head home," June says with this cheeky little smile that's a new one on me.

"Okay, no worries," Rye says, with a matching cheeky smile.

"You two have fun, yeah?" Poppy says, adding a wink.

They leave and it's just me and Rye. I feel at once both shy and excited.

The sun has completely disappeared and all that's left is the fluorescent lights from the rides and the thousands of bulb lights that are strung across the field.

"Fancy walking home with me?" Rye says, looking seemingly everywhere but at me.

My whole body gravitates towards him and I have this undeniable urge to take his face in my hands and kiss him. But instead, I say, "Yeah, I'd love that."

As we walk towards home, Rye plays some music on his phone. His playlist starts with the Eagles, followed by some soulful Sam Cooke and Etta James.

"You like the oldies, huh?" I ask.

"*Oldies*? I think you mean the 'greats'," Rye says with a smile. "Mum brought me up right. We've listened to vinyls for as long as I can remember."

We carry on walking but don't talk. We just listen to the music. Occasionally our hands brush each other and we both step apart a bit before finding our way back to the middle again.

A song by Bleachers comes on and Rye starts singing along.

"I said *la la la la la la la* ..."

With a rock-star attitude, he plays pretend drums with some twigs he's just found on the ground. He's effortlessly cool. Whereas my heart is busy now on a series of somersaults.

"You know, I never got to thank you properly," Rye says, turning the music down and looking over at me. "For yesterday."

"You did. You've thanked me more than enough. Which was unnecessary," I tell him.

"No, I'm serious, Fin." He stops and turns to me. "What you did was ... It was so sweet. You're a real great guy."

I stare at him, doing my best to stop a huge grin from spreading all over my face.

"You're pretty decent too," I say.

We catch each other's eyes for longer than a beat before starting to walk again, Rye's music coming back a bit louder than before.

We're at the turn off between Kettle Lake and the road to either our houses or into town when Rye grabs my hand and leads us through the shrubbery towards his spot. The crickets scatter underneath our feet as we crunch over branches and leaves, finally getting to Rye's little cove.

"I'm sorry," Rye says, getting comfy on the floor and patting the ground next to him: "I just wanted you to see this."

I hesitate and then sit down next to him; I don't realise how close we are until the musky fragrance of his cologne wafts over me.

"Look," Rye says, motioning in front of him and smiling like it's the first day of summer.

I glance up and the entire lake is bursting with light. Hundreds of fireflies dance through the reeds, along the surface of the water and into the shrubbery.

"This is amazing," I say, bewitched by the magic unfolding in front of us.

I sense the movement of Rye's body as he turns towards me, clearly no longer focused on the fireflies.

We lock eyes and my body does this thing where it's like a thousand currents of electricity shoot through each atom of my flesh. I look at his smooth dark skin, his almond eyes, his big beautiful smile and I'm overwhelmed with the want to kiss him.

He smiles shyly but doesn't break eye contact. Neither do I. I don't want to. I want him to know how amazing he is. I want him to know that he's worth every firefly in this whole damn lake.

My body is alive, tingling.

The crickets click in unison and I lean towards him, aware of every tiny movement I'm making. He smiles again, a simple, genuine smile, which turns to soft laughter as he also moves closer.

The gap of air between our bodies get smaller. But instead of the kiss I'd been longing for, I realise that Rye's hands are on me and he's …

What?

Pulling me to my feet – and before I know it we're running, splashing, into the shallow blue waves at the shore of the lake.

24

Rye

First thing the next morning, I'm sitting opposite Poppy in McElroy's Fish & Chippie, nursing a cup of chai latte. They are probably the only fish and chip shop in the world with chai on the menu. I'm here for it. Poppy's busy eating yoghurt – an off-menu choice – and her preferred method consists of dipping her finger in it and licking it off.

"When he … I just … I don't know … I felt something happen inside and –"

"Like diarrhoea?" Poppy asks, matter of factly.

I stare at her for a second then burst into laughter.

"No, Poppy. Not diarrhoea."

She shrugs.

"Also, do you want me to get you a spoon? You look like a gremlin."

Poppy smiles and lets the yoghurt seep through the gaps in her teeth.

"Gross," I say, taking a sip of my chai.

"*You're* gross," Poppy says. Then, going straight for the jugular:

"So, you like Fin, then?"

I wrinkle my nose. "Maybe."

Once Poppy finishes her yoghurt, we grab our bags and leave for school. The weather is fresh and sunny and everything smells like cut grass and saltwater. I love days like this.

When we arrive, June is waiting at the entrance and we link arms together through A-block. I make a beeline for Fin's locker, thinking I'll catch him there before class but when I get there he's nowhere to be seen. I check my phone again but nothing. He hasn't been online either.

The day drags on, and I cannot get him out of my head. I check my phone a million times a minute, but not a peep. I feel myself obsessing and so instead I head to the track at lunch and run laps. It's something I actually enjoy. Running seems to calm my mind (and hurt my calves, but whatever).

June and Poppy meet me at my locker before fifth period and I spot straight away that June has a look of concern plastered on her face.

"Rye, are you okay?" she says.

"Mmhmm," I say, grabbing my science textbook and chewing a hangnail on my thumb. "Sweaty, but okay."

"Rye, c'mon. The whole Eric and Fin thing must be a lot to deal with right now," Poppy says, half a smile, half a look of pity on her face.

"Uh-uh, I'm fine," I say. Even I don't believe me. "Okay. Not fine. Have either of you heard from Fin?" I say, sounding more desperate than I intended.

They both shake their heads no and my shoulders slump.

"Hey," Poppy calls, as I turn to go to my science class. "Meet here after last period. We'll go see where he's been all day."

*

The final bell rings and I practically throw myself through the door towards my locker. Poppy and June are waiting with expressions on their faces that I can't quite read, but I'm hoping mean they think going to Fin's house is as great an idea as I do.

As we climb into Poppy's car and head off, I have this uncomfortable feeling in my tummy like I know I shouldn't be ambushing Fin like this – the last time we turned up at his was *so* weird – but it's countered by a stronger urge to see him. Since last night, I haven't been able to get him out of my head

We turn left onto Crescent Boulevard and right up Fin's street and June turns around to face me.

"Okay, what's your game plan?" she asks.

"My what?

"Game plan. What are you going to say to him?"

"Um. 'Hey, Fin, why weren't you at school?'" I say, shrugging.

"Smooth, Rye." June rolls her eyes playfully.

"Real smooth," Poppy adds, turning the ignition off and turning to face me as well.

"So, you like him, yeah?" Poppy continues.

"I guess. Is it weird? That I do?"

"Why would it be weird?" June asks.

"I dunno. Eric and I were –"

"Rye, don't go there," Poppy says. "You have every right to be all gooey about Fin. Don't even think about Eric. He's the president of the ass-hat society."

She's not wrong about that.

"Do you want us to come with you?" June asks.

"No, it's okay," I say. Then: "Actually, yeah."

They share a knowing look. And then we're walking in a line up Fin's path to his front door. There's a car in the drive and a light on upstairs so I'm certain someone's home.

"Maybe we should just leave it," I say, my anxiety kicking in big time, my heart pounding.

"Don't be dumb," Poppy says.

"Wait, Pops. Is that what you want, Rye?" June asks, a look of genuine concern in her eyes.

I go to say something but decide against it. "No. No, I'm being stupid," I tell them.

I knock a few times on the door and wait, my forehead breaking out into a waterfall of sweat.

"Relax," Poppy says and adds, "Chill, man," with a giggle under her breath.

The silence that follows my knocks seems to last a year. Finally, a door shuts somewhere inside, and the creak of stairs lets us know that someone's on their way.

The door swings open and I realise I haven't taken a breath in a really long time. I inhale and exhale slowly as a guy who looks like Fin, only older, stands holding the door open with one hand and a protein bar in the other.

"H-hi," I say, looking at him and then into the giant interior of the house behind him.

"Hey, dude," he says. "Elliot." And he stuffs the bar in his pocket, then holds his hand out, which we all shake one by one.

"I'm … We're friends of Fin from school. We were just wondering if he was home?" I say, my voice sounding oddly unfamiliar.

Elliot goes to say something but before any words leave his

mouth, a man is standing beside him. He has the same eyes as both Fin and Elliot – obviously their dad.

"Evening," the man says.

"Hi, Mr Whittle," Poppy says, stepping up like a badass. "My name's Poppy and –"

"Poppy?" he says. "So great to finally meet you."

We all give one another a puzzled look as Mr Whittle extends his hand to Poppy and only Poppy.

She shakes it with a half-smile. "Hi," she says.

"Fin's told us all so much about you," Mr Whittle says.

"Well, that's sweet," Poppy replies, with a laugh. "I am kind of amazing I guess."

Mr Whittle's bemused smile doesn't reach his eyes – he clearly doesn't get the gag. "Well, it's certainly a treat to finally meet Fin's girlfriend."

Poppy, June and I snigger in unison.

"What's so funny?" Mr Whittle enquires, the initial warmth on his face rapidly fading.

"Oh. Fin's not –" Poppy starts, but Elliot scrunches his face up and cuts in.

"– Here. Fin's not here. He's at church with Mum. Had a workshop thing." Elliot looks between Poppy and his dad like one of them might be about to spontaneously combust.

Then it's as if Mr Whittle finally realises that June and I have been here the whole time. He stares at us both, looking intently at June like he's trying to decode a safe.

"What did you say your names were?" Mr Whittle asks.

"They didn't," Elliot says affably. "You were too busy acting weird." He's clearly trying to smooth over whatever it is that's happening right now, but his dad doesn't seem to want to play along.

"We should get going. Will you please tell Fin we stopped by?" I say, grabbing June by the arm, who then takes Poppy's arm. We head back down the path to the car. I feel panicky, like we really shouldn't have done that. Something about the way Fin's dad was refusing to engage with us makes me horribly uncomfortable.

"Well, that was fun," Poppy says as she turns the ignition.

"Define 'fun'?" June deadpans.

I put my seatbelt on and we are just about to pull out when Elliot is there at the passenger window, knocking.

June smiles and rolls down her window.

"Hey," Elliot says. "I'm really sorry about that."

June shakes her head. "What exactly *was* that?" she asks.

"My dad…he's…I dunno." Elliot's clearly struggling to work out what he needs to say. "He's – he's not making life easy for Fin right now."

Poppy leans over June to get a better look at him. I sit quietly in the back seat avoiding eye contact.

"Does your dad think Fin and I are…what?' Poppy asks. "A thing?"

Elliot gives us all a look that resembles pity. "Dad doesn't know what he's talking about…With a lot of stuff," he adds, vaguely.

"Gee, that's helpful," Poppy says. "Thanks."

June gives her a glare before turning back to Elliot. "Will you tell him we stopped by?" she asks.

"Yeah, I will…I'm sure Dad will too," he adds grimly.

Poppy puts the car into gear and we leave. As we turn onto the main road, charcoal-grey clouds hang heavy in the sky.

25

Fin

That workshop's exactly as bad as I imagined it to be. Nothing but a bunch of uptight ancient old guys telling young men how much more "manly" they all were back in the day. Their dreary prayers for our "healing" were the worst. I roll my eyes so many times I give myself a headache and I practically fall off my chair with joy when I can finally leave.

Outside, Mum is waiting with milkshakes by the car and asks me how it was before we're even on the highway.

I shrug. I can't be bothered talking. I can't believe they thought it was a smart move to send me to something like this horror show of a "workshop".

"So?" Mum says, lifting her eyebrows up with a hopeful smile.

"Do you want the truth or a well-acted lie?" I ask, the anger in my voice coming out sharper than I perhaps intended.

Mum shifts in her seat and puts her blinker on to turn right as I take a gulp of my milkshake.

"You know, we're only trying to help you, Fin," she says, looking straight ahead.

"Help with *what* exactly, Mum?" I ask, genuinely unsure of what she's talking about. Wasn't their idea of "help" moving us to an entirely new town? Making me start my life over? What more "help" do they think I need?

"Your father and I are doing the best we can considering the circumstances –"

"What circumstances, Mum? Can we *please*, just for once, address the big fat rainbow elephant in the room? *Please*?" It's incredible to me that I'm challenging her on this, but I'm so glad that I am.

Mum sighs and shakes her head, never taking her eyes off the road. "All things aside, Fin. Your choice of sexuality has made –"

"Mum, please, you can't be serious," I say, my legs trembling and my throat tightening up. "Choice? Get real. I've had a whole day of listening to uptight old bigots drone on about 'unnatural choices' and right now I'm honestly considering throwing myself out of this car –"

"Don't, Fin," Mum says, looking over at me. "Honestly, please don't imagine for a minute we *enjoy* this. This town is our home too. Do you think we *like* having people talk about you – about us – behind our backs?"

What am I hearing?

"Mum, *people*? What does it matter what *people* are saying?" I say. "I'm your son." I choke on the last word.

"Then behave like it," Mum says, straightening up in her chair and brushing away what I think is a tear. I'm about to ask what exactly behaving like a son looks like when she says: "I know Poppy isn't your girlfriend, Fin. I know, okay?"

Oh.

"This is such a mess." Mum sighs. "It's not *normal*. This sexuality thing will ruin your life ... Everything we've ever dreamed of for you, everything we've worked for –"

"What are you *talking* about!?" I slam the milkshake down on the dash. "What makes you think I'd let you down? Why –" But what am I even saying? It's so pointless trying to get through to her. Am I speaking a language she can't understand? "I give up," I mutter under my breath.

"On what, Fin? What could you possibly give up on? You haven't even tried to see where we're coming from." Mum's voice is deflated, resigned, like she really has been in a wrestling match with her whole belief system.

"Please just don't in any way indicate to Dad that Poppy and I aren't ... whatever. Okay? I can't deal with him," I say. I feel numb. But at least we've somewhat addressed the fact that I'm not into girls without ever actually talking about it at all.

Mum stares ahead and turns the radio on. Dolly Parton's "Tennessee Homesick Blues" is playing and I'm glad because Dolly's upbeat vocals help alleviate the miserable sinking feeling that now engulfs me.

We pull into our drive and trudge inside. Elliot gives me a proper hug, which is kind of odd because he's not really a hugger, and we head into the dining room where Dad has made a casserole. It's his specialty and, in fairness, it's always really tasty.

We sit down and Dad says Grace and we dig in. The sound of cutlery on plates is a nice way to break up the blistering silence that's for sure.

My fork is halfway to my mouth when Dad wipes his mouth and stares at me.

"How was today?" he asks.

"Great," I say, lying through my teeth like a boss.

Mum looks over at me before distracting herself by taking a sip of water.

"You feel like you have more of a foundation now, yeah?" Dad says, cautiously.

All I can do is nod.

"So, I met your girlfriend this evening," he goes on, before taking a bite and chewing slowly.

I nearly spit my own food across the table. "My … what?"

"Yes." Dad looks at me so forcefully I feel like I'm being X-rayed. "Poppy, Rye and … June, was it?"

"She's nice, Fin." Elliot clears his throat. "Your other friends are sweet too."

I feel myself tense and my hands are suddenly so sweaty I need to wipe them on my jeans.

I see Mum cast an anxious look around the table. "Can you pass the salt?" she asks.

I wipe the Niagara Falls of sweat from my palms again and I pass Mum the salt. "Well, I'm glad you think so," I say, doing my best to sound nonchalant.

Dad is still boring into me with his X-ray eyes, but I breathe my way through dinner and somehow we manage to avoid any further controversy.

When I finally escape to my room, I collapse on my bed, my mind a complete and utter blank.

∗

I spend the weekend hibernating. After the "workshop" on Friday, all I want is to be left alone. By the time Monday comes around,

I'm dreading school. For the second time, I have to justify my family's super weird behaviour to my friends.

Poppy arrives at school sporting a knowing smirk which I know is harmless but I really don't want to have to explain anything right now. I'm not in the slightest mood to account for myself and my absurd family, but by the look on her face, she can't wait.

"Hey, boyfriend," she says, throwing her arm across my shoulder and giggling.

I shake my head. "Hey," I say, taking some chewing gum from my pocket and offering her one.

"I could share yours!" Poppy says leaning in to give me a kiss which makes me laugh as I push her away.

"Get off me, you big hetero weirdo," I say, handing her her own piece which she pops in her mouth with a grin.

"Have you seen Rye?" she asks.

I shake my head. "Nope. How come?"

"No reason," she says, taking her phone out of her pocket and sending a message.

"I'm sorry about the other day," I say awkwardly. "Heard all about it when I got home."

Poppy scoffs. "Don't be dumb," she says. "*I'm* sorry. We shouldn't have turned up like that."

"No, I'm sorry. It's just –"

I'm cut off by June who, appearing out of a nearby classroom, spots Poppy and gives her a kiss as they entwine their hands – completely unconcerned about the looks some students still throw their way. I have to admit, seeing these two so in love makes me feel both all mushy inside and also like I want to set myself on fire. Especially because I'm here all on my own with nobody. Life's fun like that.

"Hey, Fin," June says.

"Hey."

"What were you saying?" Poppy asks, smiling.

"I dunno. All good," I reply, stuffing my hands in my pockets.

We round a corner and stand near a bubbler as Poppy laps up water like a cat.

"So, word on the street is you're out for my girl," June says, sending Poppy into a laugh-choke at the bubbler and causing her to spit a mouthful of water at the wall.

I burst out laughing. June is a riot and, if I'm being honest, it is kind of hilarious. The thought of me and Poppy (even if we were in any way "compatible") is just ... no.

"Yeah, about that," I say, my grin fading. "I'm really sorry. It's just my dad ... he's ... not the most supportive." It's so hard to explain my family situation. For the first time it hits me how impossible it would be for these two, with their chill and ridiculously on-side parents, to understand where I'm coming from. So, I go quiet instead.

They look at me and their sarcasm and playfulness disappears to be replaced with this sweet look that reads *it's all good*.

"We love you, man," Poppy says, giving me a kiss on the cheek.

"I mean, you're quite the dish," June says smiling. "I could see it." She motions to both of us and laughs.

"A dish?" I say. "Yeah, like McDonald's."

Poppy makes a heart shape with her hands and, as we round another corner, we see Rye walking towards us.

He looks sheepish and almost embarrassed to see me. It's suddenly beyond awkward and I have no idea why.

Poppy and June sense it too and decide to scoot off and leave Rye and me alone together. Thanks a lot.

"So, about the other night," Rye says, kicking his boot gently on my shoe. I feel my tummy go over at this simple touch from him.

"I'm really sorry," I say.

His eyes finally meet mine and he looks genuinely confused. "Sorry?"

"Yeah, about … well about the whole awkward thing at mine. I didn't –"

"You don't have to be sorry. My god, I'm the one who's sorry. We shouldn't have just turned up like that. It was a bad call. And stupid. And –"

"No, it's … I'm –"

We both stare at each other and next thing we're both doubled over, hands on knees, laughing.

Something's shifted and it feels like the air is alive between us.

"Do you want to go to the beach? We could get fish and chips?" he asks and I smile the biggest smile the world has ever seen.

"I would love that."

He smiles back.

"Now?" I ask.

He laughs some more. "Tonight!" he says.

The day rolls by and I'm a bundle of nervous energy and tingly happiness from the top of my head to my toes. It's the most awesome yet terrifying feeling in the world. This all-encompassing, all-consuming feeling that I want nothing more than to be around someone. Even if we're just passing in the halls or sharing a glance, every time I'm near Rye my heart beats faster.

*

Before I even realise it, it's six o'clock and I'm standing outside McElroy's Fish & Chippie wearing my skinny jeans, white tee and sweater with the Looney Tunes logo on the back. I feel pretty cute but nowhere near as hot as Rye as he rolls up looking like the drummer from an indie rock band.

"Hey," he says, slowly walking up to me and going in for a hug.

I let my arms wrap around his waist and breathe him in. He smells of incense, lavender and some cologne that's earthy and sexy as hell.

"Hey," I say. "You look nice."

He smiles and even though the sun is almost gone I can see a sprinkle of a blush across his cheeks.

"You do, too," he says, kicking his shoe at the gravel.

We head inside, keeping an eye out for Poppy but no one's here but her mum, Isla, who serves us enough chips to keep us going for a week.

I'm doing my best to not look at Rye as we wander back outside and head towards the beach, but I can't help it. He's ridiculously attractive tonight. Maybe it's not *tonight* that's making him attractive, but the energy shift that's happened today. Just by the outline of his dimples, I can feel him smiling without looking at him. He glances up and catches me staring. My face tingles and I look back at the beach ahead of us and pretend like I'm searching for a good place to sit.

"So," he says.

"So," I say, looking back at him.

"You good?"

"I'm great," I say.

"Good."

"Good."

"Yeah."

"Yeah."

We grin at each other and I think my face might actually seize up from how much I'm smiling.

"What are you thinking?" Rye asks, as we glance around at the picnic benches.

I'm thinking I want to lean over and kiss you, that's what I'm thinking.

"Over here," I say, instead, leading him over to a secluded bench right on the sand. I gallantly wipe some old seaweed off the seat. The air is still warm and the light is gently fading; the perfect night – made even more perfect by Rye looking so outrageously gorgeous next to me.

"Oooh, I like your style," he says and cracks another one of his ridiculous smiles. "Thanks for coming," he says, once we're settled down and tucking in.

"Are you kidding? This is *awesome*."

"Woah, someone must really like fish and chips."

"Something like that," I say.

Rye shifts and one of his curls falls across his eyes which he shakes away with a flick of his head.

Neither of us are precious about our table manners. Firstly, we're on the beach. Secondly, I'm not about to care about whether I look like a rabid dog when something that tastes this good is in front of me. We both eat like dingoes and throw random questions at each other in between bites of fish and salty chips.

"Favourite movie?"

"*The Goonies*."

"Least favourite food."

"Celery."

"Running or swimming?"

"Swimming."

"Hot or cold?"

"BOTH, that's impossible."

"East or West?"

"What?"

We laugh, eat and stare at each other every once in a while, the banter flying easily back and forth between us.

Eventually Rye eats his last chip, wipes his mouth with the back of his hand. "But, really, I'm sorry about the other night ..." he says.

I'm reminded of that other part of my life. Not this. Not this wonderful beachside portion of chips and flirt-like-nobody's-business night. My life at home. With parents who want to change me. Who don't love me as I am.

"No, Rye. Honestly," I say. "Please. Don't."

"No, we shouldn't have rocked up like that. It was so uncool. Your dad ... he –"

"I need to tell you something," I interrupt and before I can help it I feel myself getting overwhelmed. I refuse to cry. Not because of some macho-masculine rubbish or anything, but because I'm worried that if I start, I won't stop.

Rye's face turns serious and his eyes lock on mine.

I take a breath and then I tell him everything. Literally everything. Emily, Jesse and Jake, my life in Pittford, the night at the bowling alley, Aunt Carla and her thousand cats, moving here like it was a national emergency, even that goddamn workshop. Right up to us now. Sitting here on Lochport beach on a Monday night over the saltiest portion of chips ever and with so much cute flirtatious energy I feel like I'm going to explode.

"So that's that," I say, wiping a tear from my eye because I said I wouldn't cry but I can't help this one rogue fighter which got too close to the surface and escaped.

We sit quietly for a moment and he just looks at me. The feel of his gaze is unlike anything I've ever experienced. Nobody has ever looked at me like this and I feel my whole body hum.

"So, I need to tell you something, too," he says, after what feels like a really long time.

"Sure," I say.

"I really like you, Fin. Exactly as you are."

All the random dog walkers on the beach melt away, the streetlights behind us seem to dim and it's just us two. My heart throws itself around my chest, my feet tingle, my arms tingle, my face flushes.

And just like that I'm hit with what I can only describe as
full
blown
fireflies.

26

Rye

Did that just actually happen?

Thelma comes waddling over to me with her tongue hanging out and when she gets to my feet she greets me with her usual wiggle dance. I bend down and give her a kiss and then sit on the floor as she jumps all over me, quickly wearing herself out and rolling onto her back for a much-needed belly rub.

"Who's my girl?" I say as she wiggles from side to side.

"Hey, hun," Mum says as she leaves the kitchen, a chakra crystal wand in her hand.

"Hey."

"Well, look at you," she adds, pointing up and down in my direction with her ridiculous wand.

"What?" I say. "Also, what is that?" I point back at her wand with a laugh.

"I've seen that look before …" Mum says, sitting down in front of me and giving Thelma a rub on her belly as well. "And it's been because of two things: my fabulous fudge brownies."

I raise my eyebrows. "Uh-huh."

"Or a boy."

Mum knows me too well.

I look down and stare at Thelma, trying not to show how difficult it is to articulate what I'm feeling.

"It's just weird because … Is it bad to have feelings for someone else right after a relationship ends?"

"What do you mean?"

"I mean, is it wrong for me to like someone so soon after …"

"After Eric?" Mum asks, her eyes scanning mine. "Hun, sometimes relationships are over long before they are actually *over* … You know?"

I actually do know what she means, but I'm still not convinced.

"You're so young," Mum says. "You think far too much for someone so young."

I shrug.

"So, spill?" Mum smiles and bounces her eyebrows up and down. "Who is he?"

I can't help but laugh. Mum has this uncanny way of always making everything better. Maybe it's just a general "mum" thing. But my particular mum is truly great at that.

"Firstly, don't do that with your eyebrows. You look kinda frightening," I say. "Second, before we get into *that*, I need to say something."

Mum looks at me with her questioning face on, then she takes a breath. "Oh no, what is it? Are you skipping school? Are you on the run from the law? Have you killed someone? Let me get my shovel …"

I laugh.

"You're pregnant, aren't you. Oh my giddy aunt, who's the father?"

"Mum. Enough," I say. "No, I want to say thank you."

"Thank you?" And she drops the joke and stares seriously at me for the first time all evening. She's smiles and waits for me to continue.

"You have ... no idea how grateful I am for you," I say, and I don't even care that I'm getting emotional the moment the words leave my mouth. I need her to know.

"Oh, hun," Mum says, taking my hand.

"No, I mean it. When I came out to you, you said all I had to worry about was making sure you liked whoever I was dating."

"Which is the truth."

"And now I have someone I think you might like, my friend ... Fin."

Mum's eyes light up. "And is this friend someone you ... like?"

I smile. "Of course. But, not the point, Mum," I say. "His family are the furthest thing from you. He has no support, nobody to tell him that everything about him is perfect and just the way it should be. Nobody to tell him life is going to be all right." I'm trying not to be an emotional wreck, but I let the tears come and Mum squeezes my hand. "I don't tell you enough how ... incredible you are and how lucky I –"

Mum scoots over and brings me in for a hug. "I'm the lucky one, Rye," she says, squeezing me tight. "You are everything and more I could have ever asked for in a son."

We look into each other's eyes, then laugh as Thelma makes a grumble to let us know there's no way we've petted her enough yet and it's totally unacceptable that we're leaving her out of our love-in.

"Now, Rye-bread, get yourself a glass of water, wipe your face and take yourself to bed," Mum says, smiling through shining eyes.

"Night, Mum. You're the best."

*

The following morning, I wake up before my alarm and jump to the shower. This is the first day since my big admission that I'm actually going to see Fin and for some reason my brain decides that now is the perfect time to question the way I look.

I get dressed, throw some product in my hair but then quickly rinse it out over the sink because my attempt at styling has made me look like I've been electrocuted. And not in a cute way. But whatever. I love my curls and everyone else can too. Deal with it.

When I get to school, I'm practically running through the halls while simultaneously trying to come across as chill as possible. As I turn the corner in A-block, I feel immediately deflated when I realise Fin's not at his locker. Mine is a few down from him so I put in my combination and throw my bag in, taking my phone out to check for texts. Nothing.

I slam my locker shut and, as I'm about to give Poppy a call, Fin, June and Poppy round the corner together. He's even more handsome than I remember him a day ago. Is that what happens when you realise you like someone? They automatically become a million times more irresistible?

The three of them are laughing about something and I hug the girls first before moving in for a hug with Fin.

"Hey."

"Hey," he says.

Poppy and June exchange a look.

"How are you?" I ask, suddenly feeling a bit sweaty and self-conscious.

"I'm good," Fin says, looking up at me and down at his shoes three times in a row.

"Good. That's –"

"Oh My. GOD!" Poppy throws her head back as she rolls her eyes at our idiocy. "Here," she says, grabbing my hand and putting it into Fin's. "Now can we *please* stop acting like you two aren't cute as all fuck and just get on with our days?"

Fin and I look at each other properly for the first time and our shoulders relax and we smile, our fingers interlocking as our palms kiss.

June looks at us and puts her hand to her mouth. "Awww, you two. I can't. Too adorable."

Fin strokes my fingers with his as we all start walking towards B-block.

"If this …" he squeezes my hand, "is too fast, we can stop."

I want to kiss him right here in the hallway. I don't remember ever being asked whether I was comfortable or okay when I was with Eric.

"No way," I whisper, squeezing back.

A few people look at us and the usual undead suspects, Paisley and Bronwyn, scoff as we walk past, but I don't have a single fuck to give. Their narrow minds are their problem, not mine.

Even so, I still can't wrap my head around what it must be like to grow up straight. To walk down the street holding your boyfriend or girlfriend's hand and for nobody to even think to give you a second glance. To have nobody judge you as an outsider or as different.

I hold Fin's hand tighter and bump hips with him as we arrive at our science class.

"I've got English," Poppy says

"Maths," June says.

We all hug, which isn't necessary. But today is a good day and, whatever, it's kinda cute.

"Remember, QSA meeting after fifth," June says as she speed-walks up the hall.

I had completely forgotten, but any excuse to spend more time with Fin and these two is a win in my eyes.

∗

After lunch Fin has geography and I have science and the girls are in food tech (which is basically a glorified baking class). We separate and when I'm sitting in science I let the day's events wash over me. I've had Fin on my mind from the minute I arrived and now, sitting here while Mr Nguyen dissects a frog, I think about how much I want to kiss him. Fin, that is. Kind of a strange place for that visual to pop up as Mr Nguyen scalpels through the frog's belly ...

The bell eventually rings and I couldn't be more grateful. The smell of frog guts is overpowering and, as we leave, I happily inhale the scent of bargain warehouse deodorant and D-list celebrity fragrances that fills the corridor from other students.

I find Fin and interlace my hand with his, as we stroll towards June and Poppy's locker.

"Ugh," Poppy says as we approach. "You two are the worst."

June finishes putting away her books in her locker and joins us as we all head for the QSA meeting.

When we arrive the rest of the group are already sitting around chatting and a few faces smile when they catch sight of

Fin's hand in mine. He seems slightly nervous but he hasn't let go of my hand (it could be the death grip I've got on his, but whatever).

We find some seats at the back and June closes the door with her foot, all business and ready for action.

"Hey, thanks for coming everyone," she says, as she takes her place in front of the giant whiteboard. "Let's get started. Now, I've good news and bad news. The bad news is the bathroom complaints haven't stopped."

We all groan. Fin and I share a glance, and I can't help my eyes from drifting to his lips.

"And up until now I've not been able to do anything besides rant and rave in here every meeting. But the good news is, yours truly has found out that Paisley, Bronwyn and their crew are geared up for their walk-out protest next Friday." She grins. "And the really good news is ... it's time for action."

Poppy hollers *woot woo* and we join in. Fin and I even stop holding hands to fist pump the air.

"My undercover mission has revealed they're planning to stage it after school," June continues. "So I say we confront them. Ask what their deal is. As my dad likes to say, 'No army is stronger than the intelligent fighting the ignorant.'"

"Can we make placards?" Poppy shouts, a bit randomly. "It's not a counter-protest without placards."

"For sure," June says. "Let's get our slogan 'Keep Calm, It's Just A Toilet' out there!"

There's a burst of excitement and plenty of others throw suggestions into the mix.

The rest of the meeting we decide on the slogans and signs we want to create, and June plots our battle strategy out on the whiteboard. Her rolled up sleeves complete the "we can do it" look.

*

When we leave the classroom, the sun is slowly departing for the day and the air smells of a strange mix of seaweed from the ocean and burnt cinnamon from the bakery nearby. Fin is walking next to me and our arms are touching – I honestly cannot get enough of him.

Fin and I are just turning to leave when June puts a hand on Fin's shoulder.

"Fin, we're sorry about Friday night," June starts but he quickly waves at her with his hand.

"No way. No. Don't be. Honestly, I'm –" he starts, but Poppy jumps in.

"I know, I know. Madly in love with me, but because I'm taken, you had to settle for Rye. I get it. I'm sorry, but June's my *numero uno*."

We all giggle. It's the first time in a really long time that I've felt so completely at ease and it's just perfect. After saying goodbye, Poppy and June head into town to buy art supplies for their placards, and Fin and I walk. It's a good night for a walk.

We leave school, turn onto Maine Avenue and head towards home. The air has a bit of a nip now that the sun has gone for the day, but it's the perfect excuse to take Fin's hand and walk close to him. Our hands fit nicely in each other's. His palm is soft and our fingers intertwine perfectly like a lock and key.

We don't talk. We are more than happy just strolling while the crickets holler at each other and the birds overhead chirp their goodnights.

Before I realise where we are, I see the turn off for Kettle Lake. We swat through the bush and the crackle of dry leaves and old pebbles underfoot makes an echo that seems to bounce off of every tree for miles.

We get to my spot and Fin looks over at me with a smile as he sits down on an old piece of driftwood.

"Well, today was a good day," I say, bumping him lightly with my shoulder and grinning.

"It was," Fin says.

We both lean into each other as much as we dare. We smile, the air between us is electric.

"It's cool hanging out with you, Fin," I tell him, my stomach humming like a swarm of bees.

"Yeah?" I catch his dimples in the corner of my eye. "It's pretty cool being with you too."

I turn to look at him. His eyes flicker to mine and then back out across the lake.

The first few fireflies blink to life and I feel my shoulders relax and my breathing slow.

"About time," I say, looking out as the lake winks and glimmers as the thousands of fireflies make their way through the reeds and across the surface.

"What do you mean?" Fin says, turning his head to face me.

"They help with my nerves," I say.

Fin smiles. "What are you nervous about?" he asks, his eyes jumping between mine and my lips.

"Doing this," I say.

And, before I let my nerves ruin this moment, I lean in and kiss him.

27

Fin

Rye's lips are on mine. I repeat: RYE'S LIPS ARE ON MINE. WE ARE KISSING. THIS IS HAPPENING.

We stop for a second and I stare at him for what feels like for ever before I lean in again and kiss him harder.

You know in the movies where people can't get enough of each other? I always thought that was just ramped up for dramatic effect. Kind of like how the robbers from *Home Alone* manage to survive falling from a three-storey building or having their heads smashed by paint cans without dying – I figured it was all just a Hollywood illusion. But get this! It's not. Not at all. I mean, the kissing thing, anyway.

I genuinely cannot get enough of Rye's lips and I'm pretty sure the feeling is mutual because he's not stopping, and neither am I.

When we finally do break apart, we smile dopily at each other and I lace my fingers with his. He is blushing and the few freckles across the bridge of his nose seem to blend into his cheeks. His curls fall haphazardly across his forehead and I grin as he shakes them out of his vision.

"You're good at that," he says which makes me snort laugh and then bury my head in my free hand in embarrassment.

"Smooth, aren't I?" I say, shyly meeting his eyes. "Kissing and then a snort. So sexy."

"Sexy enough for me." He smiles. "So, what are you doing this weekend?"

"Nothing, how come?" I say.

"You wanna come over and listen to vinyls?"

Is the earth round?

"Yes," I say. "For sure."

*

I walk through the front door and I don't even bother wiping the smile off my face. I'm ridiculously happy. The happiest I've been in months. Rye and I just spent an hour making out while watching a lake full of fireflies. It'd take the four horsemen of the apocalypse to wipe the grin off my gob right now.

I shut the door and am two steps up the stairs when I hear a "Hey" from behind. When I turn, I see Elliot scooping a giant dollop of ice cream from a tub and walking towards me.

"Hey," I say, still smiling.

"Look at you all googly-eyed. Where you been?" he says.

"Out," I say, unsure of how much I'm willing to give away. I mean, don't get me wrong, I trust Elliot. I really do. But we haven't spoken about much. I don't know how much it's safe to tell him. Or whether he is genuinely on my side or not.

"Ooooh, mysterious Fin." He laughs, shovelling up another spoonful of cookie dough ice cream. "Is it a boy?"

And just like that, Elliot breaks the ice with a sledgehammer.

He's smiling and there's not the slightest hint of malice on his face.

I nod. But my smile is a half-hearted one; I'm checking to make sure this isn't some "Gotcha" situation with Mum and Dad.

"Cool," Elliot says. "What's his name?"

I can't believe this is happening. "Rye."

Elliot smiles. "Rye? The dude on the doorstep? Where does he live?"

I'm about to answer when –

"Where does who live?" Dad appears in the kitchen doorway, his eyebrows raised in question.

I tense, immediately snapping into fight or flight mode and I feel like I'm leaning more towards flight. I'm close enough to the door to get out of here. How much did he hear?

Elliot looks at me and then at Dad.

"Fin's friend," he says, and I take a deep breath in and hold it in my chest.

Dad looks between us. He then lets out a half-laugh. More of a scoff, really. He pinches the bridge of his nose as he shakes his head.

"You know, Fin," Dad says, speaking to me like Elliot isn't in the room at all. "I really was starting to think you were coming through since being here."

I feel the blood drain from my face. "What?" I say.

"I was truly starting to think that these …" He looks at the floor and back at me. "– unnatural tendencies had been left behind in Pittford." He shakes his head again, now glancing up to the ceiling as if for inspiration. "But I'm starting to –"

"Hang on, Dad. Just –" Elliot says, to which Dad holds up his hand in a gesture that reads, *Don't you dare.*

I try to steady my breathing.

The air is icy and I don't know whether I should speak or stay silent.

"You really don't get it, do you?" Dad says, his eyes burning into me with a look that I can only describe as total disapproval.

"No, I don't," I say. "I don't know what you want from me."

"A SON," Dad yells, making both me and Elliot jump.

"Dad, this has got to stop," Elliot says, squaring off. His chest is puffed out and he actually looks ready to fight. It terrifies me that he feels he needs to. "You're being –"

"You don't know what it's like," Dad says, rounding on Elliot. "You don't know what it's like having to deal with the life Fin's chosen. To explain to people that … that your son –"

"*Chosen?*" I say, my voice louder than I expected.

Dad turns and stares at me.

"When did you *choose* to be straight exactly, Dad?" So, I seem to have decided to fight now too. I feel like I'm going to scream. I want him to listen to himself and realise how absolutely absurd he's being.

"I beg your pardon?" he says as the clogs turn in his mind. "That's not … That's not the issue here. I don't –"

"You don't what, Dad? Don't know? Or don't have an answer? Perhaps that's because you just knew. Deep in your heart and in your body who you were?"

I look behind Dad to Elliot because he's the only possible pillar of strength I have right now and if I lose sight of him I'm worried I'll collapse in a heap on the floor.

Dad's face shifts from what I think is a glimmer of under-standing to something darker. Like he refuses to grasp this. Not right now.

"You've got a nerve," he growls and I recoil at the anger in his tone. "Trying to throw your behaviour back in my face." He puts his hand to his head as if a headache just came on. "Why can't you just be normal? I can deal with you not being into the same things as me and Elliot. And I've accepted your – your *sensitivity* – but this is taking it too far."

What?

I want to say that football and *feelings* have nothing to do with being gay – that they're just more things on the list of what makes me different from him – but Dad storms out of the room before I can find my words.

I look helplessly at Elliot whose mouth is opening and closing like a clown fish, but Dad returns before either of us can speak.

"Next steps," he says, holding out a stapled booklet. "That's what we need to discuss."

I feel my stomach lurch and sink. "What *is* this?"

Dad's eyes are scanning mine. "I want what's best," he says. "For you. For us. As a family."

"So? What are these *next steps*?"

He motions to the booklet. "This is a different kind of work-shop. I did some research online and –"

I feel like the air has been sucked from the room.

"Dad, that's not a workshop. You know it isn't." Elliot takes the booklet from Dad's hands, flicks through the pages. "What exactly is this bull–?"

"It's a simple programme. A very simple programme. It's to help young people who've lost their way. Re-align themselves, if you will." He has this desperate, wild look in his eyes and I can't help but feel sorry for him. All this effort for what? Because he's scared by the fact that I like guys instead of girls? What a monumental waste of time.

"Dad, this … This thing really isn't a workshop," Elliot says, handing the booklet to me.

I only have to glance at the cover and I want to vomit. All the sympathy I feel for Dad goes out the window. Re-Souled. I know where I've heard the name before. June mentioned it at the first QSA meeting. It's a residential religious camp that practises conversion therapy.

"No," I say, more to myself than anyone else. "Just no."

"Excuse me?" Dad snaps.

"I said *no*." I want to scream it at him. "You want to send me to conversion therapy? Have you lost your mind?"

Dad shakes his head. "Fin, you're being over-dramatic, as usual. This isn't a 'conversion' programme, or whatever it is you're saying. After all, as you keep telling me, there's nothing to 'convert', right?"

Elliot shakes his head. "Dad, you honestly sound insane."

At that Dad loses any semblance of rationality. "Enough!" he bellows at Elliot, practically purple. "Fin, you will not let your mother and me down like this."

Elliot and I stare at one another. This is a new level of crazy. Even for Dad.

We stand silently.

"Is it really too much to ask to want a normal family?" he demands. Each word is deathly cold.

"You have one," Elliot says, more focused than I've ever heard him. "You're just too deluded to see it."

And with that he sweeps the booklet to the floor, then turns and leads me out the front door.

By the time we're on the front lawn I can feel my eyes burning and Elliot is already unlocking his car.

"I'm sorry. I can't take that shit any more. Do you need a lift anywhere?" he asks, looking over at me.

"No. I ..." I say. "No, I'm just going to walk."

"Hey," he says, taking me by the shoulders and forcing me to look at him. "You do not need to change."

His voice breaks and I realise how emotional he is.

"But he does." He scowls, motioning back to the house.

And then my brother jumps in his car and drives off down the street.

I think about texting Poppy or June, but instead just walk. The cool air on my face feels good and the smell of salt air from the wharf makes me briefly forget the shit storm that I was just caught up in.

I take my phone out and type a message to Rye, but I decide against sending it. Instead I just walk.

And walk.

And walk some more.

28

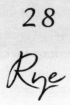

I can't stop thinking about Fin.

When he left, I went home, fed Thelma, then watched her go crazy with excitement while I looked for her harness and we headed straight back out for a walk. I know it's lame and cheesy and whatever, but Fin's kisses are the kind where my whole body melts into his.

When Eric kissed me it felt like he was trying to eat my face off like a zombie from *The Walking Dead*. Kisses with Fin are different. They're simple and perfect and I can't get enough of them.

Thelma and I are practically skipping as we make for my spot by the lake. Life seems promising for the first time in ages and I can't wipe the goofy smile off of my face.

I open up Instagram and see Poppy's story. Her and June are watching *Love, Simon* and snuggling on the couch.

"Aww," I type into the message box.

She sends back the love heart emoji. Then: "How's your night with Fin? ;)"

"Perfect," I reply. Then send the kissing emoji.

"NO," I get back in less than three seconds.

I send back the thumbs-up and a wink emoji.

I'm about to put my phone away when it starts ringing, Poppy's face illuminating my screen.

"Tell. Me. Everything," she says. Then: "June, hit pause. I refuse to miss the carousel kiss."

In the background I hear June click the remote and the room go quiet.

"You're now on speaker. We wish to know every single detail. Go."

"Hey, June," I say. "Sorry for ruining the best bit of the movie."

"Are you kidding? Shut up. Wait, no don't shut up. Speak."

"Nope," I say, hearing the grin on my face.

"You cannot be serious," Poppy says.

"There's nothing to tell."

"LIES," she shouts into the phone. I let out a giggle and give them a brief lowdown on the situation.

June is practically planning the wedding, honeymoon and golden anniversary celebrations and Poppy just keeps saying, "Um." On repeat. Eventually she manages to string a sentence together: "I love this entire thing."

I'm beaming by the time I turn off towards Kettle Lake and my phone starts dropping out.

"I'll speak to you tomorrow, okay?" I say.

"L—ve you, Rye. Keep — posted or —— have to — kill you," is how Poppy's broken voice comes through the crackly line.

I hang up and keep walking, Thelma snuffling around in the trees like she loves to do.

When we get to my spot I take a deep breath in and settle

myself down. I want to jump around I'm so happy. I check my phone on repeat, just to see if Fin's online but the signal is so bad here I can't figure out a thing.

Thelma and I snuggle up on a blanket under the string lights and just breathe. I can't get over how funny life is. When I was with Eric, I thought that was the best I could hope for. The fact that I had someone who was somewhat into me was enough. I guess I don't have the highest self-esteem, especially considering I thought Eric was as good as I could get – a guy who would rather chug beers with his rich-kid party friends than hang out with me – but I always tried to make the most of our situation. I never realised how it could feel to be with someone who actually *likes* me, someone who I wouldn't even think to doubt or mistrust.

I take out some almonds I brought along from the inside pocket of my denim jacket and have myself a snack. Thelma's snoring like a little tank. The lake is completely still; there's not a hint of a breeze in the air.

I take in the surroundings and listen to the crickets and bull-frogs. Nothing beats this. Other than kissing Fin, of course.

*

After an hour or so I stand and brush the dried leaves and dirt from the back of my jeans. I'm about to wake Thelma and make tracks when I hear the snap of a branch somewhere to the left of where I am and my heart sinks.

I hold my breath and stand rooted to the spot. Nobody comes here. Nobody knows about this place, which means this entire situation is now feeling like the beginning of a B-grade horror movie.

"Is … Is anyone there?" I say into the overgrown shrubbery, then hate myself for using the most basic line that always gets the character killed off immediately. Rookie mistake.

Another rustling noise makes my knees lock and I realise I can't move. This is extremely inconvenient considering I should be burning a trail through the bush towards home, but nope. Pesky legs are stuck and I am frozen with fear.

Some more rustling and then footsteps have me all about ready to drop dead on the spot, but then out pops something equally as terrifying as a mass murderer.

"Hey," Eric says, looking down at the floor and back up at me like a kid who's been given detention.

"What do you want?" I ask, my gut doing all kinds of unpleasant things as I stare at him.

"I want to talk," he says, giving me the puppy eyes that I once thought were adorable, but which now just really annoy me.

"I'm done talking with you," I say, feeling myself coming apart.

"Rye, you don't mean that." He smiles. "I miss you."

"Really?" I ask, tears rising in my eyes, despite myself. "Chad not such a hotcock as his Grindr profile claimed?"

I'm so not here for a conversation. I'm exhausted by his head-games.

"Rye, c'mon, I was an idiot. A complete idiot. I see that now. I don't –"

"I don't want to speak to you," I say, finally letting my breath out.

"Rye – just …" Eric starts.

"No, don't 'just' me, anything. What are you *doing* here?" I can't believe he's invaded my haven. The sight of him makes me want to bang my head against a tree trunk in frustration.

"I came to see you," he says, looking down at the ground again.

"Yeah, I figured as much what with you wandering around the bush in total darkness," I say.

"I'm here to apologise," Eric says, looking up and meeting my eyes. "For everything."

I try to hold my anger tight, but for some reason I still feel some form of empathy.

Maybe that's because he sounds the most sincere he has ever sounded and for a brief moment I remember why I fell for him in the first place.

"Great. Thanks," I say, holding my own. "I'm going now," I add, but my feet don't move. Who knows why, but I want to hear what he has to say.

"Rye, I was such a dick to you. A total jerk. I didn't mean to upset you –"

"So why all this now, Eric? What's the go? Did you have an actual epiphany or are you simply bored?" I say, breathing in the air of the lake and staring at him without blinking.

"I'm not … It's … I'm not like you, Rye. I'm not good at expressing –"

"Don't turn this around, Eric," I say, my thoughts crystal clear. "This has nothing to do with how I behave. You chose to chase some guy because I wasn't ready to go all the way. That's just point blank, textbook douche-baggery and you know it."

Eric looks down at his sneakers. "I know," he says, and for a second I think he's crying, but when he looks back up at me there's no tears.

I'm not enjoying this. This isn't what I had in mind. I don't like making anyone feel like garbage, but I'm not about to tell him it's all okay when it's not.

"Look, Eric. Just ... I'm fine. Okay? If that's what you want to know?" I look up at the branches overhead and the sprinkle of stars that shine through them and I feel completely at ease. "Honestly, I'm completely fine," I repeat.

Eric gives me an awkward half-smile. "Good. Okay. Good," he says.

We pause for a second that feels like a hundred years and I turn to leave, Thelma shuffling sleepily along next to me. I'm three steps towards the path home when I feel an overwhelming loneliness. Not for Eric, but for the situation. For the fact that you can one day think everything will work out, only to be floored the next when it all goes to shit.

I'm so in my head that I don't realise he's grabbed my arm, turned me around and is now kissing me hard on the lips. For the briefest moment I kiss him back before being knocked out of my trance-like state and unlocking my lips from his faster than humanly possible.

"No," I say, staring up at him, shaking my head. "No way."

"Rye –" He's still holding onto my arm.

I wrench it out fiercely of his grip and pull Thelma on her lead towards me.

That's when I see him.

Standing among the branches that guard my haven, his face contorted with hurt.

"Fin," I say.

But he turns his back on me and is gone.

29

Fin

I knew Rye was too good to be true. It was *such* a mistake to head for his special place, as if it could be a haven for me too.

And why wouldn't he say no to another chance with Eric?

But I honestly didn't think I'd be so stupid again.

I've barely slept – waking up this morning was a challenge – and I've swallowed more snot from crying overnight than I did when I got pneumonia in fourth grade.

This is really not what I had in mind for today. I switched my phone off after Rye's eighth attempt at calling me last night and I haven't bothered to turn it back on. I wander through the halls to find my locker – where Poppy is waiting for me.

"Dude, you look like you've been attacked," she says.

I swirl the combination on my locker and throw my backpack in, shutting it again and leaning my forehead against the cold tin.

"Are … you good?" Poppy says.

I shake my head: no.

June appears as if out of thin air. "What happened?" she asks, holding my hand in hers.

I'm about to tell them both everything, but my throat has clenched around my Adam's apple, and then Rye shows up. He's out of breath and his eyes are horribly bloodshot and swollen. Has he been crying too?

"Fin. Please, can we –"

June and Poppy exchange looks, but I'm already striding away towards D-block.

"Fin," I hear him call after me but I keep walking. I can't deal with this. Not now.

*

When I get to geography I sit at the back next to Candace "Year Captain" Dalton and immediately regret my decision.

"Hey, Candace," I say, opening my book and brushing a stray hair from my face.

"Hi, Tim," She is far too jolly for first period. But then again she is a full-blown wannabe Disney princess.

"Fin," I correct.

"Hmm?" she asks, beaming while digging an assortment of pens from her bag and arranging them in size order at the top of her desk.

"My name ... it's F–" I start, but before I can finish, she's grabbing my arm and staring at me with shark eyes.

"Oh my gosh," she says, freezing.

"I ... what?" I say, suddenly afraid to move.

"I forgot my eraser," she says, cupping her face in her hands.

"Oh. I – Here. I've got one," I say, fishing one from my backpack and handing it to her.

"No, it's – Ugh. It's not the right size. It throws the whole order into chaos," she says, motioning to the pencils placed carefully along the top of her desk.

I see her OCD has gone rogue, so I tread carefully. I know how debilitating this can be. I used to suffer from a mild version of OCD. It's no picnic. I used to not be able to leave a room my parents were in unless I'd turned the light on and off forty-four times. My parents, worried the disco-style situation I'd created in our living room would blow the fuses in the whole street, one day decided to get me to counselling and thankfully I haven't been blowing up any electrical boxes since. But still. I know what it's like. Even for someone as peppy and upbeat as Snow White herself. By which I mean, Candace Dalton.

"What size do you need?" I ask.

Candace shakes her head. "Just ... Ugh. Forget it," she says, her breathing shallow.

I nod.

"I just ..."

"You okay?" I ask.

"No," she says, biting the skin around her pinky. "I hate how nothing is ever in my control."

Wow, this is a deep conversation that I didn't anticipate having when walking into geography. I guess the universe has other plans, as usual.

"That's how it is for all of us though," I say, more to myself than her.

She shifts one of the pencils an infinitesimal amount. "Do you have problems?" she asks.

I smile. "Sure," I say.

"What are your problems?"

"Parents want to 'convert' me. Guy I like kissed his ex. My morning coffee tasted like dirt."

Candace's jaw almost hits the floor.

I had no intention of telling her all that, but whatever. I'm done being secretive about the facts of my life.

"Well, my eraser issue looks pretty pathetic right now," she says.

I shake my head. "No, it doesn't actually," I say. "You want your life to not feel like it's overflowing. I get that."

"But you have like, legitimate stuff going on," she says.

"Right, but your eraser thing is your way of trying to avoid stuff falling into chaos, right?" I ask. "Like a preventative?"

Candace smiles in agreement.

I smile back.

What I wouldn't give to be able to erase out this shit-show situation I'm now in.

The classroom door shuts and the hum of student chitchat quietens down.

"Fin, would you like to kick off class by reading from the top of page ninety-eight please," Ms Fry says, demanding my attention.

"Thanks, Fin," Candace says, emphasising my name and blushing – clearly conscious that she got it wrong earlier.

I give her a thumbs-up and start to read.

After class I turn my phone back on because it's been far too long without checking Instagram for cute dog pics and I'm bombarded with a thousand texts from Rye, Poppy and June.

Poppy has asked me to meet at her locker so I head over there and wait. The throng of students barging past reminds me of the last scene from *Braveheart* as I stand with my back pressed against the row of lockers.

Poppy arrives with a look on her face I find hard to read. "Hey," she says.

"Hey," I say.

As Poppy takes out some books and a fruit roll-up from her locker, June arrives. Thankfully Rye is nowhere in sight. I'm not in the right headspace to deal with him just now.

The three of us make our way towards the outside quadrangle as the sun puts in an appearance from behind a cloud.

"So, we heard what happened," June says, breaking the painful silence between us.

I shrug, not knowing what to say.

Poppy grimaces. "Firstly, I want you to know that neither of us think it's cool what Rye did," she says, looking over at me and then making a beeline for an empty table underneath a gum tree.

We throw our bags down and June sits on top of the table cross-legged while Poppy sits next to me.

"Right, but, from what we gathered, Eric kind of ambushed him," June says.

I look between both of them and don't really know what to say. This is painfully awkward. I'm the new guy in this friendship circle. Of course, they're going to take Rye's side.

"Ambushed or not, he looked pretty set on kissing him back," I say bitterly.

June glances at Poppy and then to me.

"We weren't there … Obviously," June says. "But we do know that Rye really likes you."

I shake my head and snort. I feel like a petulant child but I don't really care right now what they think of me.

"He does, Fin," Poppy says. I feel like it's the most sincere thing she's ever said to me. Her eyes are completely clear and she's staring at me like I'm an idiot if I don't believe her.

I take a breath. I don't like this situation whatsoever, but I also have a feeling, deep down, that Rye does actually give a damn.

"I think my parents are on to me," I say, throwing a flaming spanner in the works which I know will send this conversation in another direction.

"How come?" June asks, a crease forming along her forehead.

"Dad … He … I mean, he *knows*," I say.

Poppy looks down at her phone then back up at me. "I think I should talk to him," she says, which catapults my heart rate into the Milky Way.

"And I think pancakes for breakfast, lunch and dinner is a smart decision. It's not," June says.

Poppy rolls her eyes. "Could you for once not dismiss everything I say as a dumb idea?"

The tension just went up about a thousand notches. Dealing with their bickering is so not what I need.

"Okay, no tantrum required, Poppy," June says dismissively, which only aggravates Poppy further – but she's clearly trying her best to keep a lid on her temper.

"I'm going," Poppy announces, heading back inside. "Sorry, Fin. I'll text you later."

June looks up at the ceiling and mouths "fuck sake" before looking back at me.

"Sorry. I just … Ugh. Okay. Back to the situation at hand. We have a few options here. Your family aren't about to change overnight. But I do think there could be something to be gained from a discussion with them." June seems sincere, but I immediately shut her idea down.

"No. Absolutely not," I say. "I'm sorry, June. You mean well but that just won't cut it. I know my family. Trying for a rational discussion about my sexuality would be like chopping off a leg and walking into a lions' den. Not gonna work."

June tilts her head. I think she's about to say something else but she goes quiet, staring down at her shoes and shuffling from side to side.

I'm about to ask what the hell is going on but, before I can speak, Rye is standing next to me.

"Not now, okay?" I say, wanting to crawl into one of the lockers behind me and hide there for a while. "I'm having a tough enough time as it is."

Rye looks between me and June for an explanation.

"Fin's dad is being … difficult about his sexuality and –"

"June, please, it's not a QSA meeting," I interrupt. The last thing I feel like doing is taking part in an analysis of my "sexuality" in front of Rye.

"Fin, I really want to talk," Rye pleads, and I can't help but be touched by how genuine he sounds. But I still don't know what to say so instead I stare at the floor.

June shuffles some more and just when I'm about to walk off and spend the afternoon overthinking, Rye takes my hand in his. I look up at him and he's looking at me like I'm the only person in this universe.

But I have to pull away. I can't handle him touching me right now. June gives me a questioning look and I nod at her to let her know I'm okay.

"Please," Rye says softly. "Come with me."

So I follow him as he heads away from the quadrangle to a secluded spot on the edge of the playing fields.

The air is fresh, but the sun is warm on our backs and the smell of salt air and frangipanis is a nice change from the stale stink that fills the school.

We find a patch of grass and sit. Rye has reached for my hand again and this time I let him take it. But my fingers are loose in his. It's all too much. I want to take a nap. Or cry. Or cry while napping. I don't know.

"Fin, I need you to know that I had no idea Eric was going to turn up last night."

I extract my hand from his and pull up some grass, scrunching it up to distract myself from this less-than-fun conversation. "Okay," I say.

Rye's eyes find mine and they're painfully genuine. Annoyingly so.

"I would never deliberately hurt you, Fin," he says. "Never."

I want to believe him, but the image of him kissing Eric keeps flashing in my mind.

"So, what was that kiss about then?" I snap, not caring one bit how harsh my words sound out in the open. "I bet it wasn't a one-off either, was it? Did you ever even finish with him?"

"Steady on." Rye flinches. "He kissed me, Fin …"

"Pretty sure you were kissing him back," I spit, my stomach churning. I'm ashamed to show him this side of me, but somehow can't help it.

"Maybe I was …" he says. "Maybe I needed to be sure," and his honesty gives me a kick in the gut.

I know I need to keep quiet and we sit for a moment, both of us scrunching the grass up now.

"But I stopped … Because I know he's really not good for me," he continues. "And I think he knows that, too."

I throw the grass I've excavated behind me and pull another handful from the patch in front of us.

"I like you, Fin," Rye says and one of the layers of ice that has coated my heart since last night melts. "It scares me a bit how much I like you … Things with Eric actually really kind of screwed me up."

I look up at him and gently take his hand. I don't know why because I'm still kinda mad, but I want to hold his hand. I want him to know I get that he's trying.

"Look, I like you, too," I say. "It doesn't mean none of this hurts, but I understand." I run my fingers over his knuckles. "After what Jesse did to me in Pittford, I was a complete wreck."

Rye looks down at our entwined hands, then he looks up at me and smiles. I want nothing more than to kiss him, but my ego is making me hold back. I feel betrayed and I don't want him thinking I'm not still a little bit pissed at him. Even though, deep down, I'm pretty sure he wouldn't get back with Eric. Not now.

"Do you want to come to mine tonight?" Rye asks tentatively. "Get away from your family for a bit? Mum's boyfriend Carl is coming over and I need you to hold my hair when I'm vomiting in the toilet from their grossly inappropriate PDAs that they make me witness."

Who am I fooling? I let my guard down and snigger, which makes him smile too.

"You don't have to … I get it if you're still mad at me. I can leave you alone if you wa–"

Is he crazy?

"Talking of grossly inappropriate PDAs …" I say and with that I sneak a kiss and all my anger and hurt dissolve on his lips.

*

When we arrive at his house, Rye's dog, Thelma, greets us and Rye rolls on the porch with her and gives her more attention than any dog has ever been given. It's pretty adorable.

Thelma rests her head on Rye's chest, and I sit on the steps next to them as his mum Karen opens the fly screen door.

"FIN!" Karen says, throwing her arms around me and giving me what I can only describe as the biggest hug I have ever received. "It's SO nice to meet you! How've you been, darl'?" she asks, scooting in next to me and giving Rye a kiss on the cheek.

"Great," I say, which is somewhat the truth.

Rye sits up as Thelma trots over to Karen who happily rubs behind her ears.

"Liar," Rye says, staring at me with a hint of a smile.

I shrug and shake my head, trying desperately not to let on that anything is out of the ordinary. When adults get involved, stuff gets real and I don't feel up for that. I just want some dust to settle before I kick it up some more.

Karen seems to notice my discomfort because she takes my hand. "You okay, honey?" she asks, stroking my palm with her thumb. I only met her two seconds ago, but already feel so relaxed around her. I feel a rush of jealousy – what I wouldn't give right now for my mum to actually ask me if I'm okay.

I nod. Rye sits to my left and puts his arm around me, and Karen strokes my hair. There's no judgement or questions. We just sit for a while.

When I'm finally able to break the silence, I explain to Karen the abridged version of events going on at home.

When I'm done, the only noise for what seems like miles is Thelma's snoring. I reckon that dog could sleep through a Monsters of Rock gig.

Karen looks at me and then at Rye and then back to me again.

"You know, sweetheart, I'm really good with words," Karen says, which sends Rye's eyebrows to the top of his forehead.

"Mum, this isn't something you need to involve yourself in," he says.

"I'm just saying sometimes adults have a way of getting through to other adults and –"

"I really appreciate it, Mrs Hendrix," I say.

"Karen," she corrects me.

"Karen," I repeat. "But I think my family are past the talking stage ..."

I feel completely choked up, but not because of the shit show I'm living through. I feel choked up because I've never had anyone listen to me so intently. Not just Rye, but his mum, too. They're both so sincere; there's not a bad bone between them. If they weren't so genuinely lovely it'd be unnerving.

Karen strokes my hair back from my face, before she stands and claps her hands together.

"Okay, enough with the hangdog vibe," she declares. "We'll all end up looking like this little crumpet." She beckons at Thelma who springs to life and wiggles her butt at Karen's feet. "Carl's inside making satay tofu noodles and so I suggest we dig into that deliciousness and then play some Guess Who," Karen says, looking between Rye and me.

I smile and Rye gives a double thumbs-up.

"Oh, and Rye?" Karen says as she turns back from the front door. "Please know that I expect your Guess Who game to be strong. I have no issues with whooping your behind in front of your boyfriend." She laughs as the fly screen cranks shut and I feel my tummy burst into firecrackers at the fact that Rye's mum just called me his boyfriend.

*

Dinner is uh-may-zing and Carl keeps the conversation going with talk about his new yoga teacher in town.

"He's wonderful," he says, spearing a piece of tofu with a chopstick. "His energy is just so … ya know?"

Karen squeezes his shoulder indulgently, and Rye looks over at me and smiles.

It hasn't gone unnoticed by either of us that Carl isn't wearing any pants. No jeans or joggers. Just a T-shirt and undies. I concealed my giggle pretty well when we first noticed, but Rye has had a look of horror plastered on his face since Carl leaned across the table to grab the salt and his budgie smuggler package knocked over the soy sauce.

We wrap up dinner with a few rounds of Guess Who?, then Rye and I wash up.

From somewhere in the living room we hear a racket that sounds like tapes toppling and eject buttons being pressed. Rye looks about ready to go and suss it out when Van Morrison's *Bright Side of the Road* blasts from a stereo.

Thelma barks as Karen and Carl come dancing through the kitchen. They're technically a little inept, but are strutting their stuff with an abandon that's more infectious than the flu.

Before I realise it, we're literally all dancing.

"We're heading out in a sec," Karen says, still dancing while feeding Thelma a green bean.

"I'll just put some pants on, and we can get going," Carl says, placing his plate and cutlery on the sink for us to wash.

"I mean, it wouldn't be a bad idea to put some pants on

regardless," Rye says as he scrubs the plate and places it on the drying rack.

Carl either didn't hear or doesn't care and, while I stifle my laugh, Karen gives us both a peck on the cheek and, before I know it, we're alone.

Rye finishes off the last of the dishes and then looks across at me. His eyes hold mine for a beat longer than usual and then takes two steps towards me, his eyes still on mine and his body unmoving.

I stare back and my heartbeat speeds up. In my peripheral vision I see his hands and just as I'm about to close my eyes he taps my nose with his dishwasher hand and then paints a bubble beard on me with his other.

"Ohhh you're gonna regret tha—" I start, but he's already added another layer of bubbles and I'm chasing him through the kitchen and out on to the front porch, Thelma tumbling along behind us.

We collapse on the grass out front as I use the remnants of bubbles from my face to cover his head as best I can.

We're laughing and, as I'm about to splash some more foam on his chin, he takes my hand softly and laces my fingers with his.

Then he leans in and kisses me.

"We good?" he asks, clearing some bubbles off of my forehead. I smile. "We're good."

*

It's about eight o'clock when I turn on to my street. It's pitch black; the moon is nowhere to be seen and only a sprinkle of stars are out on an otherwise charcoal sky.

It takes me a few beats for the image unfolding in front of me to take shape and register in my mind.

Karen is at my front door. Carl is in the driver's seat of their car playing Candy Crush. My mum and dad are on the porch with Elliot off to the side.

I'm rooted to the spot just out of earshot of what they're saying. This. Cannot. Be. Happening.

My breathing intensifies and my legs take on a life of their own as they propel me forwards. I have no idea what I'm going to say but I know I need to stop whatever the hell is happening immediately.

As I near the front door I hear Karen's voice and my parents' silence.

"– and I'm just so glad because Rye hasn't been very lucky on the friend front. Well, not friend I suppose, more like a b–"

"Karen," I say in my best chirpy voice.

Karen turns to face me and beams like I'm her favourite person. "FIN!" she says, grabbing my arm and drawing me beside her. "I was just talking about you and Rye and how wonderf–"

"Have you met my brother Elliot?" I say, desperately trying to cut her off.

Dad is looking between me and Karen, and Mum looks like Karen may as well be standing butt naked in front of her. Elliot weirdly enough seems to be enjoying watching Mum and Dad squirm. For me this is about as fun as walking on hot coals.

"I have met Elliot," Karen says with a wink. "He's quite the stud muffin."

"You're too kind, Mrs Hendrix," Elliot says, grinning.

Karen waves him away playfully and just as I feel I'm about to spontaneously combust, Carl honks and gestures for Karen to hurry up.

Karen rolls her eyes and takes her leave, letting my heart rate settle and my trembling subside.

✳

When we're inside I don't bother waiting to talk to anyone, even though I can sense Mum and Dad staring at me, probably wondering why Karen felt the need to come over and tell them how delighted she is that I'm friends with Rye. To be honest, I'd be confused, too. I wonder how long it'll take them to put two and two together.

I head straight up the three flights and up my ladder to my room. I lie on my bed and push my face into my pillow and scream silently.

I think I'm safe to fall asleep when I hear a knock and the hatch to my room creaks open. I look over to see Dad regarding me with what I can only assume is despair. And anger. It looks like he hasn't cooled down since Elliot and I stormed out of the house yesterday.

"Son, I want you to think about what we discussed," he says, his brow furrowed. "It'll make you feel better."

"Re-Souled will make *me* feel better?" I say, sitting up on my bed to face him, all my fury bursting into flames. "*Really*? Or is it for you, Dad?"

"Fin," he snaps. "Don't dare take that tone with me. This family is at breaking point right now, do you understand?"

I turn cold. He's looking at me like I'm a stranger and I can't understand what it is that he's trying to say. Is he honestly saying we're all at breaking point because I've not chosen to be straight yet? As if I can shrug off being gay like it's a jacket my parents would rather I didn't wear?

"I have tried to be reasonable. I have tried to be calm. I have tried to be understan–"

"Is this some kind of joke?" I shout, feeling myself completely lose it at his self-righteousness. "How about trying harder? You're the opposite of all of those things! *You moved us to a new town!* What the hell is that even about?"

Dad looks up at me from the hatch in the floor, half suspended on the ladder. He stares at me for the longest time. It makes me want to curl up and cry. However hurt or angry I'm feeling, I can't help but want his approval, his love – his acceptance. It's horrible to see him look at me like I'm letting him down just by being myself.

Memories from when I was a kid flash in my brain like some annoying old home movie: Dad running alongside me as I learned to ride a bike, teaching me how to choose the right line when we were all fishing down at the lake, joining in with silly songs for Trick or Treating at Halloween.

I feel myself well up, but Dad's face has hardened.

"Night, Fin. You and I both know what options you have left."

30

Rye

It's three a.m. It feels like I've been rolling around in my bed for hours, overthinking.

I nearly passed out when Mum and Carl got home last night and told me they had gone to Fin's place. SO uncool. Really, ridiculously, *painfully* uncool.

Mum assured me that she didn't talk about our relationship or anything, but Fin hasn't replied to a single one of my messages.

So, come morning, I'm awake. Wide awake, and feeling as jangled as if I've drunk about nine hundred espressos. Me and Thelma are in the kitchen and I'm making waffles for myself, because waffles fix everything, and Thelma loves them so it's basically a win-win.

I decide to put my headphones in and crank up some tunes, movie soundtracks and, of course, some Cher because it feels appropriate. I mean, can you even make waffles unless you have a soundtrack? I start with "Food Glorious Food" from *Oliver!*, then as I'm pouring the batter into the waffle maker I switch it up and put on "I Want You To Want Me" by Letters to Cleo from the all-time nineties classic *10 Things I Hate About You* (Heath Ledger, my GOD).

Thelma is dancing with me in complete silence because I have my headphones in, but she loves it regardless, her little butt wagging from side to side.

When they're done, I'm onto Cher and "If I Could Turn Back Time" and I'm randomly overwhelmed with emotion. I don't think I've ever really understood just how painful it must be to have a family who don't understand you, and who don't really accept you at all. I turn the waffle maker off and sit at the kitchen table; Thelma's head rests on my knee as I listen to Cher belt out the lyrics and wonder if Fin's parents could ever know how much Fin needs them to whole-heartedly accept him.

I sit for a while and consider what I could do to show Fin that he may not have people at home who are there for him, but I care. I'm there for him.

I harpoon a bit of waffle and dollop it in some maple syrup. As I'm chewing, I decide exactly what I'm going to do to prove to Fin just how special he really is.

*

I arrive at school feeling like I've been up all night … Because I have. My eyes are carrying more bags than Anne Hathaway in *The Devil Wears Prada* and there's been multiple times that I have considered simply crawling up into a ball and napping on the pavement.

But no. Onwards and upwards. I need to find Fin.

I arrive at my locker and check my phone. Still no word from him. I don't quite know what I'm going to say but I know it needs to be along the lines of: "I'm sorry about my lunatic mother and her pants-free, Candy-Crush obsessed, yoga-fanatic boyfriend, please don't hate me."

I open up my locker and am taking out my maths books when a text from June wakes my phone up.

June: Did you bring your sign?

What is she talking about?

I start typing back but feel a tap on my shoulder and she's standing behind me.

"Hey," she says, her eyes bloodshot.

"You been crying, June-bug?" I ask, motioning to her unhappy, swollen cheeks.

June sniffs and shakes her head. "Nope. Not at all."

Lying through her teeth.

"Okay," I say.

"So, can I see your sign? I wanna make sure we have no double-ups," June says, her eyes like saucers.

"My what? I'm sorry, can you refresh my memory? It's been a day. I've been up all ni–"

"The counter-protest, Rye. Are you freakin' kidding me?"

I'm stunned, because June never gets mad at me. Like ever.

"I'm … Shit. I'm so sorry. I'll make one at break. It'll take no time and I –"

"You AND Poppy. Wow. I'm dumb."

"June, what?" I ask. I am not in the mood to have a falling out with her this morning.

"This is the first and only trans issue I've ever raised at the QSA meetings. The first one. I totally expected you guys to be there the way I am with, I dunno, every other queer issue. We've been organising this protest for *months*."

June gives me the hardest stare ever and I feel a pang of guilt in my chest.

Actually, more like a sledgehammer in the face that's rammed full of guilt. I hate it because she's right.

"June, I'm going to fix this," I promise her, but she's already shaking her head and walking down the hall. She strides straight past Poppy, whose guilty expression mirrors exactly how I feel.

"You didn't bring a sign either?" she asks, scrunching her face up. "We're total friend failures and activist assholes."

I lift my shoulders in agreement. "On top of that, my mum and Carl decided to visit Fin's parents last night." Poppy grimaces at me. "So yeah. This is really fun. I'm having such a great day so far."

"Okay. Let's tackle this one thing at a time," Poppy says, squarely facing me like we're about to do battle. "We can make the signs at break. Very simple. We'll then rally up next to June and make sure she knows we've got her back."

I nod as Poppy takes a breath before storming into more battle-talk.

"As for Fin, do you think he'll be pissed at you?"

"No, but I'm pissed at me," I say. "Well, more Mum and Carl. But still." I shrug.

"You really like him, don't you?" Poppy asks, softly.

"I do," I tell her.

"Then show him. Show the guy he means more to you than Eric ever did. Show him how much you care."

I stare at Poppy. Did she read my mind? I've never heard her talk so openly about any of this stuff. There's no sarcasm in her voice at all, which is a little unnerving.

"What's got into you?" I ask with a smile.

"I feel like I'm blowing it," Poppy says, looking down at her beaten-up sunshine yellow Converse.

"Blowing it?" I ask.

"With June … She's way too good for me."

It's my turn to be all insightful and sage-like. "Poppy, you both love each other. Very much. The pair of you need to stop this dumb-fuckery and get on with that bit. The loving each other part. I think that starts with you showing June how much you care too."

Poppy cracks a smile. "What wise being gave you that advice?" she asks with a wink.

"A wise being with such insight and knowledge she forgot she wore two different coloured socks this morning," I say looking down at her feet.

"Aw shit," Poppy says, breaking into a proper giggle.

"Catch you later," I tell her as I head for B-block.

That's when I see him. Well, I see the back of his head.

I race up and catch his arm just as he's about to enter the science building.

"Hey," I say.

"Hey," Fin says, flustered but seemingly glad to see me.

"You okay?" I ask.

"I am," Fin says.

"So, I heard about what happened last night," I start, but Fin puts his hand up.

"Don't worry."

"But I –"

"Honestly. It's cool. Not your fault. Or your mum's. I know she was only trying to be nice."

He smiles at me and my heartbeat kicks into fourth gear and revs my body into full-on tingling.

"So, you're not mad?" I ask.

He looks at me and laughs. "Mad?" He shakes his head and takes my hand in his. "Mad that my boyfriend's mum tried to convince my parents that their son isn't a complete degenerate?"

I smile.

"No, Rye. I'm far from mad."

I take a breath. "This weekend I think you should stay at mine," I tell him as he squeezes my hand. "Mum and Carl are having their annual 'Intents Barbecue'." Followed up with, "That's spelled I-N-T-E-N-T-S, because they put up a bunch of tents in the back yard so people can crash for the night."

Fin's answering smile lights up the hallway. "I'd like that."

I check my phone for the time. "Okay, I gotta go to class and then make some signs with Poppy for the counter-protest today. Did you wanna come?" I ask, stuffing my phone in my backpack.

"I got to school early and made mine in the library," Fin says.

"I'm impressed."

"But I'll come with you to your crafting session, if that's still cool?" he says.

*

At break I find Fin and we head to the library to find Poppy amid an assortment of cardboard, crêpe paper, glitter and glue.

Fin unfurls his rolled-up creation which is made to look like a bathroom sign with a male symbol, a female symbol, a non-binary symbol, followed a bit randomly by a mermaid, a dinosaur and an alien. Underneath the artwork reads:

"PLEASE! JUST WASH YOUR HANDS."

Poppy smiles. "I love it."

He blushes, which is the cutest thing ever, and I lean over and kiss him.

"Ew," Poppy says laughing.

"Now you're being homophobic," I say which sends her into a snort laugh.

We spend our lunch break working frantically on the signs and, when we're finally done, we assemble like the Avengers before heading off to our afternoon classes.

I take my phone out and text June:

Me: Please don't hate us. We love you.

∗

By the time the bell goes, and last period approaches the adrenaline has kicked in and I'm in full blown nervous mode. I really hope June forgives us. And I really hope this protest doesn't turn nasty.

On my way to the library, where June instructed us to meet, I catch a glimpse of a crowd near the oval.

Above a poster that reads "Get Your Agenda Out Of Our Restroom", I see Bronwyn's dumb head and my nerves disappear. I almost want to laugh at the ridiculousness of it all. How sad does your life have to be to bother putting up a fight against a minority using the bathroom?

When I get to the library, June is at a table fixing a trans flag semi-permanent tattoo on her upper arm and painting the colours in broad strokes across both cheeks.

"Hey," I say.

"Hey," she says, not looking up.

"Did you get my text?" I ask timidly.

She just looks at me.

"I'm so sorry, June," I say.

"Me too," comes a voice from behind me.

I turn and see Poppy walking super-cautiously towards us.

For a moment I think June is going to ignore us, but then she takes a deep breath and looks us both square in the face.

"Show me your signs," she says, her voice as clipped as a lieutenant leading her troops into battle.

We unfurl our cardboard for her approval just as Fin arrives, adding his creation to the set for June to survey.

A few moments pass as she examines them closely.

Mine says, "Trans is Beautiful", painted in the trans flag with multicoloured glitter.

Poppy's is a giant picture of a toilet with the words "Keep Calm, It's Just a Toilet", plastered across the top in rainbow sparkles.

The room is quiet when June finally looks up at us.

"Forgiven," she says, which sends Poppy off like a rocket to plant a kiss on her lips.

"You ready?" June asks as the remaining QSA squad make their way into the room holding their signs like gladiator shields.

We shout "Yes" in unison and head out the double doors towards the oval.

∗

When we get there Mr Wilkinson is speaking with a woman I'm assuming is Paisley's mum while Bronwyn stands with hers off to the left with a look on their faces like they've been sucking lemons all afternoon.

A collection of other parents and kids stomp around together holding up signs and frowning like the very idea of a gender-neutral bathroom is too heavy a cross to bear.

"Mrs Sharp, please. You are fully aware that the school supports transgender students and refuses to discriminate based on gender, sexuality, race, or relig–"

"Oh, stop being such a tree hugger," Mrs Sharp spits. "Not everything needs to be politically correct –"

"Excuse me," June says, holding her own sign up high as she marches into their midst. "But I do find it funny how those who cry about 'political correctness' are the ones who political correctness doesn't really help."

Mrs Sharp stares at her in disgust. And then in horror when she catches sight of Chrissy standing right next to her with a banner which declares: "MY FAITH KEEPS ME QUEER!"

June's parents are here now, too, and they're ready for battle. Their signs are enormous. One saying: "BACK OFF BIGOTS", and the other saying: "THE 'T' IN LGBT IS NOT SILENT".

"I mean, surely you don't *actually* care where trans students pee, do you?" June continues. "This is all about you and your outdated values."

I look over at Fin whose mouth is hanging open in admiration. Next to him, June's mum and dad lift their placards higher.

My arms erupt in goose bumps as June stands her ground like Wonder Woman.

"I simply don't feel comfortable with a *boy* using the same restroom as my daughter," Bronwyn's mum snarls, stressing the word "boy" while giving June her best evil eye.

I feel the anger ripple through the ranks of the QSA – and

the adults supporting us. Poppy squares off with her like a ninja warrior.

"But you're okay with Bronwyn sneaking into the boys' restroom to fool around with Mark Jefferson every lunch break?"

A couple of "Oooh snaps" come from behind us.

"I don't know what you're talking about," Bronwyn's mum says, outraged.

"Yeah, I bet you don't," Poppy says.

"Regardless,' she goes on, drawing herself up as Bronwyn squirms. "Our children have the right to feel safe at school. We have a right to protest."

"And we have a right to counter-protest your utter stupidity," Fin says, his voice fierce.

I look over at him and he's staring them down. I'm almost embarrassed to say that it's one of the sexiest things I've ever seen.

"How dare you –" Bronwyn's mum splutters, looking around for back-up.

"Ignore him, Van," Mrs Sharp says snidely, "He's new to this town and has *obviously* fallen in with the wrong crowd. I don't see your parents here, young man, do they not support your life choices? Ashamed, are they?"

She's way too close to home – and I instantly turn to Fin to comfort him but am amazed to see how calm and composed he looks.

"I'm not ashamed, Mrs Sharp," Fin announces. "I'm exactly where I'm supposed to be. Can you say the same? Standing outside a *school* making a fuss about *toilets*, really?"

At which point Mr Wilkinson steps in between both parties. Obviously he's decided not to let the school yard turn into an actual battlefield.

"It's very clear. Our policy is that we do *not* discriminate," he declares. "There's nothing further to discuss. Like all policies, if you attend our school, you abide by it."

I look over and see June's eyes sparkling with pride. Her dad is next to her now; one arm round her, the other holding his badass sign aloft. June's mum needs no words to destroy Mrs Sharp; her death stare does it all.

I'm amazed at how proud I feel to be at a school where our teachers can be counted on to stand up for all of us not just a select few of us.

Bronwyn, Paisley and their dinosaur crew look about ready to breathe fire but instead elect to turn their backs on us, grumbling to one another.

We all stand rooted to the spot not saying anything while we gather ourselves.

Poppy holds June's hand and I have my arm around Fin's waist.

"Right then." June mentally dusts herself off. "I think we could all use a debrief."

I look at Fin. "You okay?" I whisper under my breath.

He flashes me a smile that just about melts me into the tarmac.

I can feel the warmth of his body next to mine. "You," I tell him, "make one incredibly hot activist."

31

Fin

Well, that was one of the most exhilaratingly terrifying afternoons I've ever had. The only thing that comes remotely close is when I swam with sharks. Without a cage. Ha. I'm lying. I would never swim with sharks. I'm not crazy. But I imagine it would come close to being as terrifying as a face-off with Bronwyn, Paisley and their bigoted-on-every-level families.

Thankfully I am now nestled next to Rye in a booth at Penny's opposite Poppy and June who have made up (for what seems like the thousandth time this month), and we are about to chow down on the biggest plate of nachos completely covered in delicious gooey melted cheese, guacamole, sour cream and salsa. And, of course, milkshakes.

The stereo is playing an awesome combination of our favourite music – Poppy dictatorially commandeers the jukebox every time we visit.

"We did great today!" June exclaims while chewing on her paper straw.

"We did," Rye says, looking over at me and interlinking his fingers with mine.

I haven't had this before. This awesome feeling of belonging and acceptance where it feels okay to hold my boyfriend's hand in public. Or to have a boyfriend, period. To sit and feel comfortable around friends without fear of being judged for who I am. Or of them being judged for who they are. It's awesome.

My phone vibrates in my pocket. It's Dad. But for once he's not spoiling my vibe. I've told him I'm having dinner with some friends to which he has responded with a simple thumbs-up emoji. The coast is clear, and I can now happily enjoy my nachos.

"So, what are we doing this weekend?" June asks, surveying Rye and me like we should already have something planned.

I look to Rye who has scrunched his face up and is looking anywhere but at me.

"Hey," I say, smiling. "What's that look for?" June and Poppy glance at one another and I'm unsure if they know what he's acting weirdly about or are just as confused as I am.

"Nothing," Rye says, stroking my knuckles.

I'm about to respond when I see Poppy's face scrunch up too.

I turn to find Bronwyn and Paisley standing next to our table, looking as sinister as the twins in *The Shining*. But not as well dressed.

"What do you want?" Poppy asks, shaking her head.

Bronwyn smirks and looks around the table at all of us. I avoid her eyes to save myself from running screaming down a hotel corridor, but Rye squeezes my hand tighter and he looks truly pissed.

"Can you leave? Seriously. You've done enough damage for one day," Rye snaps, his voice on the verge of shouting.

"We just came to tell you that we're sorry," Paisley declares loftily.

All four of us stare at one another and blink a few times. June couldn't have looked more shocked had Paisley burst into flames.

"What's the catch?" Poppy asks, her brow furrowing.

"There is no catch," Bronwyn says, and for a second I genuinely wonder whether I fell and banged my head on the way in here. I don't understand what's going on, but something about Bronwyn's eyes seems sincere and I actually believe her.

"Um … Okay," June says slowly, the words hanging in the air as we all try to take in what's going on.

"Yeah. We're sorry," Bronwyn says.

I'm eyeing her suspiciously; take back what I said about sincerity, this is all a bit too good to be true.

"Super sorry," Bronwyn adds. "About this."

Before I know what's even going on, Bronwyn has grabbed Poppy's milkshake and what happens next seems to occur in dream-like slow motion.

I somehow manage to intercept the giant glass as Bronwyn aims it at June and it does this weird backflip, front flip, side flip thing where none of the milkshake actually moves until it's pointed back at Bronwyn where it lets loose in all its sugary thick gloop and douses her from head to toe.

The heavy glass bangs against the side of the table once, showering Paisley with sticky remnants of milkshake, and then bounces to the floor.

Silence.

I look from June to Poppy to Rye and then up at Paisley and Bronwyn. Paisley looks like the *Scream* mask. Bronwyn isn't moving. I'm worried she's died of embarrassment.

Everyone seems frozen in place. Then I hear a snort and I see Poppy covering her mouth with her hand, attempting to conceal a laugh.

June looks from Rye to Poppy to me and then at Bronwyn and Paisley but doesn't manage to contain her laughter.

Then Rye and I lose it.

I'm talking full-blown, wet-yourself cry-laughter.

Bronwyn stands rooted to the spot and I even catch Paisley's half-grin when she gets a good look at the banana milkshake monstrosity standing before all of us.

Bronwyn turns and leaves faster than I've ever seen dairy move and Paisley is fresh on her heels.

Jerry, who has been standing nearby watching the scene unfold, walks over.

"This. All of this. Is on me tonight," he says, grinning as he motions to the food.

"No way," Poppy stutters through a giggle as she wipes the tears from her eyes.

"*Yes* way," Jerry says, wiping down the flecks of shake from the table. "I should have stood up to that bigoted pile of garbage years ago." He looks to me and laughs. "Nice work!"

I shake my head. "I genuinely didn't even mean to. It was more of an interception than a –"

"Yeah, good job!" Rye gives me a cheeky salute. "You did great."

✳

Now it's just me and Rye, nestled in a booth together as June and Poppy have left to catch up with Chrissy, and we've decided to split another sundae because why not?

I can't stop smiling. Literally. Not figuratively like most people who use that word actually mean. I mean I literally haven't been able to stop smiling for about fifteen minutes and it's because the guy sitting next to me keeps looking at me and stroking my hand and giving me all the feels.

It's insanity and I'm loving every damn minute of it.

"So, this weekend," Rye says, taking a spoonful of ice cream and mixing it with a piece of banana. "I was wondering … Have you ever …"

"What?" I ask, completely oblivious to whatever it is that Rye is getting at.

"Um … Okay, so this is really kind of tricky for me to articulate," he says, scratching the back of his neck. "Have you ever … been with anybody?"

It takes a beat for the words to sink in and now I'm pretty sure my face, neck and entire body is fluorescent red. In fact, I'm willing to bet my life-savings on it.

"You *totally* don't have to answer that by the way. Like, at all. I just … It was just."

"No … I haven't," I say as I wipe my upper lip. "Have y–" I start, but Rye cuts me off faster than I intercepted the milkshake.

"Nope," he says, shaking his head. "Nope. Never."

I feel a smile creep across my face, a blush still hot in my cheeks. It's hilarious how dumb we're being. I feel about twelve years old. It's not like I've never spoken about sex before. This is just an entirely different scenario because I've never spoken about sex with someone I like … Or have potentially thought about doing it with. Yeah. This is strange. Cool, but strange.

"Wait. Are you suggesting this weekend we –?" I start, but

then immediately regret it because Rye's face tightens and he starts shaking his head vigorously.

"No way. No no no no. Oh god. No. No. I mean … No. Absolutely not. It's …"

I raise my eyebrows at him.

"I mean, unless you wanted to?" he says, and I can't help but laugh. "What?" he asks.

"Nothing. It's early days, but I'd be lying if I said I hadn't thought about it." My heart's kicking my ribcage like it's out for revenge.

Rye is smiling now and I can see he's nervous, but he's not taken his eyes off of me.

"Me too …" he says and my GOD I just want to kiss him right here. So I do. I kiss him and he kisses me back hard. I don't think we've kissed anywhere public but school before but I don't care. I don't care who's watching. They can go to hell if they've got a problem. Because.

We're talking about HAVING SEX WITH EACH OTHER.

When we break apart, we're both glowing and smiling.

"Okay," he says.

"Okay," I say back.

Did we just agree to … what? I don't know. What I do know is that I probably shouldn't stand up for a while.

*

The sun has set and I realise I haven't checked my phone all evening. I even put it on silent which is a major rarity considering I usually can't go ten minutes without opening up Instagram.

I take my phone out to check the time and find fifteen messages on my home screen from Elliot and a missed call.

The last message sent three minutes ago reads:

Elliot: Dude. Call me. Urgent.

I unlock my phone and don't bother reading any other messages, but instead hit dial and let it ring. My uneasiness disintegrates when I feel Rye's hand slide into mine.

"You okay?" he mouths as I hear the ring tone drone on through my phone.

I shake my head in apology as I wait for Elliot to pick up.

"Fin," comes a voice.

"Elliot, hey," I say, a bit unsure.

Then, when there's no answer, I check my screen and realise the call's cut out.

"That's so weird," I say to Rye, as we walk down the steps of the diner. "I could've sworn he answered."

Then my blood runs cold; not even Rye's gentle hand in mine does anything to warm it back up.

Dad is standing in front of us.

I feel like running. Running as fast as I can.

But, for both of us, I don't.

I hold Rye's hand tighter.

I stand up taller.

I brace for impact.

32

Rye

There are only a handful of times in my life so far where I've wondered whether my heart has physically stopped. The first being when I went on the Screamer rollercoaster at Pluto Park, the second when I ate the Carb Monster Burger at Penny's for their annual Eat It Challenge, and now. Right now. Standing here holding my boyfriend's hand while his homophobic dad takes steady, measured steps towards us, his face rigid with fury.

I don't know what I'm thinking but I take a step forward and outstretch my hand.

"Hi, Mr Whittle. It's great to see you again –"

He brushes my hand out of the way and I instead step back and take Fin's hand again. I'm not letting him go.

"Fin. Get in the car," Mr Whittle says, disregarding me entirely.

I feel Fin's hand in mine and I squeeze it to let him know I'm not going anywhere.

"Dad, I…" Fin starts, but his words fizzle out and he goes quiet.

"Mr Whittle, I know this is strange for you, but I really care about your son. I –"

"I don't know who you are," Mr Whittle spits. "But I suggest you stop talking immediately."

I feel anger burn like fire through my veins, but I keep my mouth shut for Fin's sake. I know that if I continue talking I could really screw things up for him. The way I'm feeling right now I want to go straight for his dad but I stay still, keep quiet and breathe.

"Dad," Fin says. "This is Rye and he's my boyfriend."

His words barrel straight into my gut.

Mr Whittle stands rooted to the spot staring between Fin and me like we're some circus freak show from a hundred years ago.

I look to Fin and he smiles at me before turning back to his Dad, his shoulders squared and his jaw clenched.

"Dad?" Fin says, his voice stronger than I've ever heard it. "I said he's my boyfriend."

Mr Whittle opens his mouth but I cut in before he can say a word.

"I am crazy about Fin, sir," I hear myself say. "This isn't some phase or rebellion against you. We genuinely care about each other. We're not trying to cause any trouble. It's –"

"Fin. We're going home," Mr Whittle declares icily, heading towards their car before turning back to check Fin is with him.

I don't want Fin to go but I don't know what else to do. My anxiety intensifies as he faces me.

"It's fine. I need to deal with this," he says, his face strangely peaceful. "Thank you for being the best," he adds, which just breaks me. I don't know why, because it's like music to my freakin' ears, but I bite back the choke in my throat.

"Let me know when you're home," I say.

"Sure." Fin gives me a weak smile.

He gets in the car and I watch it turn the corner.

I'm not quite freaking out. But.

This is bad.

Really, really bad.

33

Fin

Dad hasn't said a single word to me in the week since that night at Penny's. Mum has tiptoed around me like I might burst into rainbow-sparkled flames at any moment and Elliot has texted me constantly asking how I'm doing because it's too awkward to have an actual conversation at home. To be honest, I just want to sleep for a year.

School has been my only respite. Like the cheerleading squad of my dreams, Rye, June and Poppy have rallied around me to keep my spirits up.

The fact I announced that Rye is my boyfriend to my dad and that it wasn't a discussion with him directly feels a bit strange. It probably would've been a bit more special to have gotten to that point in, say, a more romantic setting, like, I dunno, anywhere but in front of my angry father in a car park while he's on a mission to turn me straight. But it is what it is.

It's Friday again, and apparently Dad is heading interstate for a job checking out a broken crane. We suffered another night of silence yesterday, but now thankfully the weekend is almost here and I can spend some time with Rye again.

That's if Mum lets me.

For days, we've barely said more than, "Can you pass the Cheerios?"

The atmosphere in the house is so bad that it's starting to make me wonder how in the hell things are ever going to be okay again. Christmas is going to be a ball at this rate.

The atmosphere outside is pretty odd, too. It hasn't rained properly since we moved here, but I'm sure that's only because it's been saving it all for today. It's coming down in giant sheets of water so I jump at the chance of a lift when Elliot offers. I'm completely drenched even in the time it takes to cover the distance between the front door and his car.

"Jeez. That is ridiculous," Elliot says, shaking his head like a dog as I'm sprayed with even more water.

"Mmm. Agreed," I say, wiping the side of my face most assaulted by the spray.

We drive in silence almost all the way before Elliot asks, "How're you doing?"

I shrug. It's hard to articulate being so happy with Rye while at the same time feeling so isolated from my family. I know Elliot's on my side, but there's not much he can do against Mum and Dad combined.

As we pull up outside the school, he looks at me. "I know it's old news, but Dad told Mum and me what happened when he picked you up from the diner that night."

I nod, not at all sure where this conversation is going.

"I'm really proud of you, Fin." I blink at him in surprise, and he smiles. "Seriously. It was such a brave thing to do, telling Dad about Rye. I hope you know how happy I am for you – even though everything else is a bit of a shit storm at the moment."

"Thanks, Elliot. It really – I really …"

He claps a hand on my shoulder. "I know." He grins. "Now, go learn some stuff."

I grin back, but my mood is very quickly reversed when I get out the car and I'm battered by another wall of water. I glance back and Elliot's laughing to himself. I flip him the bird and head inside, taking my phone out of my pocket to message Rye to ask him to meet me at my locker.

"Hey," he says before I've even finished typing. He's always one step ahead. How does he do that?

He gives me a kiss and I'm immediately calmer. It's like his lips on mine have some kind of superpower that lowers my heart rate.

"Hey," I say, smiling.

"You okay?" he asks, curling my hand into his as we head to the lockers. "You're soaked."

"Yeah," I laugh, as Poppy and June round the corner and see us.

"Okay, so, Rye," Poppy says, looking determined. "I know tonight is your mum's tent-party thing."

"Uh-huh?"

"So, we were wondering if we could come along?" June cuts in.

Rye looks between the two of them and smiles. "Of course," he says, beaming. "But we're not staying there anyway," he continues.

"We're … we're not?" I ask, feeling a little bit nervous.

"Nope." Rye shakes his head. "You and I are staying in Little Bay. About a five-minute walk from home but far enough to not have to see Carl wandering around with no pants on," he adds with a wink.

Five minutes is more than plenty of distance between us and the adults … I have a whole heap of stuff going on inside that I can't quite put my finger on, but I think this is what happens when you hit gunpowder with a match.

"Sounds good," I say, my voice a bit shaky.

June and Poppy look at one another and burst into laughter.

"Well then, maybe we'll skip the sleepover but come for the food."

Even Rye cracks a smile. I can't help but laugh. It's impossible not to know what we're talking about.

*

I have a free period last thing this afternoon so I tell Rye I'm heading home to try to convince Mum to let me go tonight. At this stage I'm considering the old sneak-out-when-everyone's-asleep tactic if all else fails, but I figure it's worth a shot at honesty first.

I take a deep breath before heading inside. I've decided to pretend like everything's normal, in the hope that Mum will do the same. I walk in to find her baking something that smells of cinnamon, green apples and cookie dough.

"Holy crap, that smells incredible," I say, opening the oven for a more full-on sniff.

"Language," Mum says, but there's a smile playing on her lips as she closes the oven and throws a tea towel over her shoulder.

"What are they?" I ask.

"Biscuits," Mum replies. "For next door. Their cat just died."

I feign surprise. I'm amazed the old bag of bones was ever alive in the first place. It looked like a barely breathing toilet brush.

"Rest in Peace, Porridge," I say, bowing my head.

I put my backpack underneath the kitchen counter and sit up on the bench, pouring myself a cup of coffee and watching the rain riot against the windows.

I'm considering the many different ways of approaching tonight and how I should go about asking to go when Mum grabs her bag and keys, turns the oven off and heads for the front door.

"Fin. Come on. We're going for a drive," she says, not even bothering to wait for me to catch up.

*

By the time Mum pulls into a car park outside a random grocery store, it's nearly four thirty and I'm completely aware of how soon Rye's "In-Tents Barbecue" is. I have two hours to somehow convince Mum to let me go, get changed, ready and presentable and head to Rye's.

But instead we're sitting in the car. In silence.

Mum keeps twiddling her thumbs and I can sense that she has something she wants to say – that's why we're here, surely? – but I also know she's finding it hard to express it.

"You okay?" I ask, catching her nerves as I fiddle with the edge of my tee.

Mum nods.

"You sure?" I say.

Mum nods again.

"Fin, I …" she starts, but before I have time to properly register what's going on I hear her sniff and look up to see her wiping her eyes.

"Mum," I say, reaching over the gearstick to hold her hand in mine.

"It's just … I …" She looks up, trying hard to stop the tears. "We're doing the best we can."

I look at her and desperately wish things weren't so complicated. Actually, no. I desperately wish the world didn't make the irrelevant so incredibly complicated.

I should be enjoying high school. I should be going on dates with guys I have crushes on and being lectured about safe sex by my parents. Excruciating but fine. Instead I'm stuck here feeling like garbage.

"Is it really so awful that I like guys?" I ask, not taking my hand off of hers.

"Fin –"

"Is it really … Do you truly believe that I'm 'broken'?"

I let the words sit between us for a second.

Mum stares at the steering wheel and I feel a lump form in my throat.

"I don't want you getting hurt …" Mum says, which is the last thing I expected to hear from her.

"Hurt?" I say.

"It's … There is so much hate in the world," she says. "I don't want your life to be any harder than life already can be …"

I sit for a while.

"Mum, as cheesy as this sounds," I say, "nothing would hurt me more than going through life pretending to be someone else." I should also tell her that nothing's hurting me more than my parents not accepting me. But I'm pretty sure she could work that out for herself.

She looks up and for a flicker of a second I'm positive I see a little smile.

"I love you, Mum," I say. "But I really want some time out

of the house. I need you to know that I'm going to stay with a friend tonight."

Mum tilts her head at me. I don't know whether this is her way of telling me that she's trying or whether she's just too exhausted to fight any more.

Either way, I have a date to get myself to.

✳

It's five forty-five and I told Rye I'd be at his at six so I already know I'm going to look like a sweaty wreck by the time I get there, but I don't care. I'm slapping the asphalt with my Converse and I have no plans on slowing down.

I make a left on Maine and another on Pasadena and just when I think my heart rate is getting to a dangerously high level I arrive outside Rye's and I'm greeted by Thelma who has a party hat strapped to her head which says, "Diamond in the Ruff".

"Hey, beautiful," I say, bending down to greet her.

When I stand back up, I'm face to face with Rye. He's standing directly in front of me, twisting his hands awkwardly together like we're on a first date.

"Hey," I say.

"Hey," he says as he leans in and kisses me, turning back into his usual bold self again.

We break apart and I lean back in and kiss him again, this time pressing closer so our bodies are touching, merging into each other along their entire length. I feel him flush against me and it drives me wild.

When we're all kissed out, his face is glowing.

"God, I love that," he says, kissing me on the forehead and taking my hand. "C'mon, Thelma, let's go."

We head through the house and to the back yard which is full of handmade tents. It looks like a bohemian art exhibition or a travelling circus and my eyes bounce from one colourful creation to the next.

Thelma plods over to her water bowl and laps up a few mouthfuls before making her way to her own personal tent and cuddling up on her bed.

"FIN!"

I turn and see Karen heading towards us, Carl trailing not far behind holding a beer and a handful of nuts.

"Honey, I'm so sorry about the other night. I ... Well, I'm sure you can imagine how embarrassed I am to interfere with –"

"It's all good, Mrs Hendrix," I say, squeezing Rye's hand which has gone cold all of a sudden.

"It's not actually," Rye says. "Mum, you know you shouldn't have done that."

Karen puts her hands up. "I know," she says. "I just wanted to say I'm sorry."

I smile.

"And call me Karen or I'll have to start calling you Mr Whittle and, let's face it, you're more of a Fin."

Rye looks over at me and winks.

"Agreed," I say.

*

Not long after, we're sitting on the back porch playing Jenga when Poppy and June arrive.

"RYE, LOOK OUT!" Poppy screams as Rye fumbles with his block and sends the Jenga tower crashing to the deck.

"Ooooh, you did that on purpose, you giant bin fire of a human," Rye says throwing a block at Poppy who catches it and puts it between her teeth.

After three rounds of Jenga, Carl sparks up the barbecue as more of Karen and Carl's guests arrive. June, Poppy, Rye and I make our way to a few logs by a fire pit and Rye sits as close to me as possible without being on my lap.

"This is nice," June says, taking a bite out of her barbecued tofu wrap.

"It is. Even if we are eating rabbit food by a fire," Poppy says, laughing at her own pretty rubbish joke.

"I like the rabbit food," I say, and I mean it, too. It's a completely plant-based menu and actually delicious. Very impressive. Karen and Carl have gone all out.

Poppy does some weird impression of a possessed-looking rabbit as June elbows her to stop.

We all nearly fall off the porch laughing and I feel pretty amazed at how at ease I am. When I'm with this bunch of lunatics it's as if nothing else matters. As if none of the stuff at home is in any way relevant or even really happening.

*

It's midnight when June's dad arrives to take June and Poppy home. He says no to a beer with Carl, who's decided to strip down to his swim shorts and crack another can, which is our cue to get the hell outta here and head to whatever it is Rye has in store.

"Night, guys," Rye shouts as everyone separates.

Waves and various whoops and hollers can be heard as he

takes my hand and brings it up to his lips. I don't know what it is about them, but these tiny gestures of affection, these minimal kisses on my knuckles, just floor me. I want nothing more than to kiss him for ever. To never stop kissing him, not even for air. Okay, maybe for a quick gulp of air, but then back to full-on pash-rash snog fest.

We've been walking for about five minutes when I see the first sprinkle of light ahead. It's faint at first and then as we get nearer I see a few more. Fireflies dash among the reeds as we head further towards more light, this kind more stable: a thousand string-lights dangle above a makeshift tent nestled between two trees. To the left flickers firefly after firefly and to the right an old rustic sign reads: "Little Bay". A couple of feet from the entrance is a small campfire, next to it some marshmallows, crackers and chocolate.

"Smores?" I ask. "My god, you're a heart-throb right out of a nineties rom-com."

Rye smiles, then looks up at me nervously. "I ... Sorry. If it's cheesy. I didn't mean for –" he starts, but instead of speaking I wrap my arms around his waist and plant a giant kiss on his lips.

"This is," I say, "the sweetest thing ever."

Rye bows his head and smiles again. "Good," he says.

We head over to the fire and make a few smores.

"Question," I say.

"Shoot."

"How long has this fire been burning for?"

Rye grins. "I got Poppy to come and light it right before they left."

"Ooh, you're good," I say, taking his hand in mine.

"Skilled, one may say," Rye says squeezing my hand in his and leaning into me.

I finish my smore and I'm about to lick the marshmallow from my finger when Rye swoops in and gently takes my fingers in his mouth.

When I smile up at him, he looks both extremely sexy and intensely terrified all at once.

"Fin Whittle, I honestly love you," he says, and I take a second to let the words hit me. It's intense and brilliant and exhilarating all at once.

I'm about to kiss him, but instead change my mind.

"I love you too," I say. "I really, really need you to know this," I say. "Because I know that what we're doing is a big deal. I know what Eric was like to you." I pause, amazed to find myself saying that guy's name without even a pang of jealousy. "And I want you to know that you are by far the most wonderful thing in my life."

Rye grins and shakes his head. "Now who's going nineties rom-com?" he says.

"Shudddupaya face," I say, planting another kiss on his lips. "I need you to know this because I don't say these words lightly. I really, truly, completely, utterly, one hundred and fifty per cent am madly in love with you."

I take a breath and he kisses me, passionately, hard on the lips.

The kissing gets more and more urgent – I'm realising I might need some chapstick as a matter of urgency – then we're embracing, hands roaming under tees and along thighs, scrambling to get as close to each other as we possibly can ... and just before we're about to start rolling along the actual ground, he takes my hand and leads me to the tent.

I feel my heart rattle, my skin burn and my breathing intensify. But here we are.

It's amazing how quickly we take our clothes off. I'm touching every last inch of Rye's body and the sensation is out of this world; it's like a million volts of electricity are sparking through my own.

"Are you okay?" Rye asks.

"Yep," I say, my breath heavy. "Are you?"

"I'm okay a million times over," Rye says, kissing me some more. "Are you sure you want to ... you know," he asks, his hands exploring my body and his lips inches from mine.

"I'm sure," I say, kissing him lightly. "Are you?"

"Yeah," he says, covering us with some more blanket and stroking my cheek.

"Do you have a ... uh ... protection?" I ask. Rye leans across to the corner of the tent and finds what he's looking for.

"Okay," I say.

"Okay," Rye says.

We both burst into giggles as we fumble with the wrapper.

"I love you."

"I love you."

Our lips are making love and our words are making love and then we are making love and it's perfect and magic and terrifying and there's a lot of fumbling and awkwardness and still it is utterly totally sexy and *oh my god* now I know why people talk about this so damn much. I have no idea if I'm doing any of this right. Or if I'm what he expected. It's almost scary but epic. Just *uh-mazing*. Yep. I'm talking movie-magic kind of *wow*. Completely and totally mind-blowing, knock it out of the park, sweet home Alabama *incredible*.

34

Rye

I cannot believe this is happening.

Wait, no, yes I can actually.

Of course this would happen. Why would anything be different? Because he told me he loves me? Because I bought it? Maybe I'm just as dumb as Eric always told me I was. At least Eric was upfront about his douche-baggery.

I cannot believe how stupid I am.

I've been pacing outside the tent for fifteen minutes and I'm struggling to figure any of it out.

So I sit down, leaning against a tree, and bury my fingers in the soft earth around it like I'm searching for treasure. But I don't find any answers there either.

Worst of all, it's all a bit of a blur after we fell asleep together. I barely woke up when he left. I caught some of his ramblings, but nothing makes sense. I mean, why would he leave like that? He must really have wanted to get the hell away from me.

Jesus, I know it wasn't as smooth as it might have been, but was I that bad? That bad for our first time that he needed to disappear before we could even talk about it?

I'm shaking I'm so upset. I can't believe I read him that wrong. I just lost my virginity with a guy who bailed before dawn. Not even a note or a text. I mean, shit. Not even a rubbishy Facebook message.

I turn and head the fuck away from the tent. I want to get as far away from it and the memory of last night as humanly possible.

I walk like the earth is on fire and when I get to the back porch Thelma is snoring with her tongue hanging out, a pool of slobber underneath her chin.

I scratch her ears as I walk past and practically knock the fly screen off its hinges.

"Hey hey hey," Mum says. "What's going on?"

I shake my head, but Mum's having none of it as she gently taps my shoulder and brings me in for a hug.

Shit. Now I can't stop crying and I'm completely soaking Mum's shoulder with tears.

Talk about a mess.

"I'm sorry," I say, swallowing a hiccup. "I just … We." I catch myself. I'm not going there.

"Where's Fin?" Mum says as she wipes my eye with her sleeve.

I shrug.

Mum looks at me quizzically and takes a deep breath. Then I think it all falls into place and I don't need to say any more. Mum knows.

"Hun, before you get yourself in a state. Take a few deep breaths and remember that Fin is going through a lot right now and –"

"What? You think I don't know that? But we're meant to be a thing. We're supposed to be there for each other. I'm supposed to … He's … Ugh." I turn and walk. I'm not doing this. I'm not talking boys with my mum.

"Rye, honey, come back," Mum calls after me, but I'm already out the front door.

＊

By the time I get to Kettle Lake my misery is at its peak. I've drafted thirty different "screw you" messages to Fin but I can't bring myself to send them. However crappy I feel, I know it's just so out of character for him.

I feel my phone vibrate and desperately plead with the universe to let it be Fin.

Poppy's name flashes on my screen.

Poppy: Hey hot stuff. How was last night? ;) Here's an eggplant emoji.

I sigh then text back.

Me: Don't even ask.

Poppy: Where are you?

Me: My spot.

Poppy: Don't move. On my way.

I kind of wish I hadn't told her. It's not that I don't appreciate it. I just sometimes need to be on my own.

Within fifteen minutes Poppy is sitting next to me and we're sharing a cheese scroll and a giant green apple slushee.

"It doesn't sound right," Poppy says, tearing apart a piece of pastry and stuffing it in her mouth.

I shrug. I don't know what to say or feel or think right now.

I feel like pulling a million blankets over my head and sleeping for a week.

"I know it doesn't. But it's what's happened," I say, taking a huge slurp of the slushee and then immediately regretting it when the brain freeze hits.

"Nope," Poppy says.

"What do you mean 'nope'?" I say.

"Nope. I don't buy it. There's no way Fin would just bail without a good reason."

I shake my head.

"Seriously, Rye. Do you honestly believe he'd do that to you? There's no way."

Poppy looks at me with this pleading look that I try to figure out.

"Then where is he?" I ask, bemused but cautiously optimistic.

"I don't know. But we're going." Poppy starts to stand. "Right now, come on. We're going to find out."

I look up at her as she dusts the dirt off of her clothes.

"I'm not sure I can."

"Not sure?" Poppy looks a little pissed but mostly confused.

We stare at each other for a beat longer than usual.

"No, Pops. I can't. I'm not getting hurt again. I'm done with being hurt."

35

Fin

My life feels like a nightmare. I'm sitting at the bottom of the stairs with my suitcase in front of me, a coffee in my hand and a plate of toast that I've taken two nibbles of. Dad is in the other room speaking quietly to Mum.

I'm going to Re-Souled.

Apparently Dad wasn't away on business assessing some crappy crane. He was away arranging my spot in the programme.

I'm set to go for a week. Then, depending on how "well" I do, I am to either act "appropriately" or I have to change schools or move to Aunt Carla's for time-out and another of my "fresh starts".

I'm too confused to cry. Too heartbroken to rage or scream. I feel nothing but numb.

Last night with Rye was the most incredible night of my life. But getting bombarded with frantic texts at four a.m. from Dad freaking out not knowing where I was and demanding I come home wasn't exactly a fairy-tale ending to my first time.

Having to dash out of our love nest, my head in a scramble

from Dad's onslaught while trying to garble at a dead-to-the-world Rye that I had to go was horrendous. I've got no idea if he registered what was going on. It made no sense to me either.

When I'd arrived back at the house, I thought of waking Elliot up but figured there's no point. Dad took my phone off me the minute I walked through the door. I didn't even get chance to text Rye. He sent me to bed, saying we had a big day ahead of us. I guess I was meant to rest, but I didn't sleep for more than a few minutes at a time. My veins are pumping with adrenaline and anxiety and I can't sit still.

Some horrible corner has been turned and I've decided there really is no winning this war. Mum and Dad think I'm broken. That I need fixing. Just as I was on cloud nine, now I've crashed back down to earth and straight into an inferno. I'm all out of fight.

When Mum and Dad come back in the room Mum's obviously been crying and Dad has this weird look on his face. Sort of like apprehension. Like he's not one hundred per cent sure of himself.

"Ready?" Dad asks, his head low and his voice softer than normal.

I shrug. Truth is, I have never felt more devastated in all my life. I've never felt more worthless, more utterly unlovable in my sixteen years on this planet as I do right this very second. I decide to try one more time.

"Do you remember when I was a kid and all I ever wanted was to listen to musical soundtracks or Cher albums?" I ask, giving a choked-up laugh at the memory.

Mum and Dad look at one another, then at me and then at the carpet.

"All I've ever wanted is for you to like me for who I am," I say, letting a couple of tears escape and hit my jeans.

Dad glances up and what I can only describe as a shadow of doubt crosses his face.

For the first time in my life I see through his tough exterior to who he really is. A man who's always feared anything that seems to be out of his control. He's scared.

"We do love you, Fin," he says, his voice just above a whisper. "I know you might not see it right now, but we are doing this for your own good."

I shake my head and I'm about to stand when Mum comes over and sits next to me.

I feel her arm against mine and it's trembling slightly.

She takes my hand in hers and I see her wipe her eye like she's brushing a speck of dust away. It's obviously an inconvenient time to have second thoughts.

"I love you," Mum says.

I turn to look at her. I want to look into her eyes and see if I can see any of that love she's talking about. I look and I look but I can't get past the sudden sheer anger I'm feeling. I'm furious at her and at Dad and this entire situation. A resigned, low-banking rage that makes me want to scream.

I blink twice, stand, breathe in slowly, then take my suitcase and walk out the front door to the car. I don't turn back. I say nothing. I keep walking until my bags are in the boot and my seat belt is buckled.

The sun is above the treetops when Dad gets in and starts the engine. I feel the car shift slowly forward when there's a bang on the window.

Elliot is standing there and knocking like he wants to break through the glass.

"Open the door, Fin," Elliot says, still knocking like a lunatic.

Dad stops the car and lowers the passenger window.

"What is going on?" Elliot says, leaning through the window like he's considering hopping in. "Where ... Dad, what's going on? Where are you going?"

Dad's about to reply when I see him stop and stare beyond Elliot to where Poppy, of all people, is standing, looking pale and terrified yet at the same time oddly badass.

"Hey, Fin," she says, leaning in next to Elliot. "Hi, Mr Whittle." She's looking at me and then at Dad, slowly tilting her head like she can't quite fathom whatever the hell is happening right now.

"Please step away from the window, you two," Dad says, his hand on the handbrake.

I hear the back door of the car open and Mum climbs in. I glance around at her; her gaze is distant and she seems far away.

"Dad, seriously," Elliot says, his voice pleading, his eyes desperate. "Where are you taking him?"

I'm out of words. I have no clue what to say but I lean forward to block Dad from view as best as I can. He's started the engine again.

"Elliot, I'll be fine," I say, biting back the pain bubbling in my gut. "Pops, I need you to tell Rye how sorry I am." That's when the tears hit. They hit fast and don't stop. "And that I really do love him." I say the last bit almost under my breath. I don't want Dad to be a part of this. This isn't his story. It's mine.

36
Fin

An ominous, heavy gate bears nothing but the number "17" engraved on a large metal plaque.

It lets us know we've made it to the right address.

Dad opens his window and presses the buzzer, which takes a few tries before it jolts to life.

A scratchy noise is audible through the intercom.

"Hello?" Dad says.

Another crackle.

"I'm …My son, Fin, is here to start the Re-Souled programme and I –"

The gate shudders and slowly opens, revealing a dismal building beyond. It's honestly prison-like. Grey walls, big black doors and not a patch of greenery in sight, this is quite literally like walking into a nightmare. There's no sign, no elaborate gesture to let us know that this is a place to destroy the lives of queer kids. It's just so grey. Unnervingly grey. Even the leaves on the trees seem washed out of colour.

Dad finds a space to park near the entrance. Mum is silent

and none of us knows what to say as Dad turns off the ignition. Deep silence.

Thankfully the quiet is broken by a knock on the window and a man, maybe mid-forties, short, dark hair, round spectacles and a bulbous nose, waves at us like we're in a fish tank.

"Hello," he says as Dad lowers his window.

The man is grossly cheerful amid all this greyness. He won't stop smiling and it's freaking me out.

"You must be Mr and Mrs Whittle," he says, leaning in the car with an outstretched hand. "And you are Fin I take it?"

He looks to me and his smile wanes at the sight of yet another rebellious child.

"We'll get you straightened out in no time," he says. "Pun wholly intended."

He laughs at his own joke, but none of us moves.

"I'm Greg. President of Re-Souled and ping-pong world champion." He chuckles again. "I'm not serious."

Yeah, I gathered.

"Let's head in and I can give you the tour."

Mum, Dad and I get out of the car and follow him inside, my one duffle bag slung over my shoulder.

Inside, the entry hall is one long corridor with a sign that says "GOD IS LOVE" on a beam overhead. How ironic given that I feel anything but loved right now.

"Here at Re-Souled the total number of our young guests at any given time never exceeds ten. We like to ensure we have all of our attention focused on a small group to achieve maximum results."

Mum takes a peek in one of the rooms and I can't tell if the look on her face is one of fear or plain indifference at how boring this place is.

Dad follows a few paces behind Greg and seems to do a double-take at everything his eyes land on.

"The days are very straightforward. Both figuratively and literally," Greg carries on and I consider taking off my shoe and lobbing it at the back of his head. Could he be any more absurd?

"We start each day with an hour of prayer followed by a group meeting discussing scripture and the word of the Lord."

We turn a corner past a dining room and head out of a set of double doors and into a bricked yard.

"All meals are served in our cafeteria and we have regular group activities outside to impose a sense of masculinity for our young men and femininity for the young women."

I shake my head and roll my eyes so hard I feel dizzy.

"Is something the matter?" Greg asks.

"A lot, actually," I say, which sends Dad's eyebrows up into his hairline. It's a warning, loud and clear.

Greg smiles in this patronising way that both infuriates me and creeps me the fuck out.

"You'll settle in soon enough, I'm sure," he says, shutting me down.

I look at Mum but she won't meet my eyes.

Greg gives us more of a rundown of the day-to-day insanity that is the Re-Souled programme before we're back at the entrance hall.

"I'll give you a moment to say your farewells. Remember, Mr and Mrs Whittle, when you see your son next, he will be back to his old self, so have no fear." Greg smirks and stands to the side.

I really want to scream but my mouth feels as dry as a desert. Up until now I've kept myself fairly composed but panic is shooting through me and I want to get out. I want to smash a window, break down a door, run as far away from this hateful, soulless place as I possibly can.

Mum and Dad don't look too brilliant either. The blood has actually drained from their faces.

"Please, I –" I start.

"Just give it a try," Dad interrupts with forced enthusiasm, as if I was a little kid and he was trying to persuade me to stick at football training. "It's not for long. A few days. It will do you good. They know their stuff." He glances down, looking anything but certain, hesitates for a moment but then turns and leaves.

Mum and I stare at each other and I can see the battle going on in her head. Her eyes are shiny and she looks exhausted.

"Fin," she says, taking an unsteady step towards me.

I take a step back. Does she really expect a farewell embrace?

"Fin, give it a couple of days. If it's not working out, call me and I'll come and pick you up. Straight away."

Is she kidding? I want to leave *now*.

"Just … a couple of days," Mum begs as she leans in and kisses me. I feel a tear hit my cheek and realise it's hers.

I hold myself together as she stumbles away.

Greg is still standing there, arms folded, as if other people's distress is his favourite spectator sport.

I barge past him into a grey corridor and sink to the floor.

My heart hammers, my ears echo with the white noise circling me.

My eyes blur and pulse into darkness.

I can't do it. I can't do this.

37

Rye

I grab my phone like it's a winning lottery ticket about to disappear down the drain.

But I'm disappointed when I see who it is.

Instead of Fin telling me what the hell's going on, it's Aunt Sandy. She's created a chat titled "Sandy's Surprise Party" and then promptly left the group.

Helpful.

I put my phone down before burrowing my face into my pillow. I manage to turn my head before I actually suffocate myself and catch a glimpse of Fin's firefly jar glowing to life. I feel another pang in my chest.

Life has a funny way of punching you in the face at the exact moment when you feel like you've got a bit of a spring in your step.

Thelma's snoring is earth-shattering even for her, so I head out to the back yard and sit on the deck, listening instead to the laughter of a family of kookaburras overhead somewhere.

"Hey, Rye-bread," Mum says from behind me.

"Hey," I say. "Where've you guys been?"

"Carl's gone home to get a clean set of clothes."

"Hopefully pants," I say.

"I'm going to ignore that," Mum says. "And I got you this." She hands me a small paper bag.

"This had better be a cookie," I say, taking the bag and immediately realising it's far too light to be a cookie. Dammit.

I open up some crumpled tissue crumpled paper and peek inside.

"Rose quartz," Mum says with an eager look that can't help but make me smile. It's so innocent and full of hope. "Great for the love life."

I smile. "Thanks, Mum."

I'm turning the pale pink stone in my hand and letting the light catch it when I hear the front door being battered like a piñata.

"RYE!"

I go to find Poppy standing looking like she's been running, which can't possibly be true because you won't catch Poppy running outside of a P.E. class.

I open the fly screen with a creak and find Elliot, Fin's older brother, standing next to her, also breathless but less so than Poppy.

"My *god*. Is there a grizzly bear on the loose or something?" I say, looking Poppy up and down to make sure we're not all about to be mauled.

"Funny," Poppy says, clutching her side. "But no. We need to talk."

At which, she barges past me and heads straight for my room. This must be serious.

Elliot stands awkwardly for a moment before reaching out to shake my hand. "Hey."

"Hey," I say, returning the gesture and motioning for him to come inside.

I don't know what's going on but I feel weirdly on edge.

"What the hell is happening?" I throw at Poppy because I can't look at Elliot. His features, his stance, everything, are so much like Fin's, and it hurts my eyes.

"It's Fin," Poppy says, her breathing calmer now. "He's gone."

"Yeah, I figured that this morning when I woke up and he'd upped and left," I say, my tone venomous as a brown snake. I'm really not in the mood.

Poppy looks up at me, puzzled. Elliot seems tired and panicked and wired all at once. Like his body can't quite process what his mind is thinking fast enough.

"Do you know *where*?" Poppy asks.

I roll my eyes. "Sure, Pops. That's why I'm feeling so cheery."

She ignores the sarcasm in my voice and Elliot cuts in.

"Rye," he says, taking a deep breath. "Mum and Dad have sent Fin away somewhere. It all happened this morning. We have no idea where, or, or … or …"

"What?" I ask, my voice catching in the back of my throat.

Guilt washes over me like a bucket of cold water.

"What, and *nobody* knows where he is? Surely *you* of all people should know something. I mean, you're his brother!" I say, practically yelling.

But Elliot stays calm, not letting me project all my anger on to him. "I never expected them to send him away. I mean, they moved him here. I didn't expect them to offload him somewhere else."

"Call June!" I scream, my blood boiling.

Frantically, I start searching for my own phone because everyone is moving at a glacial pace and it's driving me insane.

"She's on her way," Poppy says, slumping into the chair near my bed.

At last, I unearth my phone and dial Fin's number. Five times. It goes to voicemail five times.

"Shit!" I shout, feeling utterly crushed as I hit call on Fin's name yet again.

But I get nothing. Nothing but the same voicemail over and over.

*

By the time June arrives I'm sitting on my bed, my knee bouncing up and down like it's trying to detach itself from my body.

It's a miracle I haven't had a panic attack yet, but at least my body is cooperating with me for now.

"Okay, I think I'm up to date with everything," June says, rolling her sleeves up.

Her and Poppy shuggle up next to each other on the beanbag chair near my bed.

"Sweet," Elliot says, looking between the two of them and smiling.

"What is?" Poppy says, taking June's hand in hers.

"The way ... I mean. You." He stammers a bit. "You look sweet together." He blushes and then stares at the floor.

"I'm glad Fin had you," Poppy says, letting the poor guy off the hook.

"*Has*," I say. "Can we get back to what matters here?"

June brushes her hair behind her ears. "Did he say *anything* to you, Elliot? Anything about where he might be going?"

"No. I don't think *he* even knew he was going until today ..."
Elliot shakes his head. "He looked so scared and –"

His voice chokes out a hiccup and he puts his head in his
hands.

We all look at one another, unsure of the best course of action.

"It's gonna be okay, you know," I say gently, putting my hand
on his shoulder. "Because it has to be okay."

Even so, all I can think to do is to try dialling Fin some more.
We're all just listening to a pointless ringtone, when June gasps
and launches herself out of the beanbag.

"Re-Souled," she says, clapping her hand over her mouth.

"No way," I say, dismissing the idea as my stomach flips over
and over. "Fin's parents aren't exactly gay-friendly, but they're
surely not that crazy."

"I'd put money on it," Poppy chimes in. "It makes sense. Just look
at how Fin's dad's been behaving since he found out about you guys."

Elliot lifts his head and looks between all three of us.
"Re-Souled?" he says carefully. "You're right. Dad had a booklet
from there."

"It's dangerous." June's face is rigid with horror. "Conversion
therapy disguised as a self-improvement camp. One of the most
deadly, irresponsible forms of torture for queer kids masked as
beneficial therapy. How it's still legal is beyond me."

"So ...I mean. What do –?" Elliot asks, but June hasn't finished.

"Everything from faux-therapy, to aversive conditioning, from
'praying the gay away' to straight up abuse."

I feel the walls closing in on me. The thought of Fin in a living
hell like that really makes me heave.

"No ... There's no way," I say, closing my eyes.

"We need to be sure," Poppy says, taking her phone out. "June, quick, google the –"

"I'm on it," June tells her and calls the number out.

We all sit watching Poppy like we're waiting for the executioner.

"Hello?" Poppy takes a breath, then puts on her best "adult" voice. "Hi, yes, it's Sally? Mrs Sally Whittle?"

My mouth goes dry.

"I just wanted to check how my son Fin is settling in?"

There's silence and I think my heart has stopped beating entirely.

Poppy is gripping the phone like she'll crack it in half. "Okay. Okay. Thank you." She hangs up and looks directly at me. "He's there."

June looks at the floor. Elliot shakes his head and stands.

I just sit still.

A moment passes. Then another.

Then I sink my face into my pillow and scream until my lungs burn and the world disappears.

38

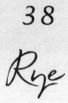

"What!? What!? *WHAT!?*"

When I look up, I'm dizzy and I can see little yellow flecks from the energy it took to scream like that. Mum is staring at all of us.

"What is going on!?" Mum demands, her eyes like saucers.

June takes her aside and explains everything while I go to the bathroom and splash some cold water on my face, taking deep breaths to steady myself.

When I get back Mum seems nervous – out of her depth, which isn't like her at all. Elliot is staring out the window, tapping his foot, seemingly full of frantic energy.

"Rye?" Mum says to me as I rub at my face with a towel.

"Doesn't matter about me," I say. "We just need to get him out."

"Too damn right," Elliot says, turning to look me in the eye. "You really care about him, don't you?"

Hearing that from Fin's big brother almost shatters me. "More than I could ever explain," I tell him. "But right now I really need to talk to your parents." The words sound strange out in the open; they've been on repeat in my mind since I grasped the reality of this situation. I need to speak to them. I need to make them listen.

"Look." Elliot's voice is unsteady. "I'm the first to admit they need a talking to. I've never really seen this side of them. Since I've been back, their stubbornness is off the scale. It's that different ..." he says, barely blinking.

"I think Rye's right," Poppy says, standing up, too.

Mum looks at all of us, her expression troubled. "I'm really worried, Rye," she says. "I mean, this could all turn very nasty."

"Mum, Fin is in *conversion therapy*. This is already nasty. Really, *really* nasty," I say, my voice getting louder. "And I'm not waiting around for him to come back broken. I'm getting him out. You can join me or not. Up to you."

"I'm in," Elliot says as Poppy and June link arms with him.

Mum takes my hand, her fingers interlacing with mine. "Me too," she adds.

∗

By the time we get to Fin's house I feel like a gorilla is sitting on my chest. Anxiety is one thing. This is on par with a full-blown panic attack.

Elliot, Poppy and June sit huddled in the back seat. Nobody moves.

"Are you sure you want to do this?" Mum asks.

"Yep. For sure." I smile, my lame attempt at coming across nonchalant failing majorly. "But," I add, "I'd like to do this on my own." I can hear the tremble in my voice but I'm not sure if the others notice it.

I get out the car and head up the path to their front door.

It's windy and the gravel crunches underneath my feet.

When I am finally standing on their front step I nearly turn and run back. I'm halfway spun around when the door opens and Fin's dad is standing there, on his way out by the looks of things.

I swallow and feel my tongue go numb. It's as if everything I've planned to say has decided to hop skip and jump the fuck out of my head and leave me stranded here staring up at him like a fat walrus on a beach.

"May I help you?" Mr Whittle asks, his voice sounding as scratchy as the gravel of the driveway.

"I … There's …" My words are bumping into each other.

"If you don't have anything to say, I have things to be getting on with," he says, readying himself to push past me.

"Wait," I say. "I …" I take a breath and glance back to the car, where everyone is looking on and Poppy seems like she's about to get out and join me. "My name is Rye Hendrix –"

"I know exactly who you are –"

"and your son Fin is really important to me," I finish.

Mr Whittle rolls his eyes, but I can't miss the flash of alarm in them. He goes to shut the door but I stick my foot in it before he can.

"Sir." I put my hands up. "Please. Hear me out."

There's a beat where I worry he's going to slam the door shut, but just when I'm about to brace myself he opens it again.

"I know you've sent him to Re-Souled. But that place is awful, a cruel scam. I'm begging you to reconsider," I say, my voice wobbly but doing good considering I feel like I'm sinking into quicksand.

There's movement behind Mr Whittle and then Mrs Whittle is standing there, her whole being crumpled and pale.

"What's all this?" she asks, wrapping her cardigan tight around her.

"Nothing, Sal. This young man here was just leaving –"

"No, I wasn't," I say. "I really need you to listen to me. Conversion therapy is dangerous. It's a form of torture. You know that right? People have *died* from it."

I can't believe I'm having a standoff with the parents of the boy I'm in love with, but they look at each other for a moment, as if my words are striking a chord. Perhaps I can get them to realise the magnitude of the situation.

Fin's mum stares at me like she's unsure whether to take my side or throw me across her front yard. I wouldn't know where to start with what Fin's dad is thinking, though. But that expression "if looks could kill" seems pretty spot on.

"Please …" I start. "You need to think about all of this."

Fin's dad opens his mouth to speak, but I carry on.

"Fin isn't broken. He isn't confused. This isn't a phase." My heart's beating faster and faster. "This Re-Souled place is wrong for him. For anyone. He doesn't need to change. You know he's perfect exactly as he is."

Mr and Mrs Whittle look at me and for the briefest moment I think I've gotten through to them.

"Charles," Mrs Whittle says, gently touching her husband's arm.

I hold my breath, desperate to open the dialogue. To start a genuine conversation.

"Enough. That is enough," Mr Whittle says, shaking any reconsideration from his mind as his hard shell closes over again. "Please get off the premises right now."

And he shuts the door.

I stand for a beat longer and then look over to the car where

Mum and the rest sit, expectant. Emotion is bubbling to the surface but I press it down. I'm not done fighting yet.

"I need paper and a pen," I say as I throw myself into the passenger seat.

Mum tears a page from a notebook and extracts a sharpie from her bag.

I scribble:

"Penny's diner. Tomorrow night. Six p.m. Please come."

I fold the paper over, go over to Fin's parents' car and stick it underneath the windscreen wiper.

When I get back, Elliot is shuffling in the back seat. "I'm coming with you guys," he says, determined.

"You sure you don't want to go hang with your parents?" Poppy says, far too sarcastically.

"Not yet," he says, grimly. "We need all the artillery we can get."

"Thanks," I say, turning around in my seat to stare at everyone. Mum turns the ignition and we hit the road. "We're going to get him out of there if it kills me."

39

Fin

Sterile and unnerving are two of the less negative words I'd use to describe Re-Souled.

One of Greg's minions gave me a tour and I saw "motivational quotes" lining the walls; segregated male and female dorm-style areas for sleeping (are they total idiots?); and a canteen with a fluorescent white light overhead, giving it the feel of an old-school asylum. Once that excitement was over, I was taken to the recreation room. A stark, basic space with nothing more than the Ten Commandments on the wall, a scruffy couch and a side table with a Bible on it. It looked like a sad motel room in a stage-set for a horror movie.

From there I was given a sandwich and a glass of milk, like I was at nursery school, and then taken to my first "counselling" session. It consisted of an introduction to the team – a ragtag, joyless bunch of apparently "transformed" and now straight people who came through the programme previously and are here to teach us how it's all done. It made me simultaneously want to pull my hair out and punch a wall.

There are four other people in my group. Two guys and two girls. None of us wants to meet one another's eyes, and so I've only spoken to Clare, a girl with blue eyes, straggly pink hair and more piercings than a pin-cushion. She told me how, since coming out as gay to her family, she was given the ultimatum of "check in or get out" which led her to here, with me, in this toxic mess of a place. The worst part is, Clare seems to be actually buying this bullshit. It's like she truly believes she can be transformed.

It's midday when I'm asked to join another group "therapy" session. Clare is waiting in the hallway for me and, when I get closer to her, I realise she's been crying: her eyes are bloodshot and watery.

"Are you okay?" I ask, knowing the answer. How can anybody be okay in a place like this?

Clare nods.

I don't buy it, but I also don't push it. I'm hanging on by a thread. I don't need to make her re-live anything she doesn't want to.

We head to "assembly" where Greg is waiting to address our group. He's stood on a low podium and the way his creepy-clown smile bears down on us sends a severe shiver along my spine.

"Welcome, gang," he says, his pebbly eyes alight and his cheeks rosy.

Violence has never been my thing, but I really want to smack that stupid faux-angelic smirk off his face. He's loving the fact that this is destroying us.

"As you know, the next few days might be tough," he goes on, his face switching to caring and sombre now. "As we make those all-important changes to ourselves. But come the weekend, we will celebrate with our transformation ceremony. This marks the moment at which you truly turn over a new leaf and start your lives afresh as normal and wholesome members of our society."

I flinch as he claps his hands together and beams.

"The Mountain Song Choir will join us for a special performance in which, I can assure you, you will hear the healing grace of God in their divine voices."

I grimace at the thought, shuffling my feet in a mix of boredom and anxiety at what's to come.

"Now, for the remainder of the day we will join into groups for our prayer therapy sessions," Greg concludes, thumbing through a booklet as if searching for a prayer to bring this nightmare assembly to a close.

I try to tune out of the garbage that is pouring out of Greg's mouth, but when I glance at Clare she seems to be hanging on his every word.

"You're not seriously believing this guy, are you?" I whisper under my breath.

"Yes. Yes, I am," she says, her face intent as she averts her eyes from mine.

"Listen," I tell her. "I have a boyfriend. A boyfriend who loves me and who's waiting for me to get the hell out of here," I say, feeling my chest puff out with pride.

"So, where is he?" Clare asks, turning to me.

"What?"

"Where is he? If he loves you so much, why isn't he here?" Clare says, a hint of a dig in her voice mixed with uneasiness. "Why isn't he rescuing you?"

"I … I … what do you mean?" I stutter.

"This is my third time here," Clare tells me, her voice trembling. "No one loves me anymore. I need to get it right this time."

I shake my head, horrified. "No. No you don't," I say, urgently. "Plenty of people will love you exactly as you are."

These words seem to get Greg's attention. He breaks off from his droning prayer to focus his beady eyes on us.

"Sorry, Fin. Is there something you'd like to share?"

He gives me a patronising, bland smile.

I'm about to say no, to stay silent, to get through this nightmare as quickly and quietly as I can.

But then I think of my friends. I think of Poppy calling out Bronwyn and Paisley at the wharf that very first time I met her; June valiant with her "Keep Calm, It's Just a Toilet" protest. I think of everyone at our QSA meetings and what they'd want me to do in this situation.

I take a deep breath.

"Yeah, actually," I say, standing up, never mind how badly my legs are shaking. "I'd love to share something with you all."

Greg's stupid smile stretches wider. "Please go ahead, Tim."

"It's Fin," I snarl. "And I'd like to share that I don't buy into a single stinking piece of your steaming pile of bullshit."

There are a few bewildered gasps behind me and even Clare stares at me in shock, but I absolutely don't give a –

"Oh what?!" I say, looking around. "Not a fan of the word bull*shit*, but happy to listen to it?" I choke out an angry laugh. "This place is a vile joke. Greg is a scam artist. And you're here swallowing his pseudo-scientific religious *crap*. Face it. He doesn't have a clue what he's talking about."

I stop, aware that Greg is simply looking on calmly, which only pisses me off more.

"I mean, seriously?" I challenge, my legs shaking harder than ever. "A *transformation* ceremony? That has got to be one of the dumbest things ever. If God is so powerful and wise and all-loving, how come He gave me such a gorgeous guy to fall in love with?"

These last few words rattle my throat and I realise how much pain each word holds, but also how strong I am – how strong I have to be. This is about more than me now.

I've got to stand up for every single person who's not been accepted for who they are. I need to fight.

Clare looks up at me. "Fin … shut the fuck up," she whispers. "Please, sit down."

But Greg keeps gazing at me calmly. "Is that all, *Fin*? I am more than happy to start aversion therapy immediately if that's what you'd prefer? It's a process usually reserved for later in the programme, but since you're so … passionate, it would be most appropriate if we were to bring this helpful technique forward."

I feel like I've been plunged into icy water.

We had a whole QSA meeting about aversion therapy only last week.

But I won't let Greg's threat break me. I refuse.

"I'm not doing shit," I yell. "Call my parents. Right now. Call my family and tell them I don't care if they throw me out –"

"Ahhh, Fin, my impulsive little firecracker," Greg says, his voice syrupy. "Surely you understand what sort of life awaits you and your family, should you decide to leave?"

"I … what are you talking about?"

"Where will you go, exactly? Your family want you to have a fresh start. Put this madness behind you, Fin. Embrace a healthy, wholesome life not a sinful, perverted one. They will not have you back until you have given Re-Souled your all." He pauses and his eyes drill into me. "Where would you go? What would you do? Drop out of school?"

How can he say this stuff? It's one big mind-game. I'm so angry, but still I feel it getting under my skin.

"I ..." I force myself to speak. "My boyfriend. I'll stay with my –"

"Oh, your boyfriend?" Greg says with a sneer that absolutely terrifies me. "And where is he right now, exactly?"

My heart sinks. Why does everyone want me to feel like Rye has abandoned me?

"Now then." Greg comes over and stands right in front of me. I lean as far back in my chair as I can. Please, *please* don't let him put his hands on me. "You'll be good as new in no time. Or as long as it takes until something clicks." He smirks again. "And trust me. It always clicks."

I can't look at him.

I dig my fingernails into my palms until I break the skin.

*

It's evening when the weather changes, bringing with it a nice breeze, but even that doesn't banish the grey cloud of despair hanging over this place.

I have an hour to kill before the day is over. I've never felt so beaten up emotionally.

After the assembly from hell I joined in the "pray the gay away" session, which I had no choice but to try to block my hearing to. Then I came straight back to the Rec Room and laid down on a lumpy beanbag and tried to slow my breathing.

I need some space to myself, so I head to the toilet block. It's outside near a pile of old abandoned tyres against a wall. There's a small fountain built into the bricks to wash your hands in.

I find a cubicle, put the seat down and sit. I don't actually need to use the bathroom, but the thought of being among the people here makes me want to hurl.

I put my head in my hands and take slow breaths.

As I sit and breathe deeply, I think of next week when I won't be here anymore. I don't care how hard they try, I'm not succumbing. I won't give in. They're not breaking me.

My hands are starting to feel clammy when there's a knock on the tin door.

"Just a sec," I say, pushing my palms hard into my eyes.

Another knock.

"I said just a sec," I say again, standing up and flushing the toilet needlessly.

Another knock.

"Seriously, what's the go with –"

I open the door and he's suddenly in front of me, cheeks flushed like he's been sprinting, his breath coming out in shallow puffs.

40

Rye

I pull Fin close and he clings to me, his skin warm against mine.

Oh my god, it's good to kiss him again. To hold him.

But he seems so different. Like the air in this place has sucked the very life out of him. His eyes are hollow and his lips dry and cracked.

"We need to get you some chapstick," I say stupidly, as I gently lift his chin up to get a better look in his eyes.

"I … You're here," he says.

"Of course I am," I say.

We sink into each other's arms, but then we hear what sounds like a car backfiring and both of us freeze. I don't know what it would mean if they found me with Fin, but perhaps I should grab him and run. Now that I'm here, I can see how toxic this place is. The thought of leaving him is unbearable.

"We're breaking you out," I say, a shiver in my voice. "Not right now. I'm sorry. But I promise you we'll come as soon –"

"I can leave now … I can grab my bag and … No, scrap that. Forget my bag –"

"I'd love that," I say, kissing him. "But, Fin, be patient. We have a plan for bringing your parents round. To get your family on side, accepting you one hundred per cent."

Fin says nothing and I gently kiss the tears from his cheek.

"Is it really bad?" I ask.

"It's all talk." He shrugs. "Then there's some weird transformation ceremony on Friday … They even have a choir coming. Then …" He stifles a sad laugh and looks at the floor. "How does a place like this even exist?" he whispers.

I have nothing. No words. Nothing makes sense and it hurts to try to comprehend the question. How *does* somewhere like this exist in 2020?

"But I'm going to stop it existing. When I get out of here, I'll tell the world exactly what kind of 'therapy' this shitty place offers."

"I'm all here for that," I say, encouraged by the strength in his words. "Wait, go back," I add, gathering my thoughts. "A choir?"

"Apparently." Fin sighs.

My mind goes into hyperdrive. "Can you hold out until then?" I ask, a punch of excitement running through my belly.

"I guess …" Fin says. "Yes –"

I gather his hands in mine, as if I can give him the energy to carry on. He leans into me, covering the side of my neck with kisses …

"OY!"

We flinch as a man with a pinched face and a "All You Need is Jesus" hoodie comes striding round the corner, glasses falling down his nose. He's accompanied by a man as wide as he is tall in a lame security baseball cap.

"OY! Stop that!" they shout.

"I love you, Fin," I tell him, as the security guy starts to barrel towards me. "I love you!"

But then, like a coward, I sprint up over the tyres and over the wall. I turn as I flee that hellish place to see the security guy grapple hold of Fin, pinning his arms roughly behind his back.

*

I've barely slept, but I have so much adrenaline coursing through me that I could keep going for a few days without a wink of it.

Fin's pale face outside that miserable building has been on a loop in my mind like an old film since I abandoned him there and I have this sick feeling in my stomach that won't budge. Please, please let him be all right.

When I get to the school car park, I find a bench and wait for Poppy and June to arrive. We've decided to convene here before we head to the lockers because it's easier to talk without a bunch of eavesdroppers around.

Last night when I got home, I called Poppy and June to tell them everything Fin had said.

They both looked genuinely scared, but we convinced ourselves Fin would be strong enough to survive the bullshit "talk" going on over at Re-Souled until we got him out.

June was all for organising a full-on QSA demo outside "that evil place". It took everything I'd got to convince her to hold fire; we'd need a protest once Fin was out of there – to close Re-Souled down once and for all.

We then put our energy into planning the perfect rescue mission Trojan Horse-style … Well, if the horse and its bellyful of warriors were as gay as *Kinky Boots*. These creeps want to play preacher, we'll give them something to preach to.

When at last she arrives, Poppy looks shattered, but June seems much more together.

"You okay?" I ask, gesturing to the jumbo can of energy drink that Poppy has clutched to her chest.

"Completely fine," she says, waving me away.

"Really?" I ask. "Because you look like you're three sips away from a meltdown."

"You know this stuff wakes me up," Poppy scoffs.

"Prescription amphetamines would too. Doesn't mean they're good for you."

"Okay, Oprah. Can we just get going? There's a lot to do."

June has her usual backpack as well as another duffle slung over her shoulder.

We find a place in the shade to sit and I check my watch. We've got exactly eighteen minutes to discuss our master plan before we start another day of school and I'm not wasting a single second.

"Are you coming to the diner tonight?" I ask, opening up my backpack and taking out a notepad and pen.

My fellow conspirators give me the thumbs-up.

"What are you planning on saying if Fin's parents actually show up?" June asks.

"Everything," I say.

"That's nice and specific," Poppy says, taking another gulp of her liquid caffeine.

"I'm on it," I tell her before motioning to June. "What's in the bag?" I ask.

A mischievous grin lights up her face.

"What's in the bag, June?" I ask again.

She throws it over to me and I hurriedly unzip it.

It takes me a moment to realise what I'm looking at. But still it's only once I finally take it out that it all makes sense.

"How in the f–" I start and Poppy bursts out laughing.

"Who is this chick?" Poppy says, wrapping her arms around June and going in for a peck on the cheek.

"HOW!?" I ask.

Poppy and I are seriously laughing now.

"Last night when you told me about the plan, I … well, let's just say I liberated these beauties."

Poppy and I lose it and soon enough June is laughing too.

"Well, regardless. We're tweaking the hell out of these *beauties* and turning them all the colours of the rainbow," I say, stuffing everything back into the duffle.

"Agreed," June says.

Poppy rolls onto her back and stares up at the sky. "Mum said she's in."

"Good," I say. "Mine too."

"And mine," June chimes in. "Dad too."

"Awesome," I say.

With six minutes to go, we move on to discussing logistics. The logistics of how we're going to rescue Fin. How we're going to show that Re-Souled bunch of losers what real soul looks like.

I feel a rush of energy pulse through me and then a break in my heart when I think of Fin. I can't believe he's stuck there. Whenever the thought of him in that place creeps in, the horrible reality of it absolutely floors me.

"Let's go," I say, standing. "I've got food tech and could really use a nap."

*

The smell of bacon and cheese sticks is overpowering when we arrive at the diner. I have barely eaten a thing all day and the stench from the over-processed dairy products turns my stomach.

June and Poppy seem way more composed than I feel and when we finally find a booth, I'm almost annoyed at how cheery Jerry is. I know he doesn't know what is going on with us. I have no reason to bristle or be upset. Yet I can't help it. It's almost obnoxious that his life is unaltered. That he can carry on with that big smile of his and take our orders without a clue that my boyfriend is being held captive across town in some nightmare camp for queer kids.

"What can I get you tonight?" he says, all fluffy blond curls and baseball cap and strong white teeth.

"The usual, J," Poppy says, offering her most minimal of grins.

"Sure thing," he says, beaming some more.

June smiles and hands her menu to him. "You been good, Jerry?" she asks, always the decent human being among us to bother to ask the normal questions while Poppy and I stare on like idiots.

"Can't complain," he says.

Of course he can't.

"How's your sister?" June asks.

"She's better. Definitely on the mend, thanks," Jerry says, and it's the first time I've ever seen his smile waver.

"Good to hear," June says, offering him a fist bump.

"Be right back with your stuff," Jerry says, heading back down the aisle and past the jukeboxes to the kitchen.

"What was that all about?" Poppy asks.

"His sister. She was physically abused over in Richmond just for holding her girlfriend's hand. On the freaking bus," June says, folding up the side of the tablecloth into ever smaller shapes.

A wave of guilt washes over me and realise just how dumb I am to think I'm the only person on the planet with an issue right now.

"My god," Poppy says. "It's at times like this when I lose faith in humanity. To know that all this badness goes on just wrecks my soul."

June puts her arm around Poppy's shoulder. "Can you imagine what a breeze it must be like to grow up straight?" she says.

"And white?" Poppy says.

"And cis-gendered?" I throw into the mix.

Poppy looks up at the ceiling and we all sit quietly for a moment.

"Yeah, but like … Imagine seeing yourself represented every-where," I say. "Doing your own stuff. Everyone assuming you're completely *natural* and *normal*."

*

Jerry brings us our double burgers and cream sodas and his smile is back and brighter than ever. Some people are better at holding back their hurt than others. I, for one, am shockingly hopeless at it. I'm missing the hell out of Fin and wish his hand was here to steady me.

"How long do we plan on waiting this out?" Poppy asks, nibbling on an onion ring.

"Until closing if I have to," I say.

"I don't think that'll be necessary," she says, using a sweet potato fry to point over my shoulder.

My guts tighten and my knees start to shake as I turn to see

Mrs Whittle in the doorway, looking around the diner. I stand, then sit and then stand again; my attempt at attracting her attention must be coming across as almost insane.

She eventually spots me and keeps her eyes to the floor as she walks over. I feel my heartbeat intensify as she nears us and then, just as I think my body is about to shut down, Mr Whittle walks through the door. He strides over, his face a picture of exhaustion.

"Seriously, Rye," Poppy whispers. "Are you sure you're up to this?"

I don't move. I can't believe they came.

"Mrs Whittle," I manage to say, as she arrives at our table.

June and Poppy have stood up as well and we're all just sort of standing there like a bunch of little kids on their first day of school.

When Mr Whittle joins us, I don't know whether to smile, cry or just take a running jump through the plate glass window next to us.

"Evening," Mr Whittle says, motioning for us all to sit, which we do.

Mrs Whittle's eyes are darting around nervously like she's never been to a diner before and Mr Whittle looks like we've invited him here to take part in a seance.

"Thank you for coming," I say, quietly. I nearly repeat myself as I wasn't sure if they heard me when I see Mr Whittle nod politely.

"With all due respect, sir," June says, her posture tall and professional, like she's ready to give a presentation. (Then again, she very well might be. It is June after all.) "My name is June … I have done a lot of research of conversion therapy and … your son Fin shouldn't be at that camp you've sent him to."

The tension in the atmosphere builds and builds until Mr

Whittle gives this resigned smile like he's dealing with a preco-
cious toddler who has no idea what she's talking about.

"Well, we came here tonight to advise you that we know what
is best for our son," Mr Whittle states, but I'm certain I can hear
a hint of doubt in his voice.

"Are you sure?" I ask. I can feel anger bubbling up inside me,
but I don't want to lash out. I don't want to go there. This needs
to be as straightforward as possible and going off at him won't
achieve a thing. "It's just …" I start. Then I see Mrs Whittle look
at me and I take a different approach. "Mrs Whittle, what was
Fin like as a kid?"

She smiles softly and a warm blush colours her cheeks,
defining a sprinkle of freckles that I've never noticed before.

"Sweet," Mrs Whittle says. "The sweetest boy you could have
ever met."

I recognise that boy, I think. "Would you say he was different
from the other boys back then?" I ask, looking over at Poppy and
June who are holding hands and sitting closer to one another
than before.

"Yes," Mrs Whittle says, sniffling quietly. "I used to call him
my special boy."

"Why?" I ask.

"He …" She pauses, as if suddenly overwhelmed by memories.
"He was always special to me … Sensitive and thoughtful. He
used to love music … He'd dance around our living room whenever his favourite songs came on the radio." She laughs properly
and I can see Fin in her now. "To be honest, I always kind of
knew he was different," she adds, glancing at her husband.

Mr Whittle doesn't react – I can't tell if he also always knew
that Fin is "different" or if he's always refused to see it. Until it

was staring him in the face and he couldn't choose to look away anymore.

"Then why are you wanting to change him *now*?" I ask, which stuns both Mr and Mrs Whittle for a second; they didn't see that coming.

"We're … We –" Mrs Whittle stops; she doesn't seem to know how to finish her sentence.

"We aren't trying to change him," Mr Whittle says. "We're trying to get him back to being himself." He shakes his head. "I mean, surely. I want his life to be normal, I don't want his life to be any harder than –"

I'm not having that.

"I'm sorry?" I say. "Have you considered how hard Fin's life is because of you guys not accepting him for who he is? For forcing him to conform to your idea of normal?"

Mr Whittle sits upright in his seat.

"If what you're saying is that you care about life being hard for him," I say, taking a breath to calm myself. "Then maybe start here?"

They look at one another.

"It's … We want him to have a full and happy life. We want him to have every opportunity. We want him to have the best life that he can."

"Do you think he can't have that if he's gay? Have you ever asked Fin what he wants?" June steps in, her voice soft and slow, doing all she can to contain her simmering anger.

Mr and Mrs Whittle sit in silence for a moment.

"That place you've sent him isn't just a bad idea … It's dangerous," Poppy tells them. "It won't make his life full or happy, that's for sure."

I have a feeling some of what we're saying is getting through to them, but Mr Whittle is about as easy to read as *War and Peace*. In the original Russian.

"He's not in prison," Mr Whittle scoffs, looking between June, Poppy and me.

"No," June says, "He's somewhere much worse."

"We just want him to be okay," Mrs Whittle says, looking genuinely frightened, but I've had enough. I don't care what it takes. They need to hear me out here.

"Then you need to get him out of there," I declare, my voice louder now that I no longer care to hold back. "People die from conversion therapy. Maybe not right away, maybe not when they first get out. But ..." I shake my head. "It's a form of abuse. It mentally breaks people. They can kill themselves because of it. Surely you know that."

They look at each other and I wonder if I need to climb across the table and shake them.

Mr Whittle sighs, warily. "Fin is *not* in the kind of place you are talking about. This is an established, recognised programme and –"

"It is a recognised *conversion camp*, Mr Whittle!" June cuts in.

But he simply raises his palm to silence her.

And, as he stands, I see Mrs Whittle hesitate and that small moment makes me want to grab her arm, but I don't. It's like I've got a gobstopper in my throat that I just can't swallow.

"Enough," Mr Whittle says. His voice is still stern, but he looks drained of colour – as if this talk has sickened him. "We're his parents and you have to understand that we know what's best for our son."

41
Fin

My head feels like it's full of dirty cotton wool and I've got that sick feeling in my stomach.

It takes a solid sixty seconds before I remember where I am. Horror seeps slowly through my body.

But I ignore it.

After seeing Rye yesterday, I came to a decision. As messed up as this place is, I know I'm strong enough to survive it. And when I get out I can actually do something to help. I can expose Re-Souled for what it really is. These programmes happen all over the country and I can stop them. I have to. My days here won't be wasted if I spend them gathering as much damning evidence as possible.

I shake the heavy feeling out of me, head over to the breakfast room, grab a bowl of sawdusty cereal, an equally sawdusty coffee and find a seat in the corner.

The other people in the room all have their heads down and are eating in silence. Talk about a jailhouse vibe. I need to focus all my energy on ignoring the message this hateful place is throwing out.

Today's first session is the "praying the gay away" prayer circle, and I steady myself for blanking out an hour of what they call "repelling sin".

Later, I sit on the hallway floor, my back against the wall, thinking of Rye. I can't help wondering what Elliot is doing, too. Has he tried getting through to our parents, or has he resigned himself to the fact that they will never change?

But none of that really matters.

There's no doubt in my mind what's going to happen. I can see it all playing out like a depressing film. When I get out of this place, I'll have two choices. Fake it until I leave home or leave home immediately. Somehow. Both options seem pretty dismal. Either way, there'll be no real relationship with my family. I'll be cut off from everyone.

I'm lost in a whirl of dark thoughts when Clare arrives.

She sits down next to me. "How are you doing?"

I look at her and up at the poster above her head that says "REPENT". I can't quite put into words how I'm feeling. It's like describing what a kiwi fruit tastes like. Impossible. So I just shrug.

We sit in silence for a moment.

"You?" I ask.

"I'm good," she says, but her hazel eyes tell another story. I immediately call bullshit. There's no way anyone can feel "good" in a place like this.

"Really?" I ask. "How?"

Clare smiles, a closed-mouth smile. "Like I said, I've been here three times now. I want it to sink in this time. Because, y'know, it's about how I view it rather than –"

"No, Clare. This isn't about your attitude," I tell her, like a

QSA boss. "Re-Souled is poison. They're the ones who need to change, not you." I can imagine June punching the air at my words, and Poppy doing her *woot woo* thing. Courage fills me. My real family might have rejected me, but I have a whole other family who've got my back.

"I don't want to feel like this anymore," Clare says, her eyes bouncing from me to the floor like she can't decide what's easier to look at.

"Like what? Queer?" I ask, treading carefully. "Or hating yourself?"

Clare pauses. "The last time I was here I lost someone close to me," she says, and I wonder if she's confiding in me or just getting something off of her chest to the universe.

"I'm sorry," I say.

"She was in here with me. Both times."

For the first time, I feel a ton of empathy for her. I realise how hard she's trying to live up to an ideal that's expected of her and it kills me to think that maybe this is her breaking point. This is my first time here. Maybe Clare fought against it the first time. And the second. Maybe there comes a point when something sinks its claws in and grabs hold of you and you have no choice but to let the ignorance take hold.

"Were you close?" I ask.

Clare flinches, like I've poked her in the side. "We were together," she says.

"In ... in here?"

Clare nods. "Both times. We held on and we said we wouldn't listen. That we'd fight against ..."

I look to her, but her mind is elsewhere, her eyes watching something only she can see.

"And she left?" I ask.

Clare wraps her arms around her knees. "Sara ... she killed herself."

I feel like the walls around me have turned to molten rock and lava. I feel like the roof is slowly caving in and I struggle to remember how to breathe.

"She ... My god. I'm ..." I start, but Clare shakes her head.

"I don't want this, Fin," she says, her voice quiet and focused as she fixes her eyes on me for the first time today. "I need this to work."

I snap out of my trance and grip her hand. "No," I say, squeezing her fingers too tight. "No, we need to expose this place. And you're getting out of here with me. I won't leave without you. Promise."

I'm serious. I'm not leaving her alone, not with what she's suffered. Whatever plans Rye has, Clare has to come too.

Clare squeezes my hand back, but then whispers, "And go where, Fin? Where would I run to? I don't have anyone out there waiting for me. It's my parents – who want me changed – or the street."

I let this sink in and I'm unable to come up with a response. Then I remember June and all her talk about support groups – people who will be on Clare's side.

But, just as I'm about to tell Clare this, a woman sits down opposite us. I've seen her around, she's one of Greg's cronies. Her name's Taylor and, although she has the personality of a cardboard box, she gives me a serious case of the creeps. The word is she's an "ex-gay" tutor who owes her "salvation" to Re-Souled.

If the hobgoblin spawn of the underworld sitting in front of me is what "salvation" looks like, then they really need to update their brochure.

"Clare. Fin," Taylor says. "How are we both?"

I pick at a loose thread in the knee of my jeans. Clare is suddenly very interested in re-tying the laces of her sneakers.

"I couldn't help overhearing your chat just now," Taylor says, mock sincerity plastered over her face.

My temper flares. "I couldn't help noticing you listening in where you're not wanted," I snap back.

Clare is half smirking and I hope my little dig has cheered her up.

"Your insults won't hurt me," Taylor says, her voice icy. "But I'd like to remind you that it is unacceptable to speak of such matters while you are under the care of Re-Souled."

Clare goes back to her sneaker laces, but I've had enough.

"Hmm … And if we don't obey?" I say. "You'll what? Throw us out?"

"What?" Taylor chuckles. "And hinder all your progress?"

I roll my eyes. "Okay, message received. Can you leave us alone please?"

"Of course. But don't forget, we have ways to punish those who continue to choose a sinful path."

My face flushes with anger, but next to me Clare turns as grey as the hallway walls.

I have to be strong enough for the both of us now.

*

After a miserable lunch of greasy stew and dry bread, Greg makes the unexpected announcement that we are each allowed a telephone call home. How kind. This place truly feels a prison.

I trudge my way through the musty halls and find the old cord-phone in a room with those grim motivational posters glued to the walls. Sunsets, lighthouses, paths through woodlands. Tasteless as all hell.

Taylor is there to stand over me as I dial home.

She backs off when Dad answers, but I nearly hang up. I don't even know where to begin.

"Hello?" I hear him say. "H-hello? Is ..."

"It's me, Dad," I say, letting all the air in my lungs out in a rush.

"Fin ... Hi," Dad replies, his voice softer than usual. "How's things?"

I pause.

I could lie and tell him how much "progress" I'm making. Let him believe this place is changing me. How great it is they sent me here.

But why would I do that?

"Shit," I say. "Total shit."

There's silence and I wonder if he's hung up.

"Fin ..." Dad starts. "You know it's ..."

But I can't handle another lecture. "Dad, no. This is the one time in my life I'm going to tell you, politely, to shut up," I say, and already feel better for it. "Sending me here was the worst thing you could have done. In fact, it's the worst thing anyone could do."

Silence, and so I speak into it.

"A girl in here died last year," I say, throwing the truth grenade down the phone as hard as I can. "She killed herself. She killed herself because she hated herself because of all the bullshit this place spews out." I feel myself growing more and more furious with every syllable that leaves my mouth. "Is that what you want,

Dad?" I spit. "For me to *die*?"

I hear his sharp intake of breath. "Fin … No … Don't be vile. Of course I don't want you –"

"Then what? What do you *want*? To put me through this living hell?"

Dad is quiet and I put my hand to my chest in an attempt to calm myself. The cupboard-sized room is spinning and I'm starting to sweat and tremble.

When Dad speaks again, he sounds exhausted, fragile. I've never heard him like this – my whole life, even before I told them I'm gay, he's always been in charge. Assertive. And now, recently, cold and angry as well.

"Fin, we just want you to have … A good, *normal* life and –"

"Dad, the only thing that's not normal about my life right now, is my parents trying to change who I am," I say.

"Wait, Fin –" Dad says, desperate, as if he's searching for an answer. "Please, speak to your mum."

I hold the phone tight, and wait.

"Fin?"

"Hi," I say.

There's quiet, nothing but the faint buzz of static. I let it happen. I have nothing left to say. To either of them.

"I …" Mum starts, and I hear a hiccup in her voice. "I want you to know I love you …"

I swallow twice to stop myself from crying. I'm not breaking. I can't.

We are quiet for a moment longer. I debate whether to reply.

"Not now, Mum," I say and hang up.

*

A day later and I'm about ready to burn this place to the ground. I've decided that I can't deal with life today. Anything. I haven't showered. I haven't eaten. I haven't even brushed my teeth and I'm pretty sure they've started to grow fur. Very attractive, I know.

Clare and I have shut ourselves in the recreation room. I've told her I'm serious about my promise – I'm not going anywhere without her. And I'm going to let everyone know exactly what a hellhole Re-Souled is.

We've found an old pack of cards and she's teaching me how to play Crazy Eights. It's a good way of ignoring Greg's lame attempts at getting us to participate. I'm not doing it. I'm not pretending and I'm not listening to any more of this ignorant dumb-fuckery.

Even when Greg sidles up to tell me my dad has called to "take me home" – total bullshit, I know – I refuse to come to the phone. Mind games won't fool me. I tell Greg I'm not leaving. Not now.

He can smirk all he likes, but I have a plan. Re-Souled is a story that needs to be broken.

*

It's just after dinner when I go outside. There's a fire pit with a few benches around it. The staff here don't miss a beat: every bench cradles a small Bible, each with verses dog-eared to remind us of all the ways a sinful human can burn for eternity in the fires of hell.

There's a breeze in the air, and the sky is a blaze of colour. I think for a moment how great this would be if Rye were here with me – if we were anywhere but here. Just us two, around a fire. No Bibles. Thinking of nothing but each other and dreaming of the future.

That thought evaporates when I see Taylor wandering slowly over to me.

"Fin," she says.

"Taylor," I ape, imitating her ghost-like voice.

She smiles at me like I'm stupid. "You know, you're only making this harder for yourself," she says, perching next to me.

"Hmm. Really? I don't actually think that's possible. This place is toxic and I'm already at rock bottom."

The fire in the pit flickers and her eyes narrow at the smoke.

"Fin, is this what you want?"

I scrunch my face. "What?"

"This," Taylor says, motioning to the fire.

"Taylor, you're going to have to be a bit more specific."

"Fire," Taylor says, solemnly. "For eternity. Is that what you desire?"

"I'm not listening to this," I say, and I stand.

"The doors are locked, Mr Whittle. You can engage in adult conversation with me, or you are staying out here all night." Taylor clasps her hands together in her lap like some sort of holier-than-thou church statue.

"You want an *adult* conversation?" I say. "Seriously? Did you hear what you just said?" I snort. "Just work, church, sleep, repeat until we kick the bucket in the hope that heaven is waiting for us?" I'm almost snarling at her when I say, "You're delusional." I can't quite believe the fire coming out my mouth. Since entering Re-Souled, I've become that hot activist after all.

"Delusional to believe that God has a plan? And your lifestyle choices are not part of it?"

I hate how calm she is. How unperturbed she is. How she truly believes this shit.

"My choices?" I look to the floor, gathering my energy. "We can't have an adult conversation because you're not an adult," I say. "You're a grown-up baby who's so terrified of being who you truly are that you're determined to spend your life pretending. Do you really think that God or the Holy Spirit or whatever is paying attention to what a good 'normal' girl you are?"

Taylor twitches and for a second I think I've hit a nerve. I press on, driving my point home.

"Seriously, Taylor. Do you *honestly* think God would want you to be anything other than who you are?" I ask. "You *know* who you are. You can try and fake it and act like all of this conversion crap worked, but deep down you know."

Her hands grip the bench so hard her knuckles turn white. "That's the devil talking in you," she intones, her voice flat.

"Oh, get *real*. If your God exists then he made me exactly the way I am. And I'm *fucking* proud of it," I say, and I mean every single word. No one at Re-Souled, Taylor included, is going to break me. And as soon as I'm out of here, I'm going to make damn sure that they don't break anyone else either.

The fire has turned to embers. I wonder if any of my words have made the slightest bit of difference.

"You'll spend the night in the chapel," Taylor says with a long-suffering sigh, but her voice is deadly and there's an eerie glow to her eyes.

"But where will I sleep?" I protest.

The chapel is converted from an old garage. It stands by itself. No lights or warmth. A cold stone building with a wooden cross on the door.

"Find a pew." Taylor gets up with a triumphant smile. "Pray hard and emerge cleansed."

42

Rye

It's been a day since I saw Fin and I am going full-blown stir crazy. I've had to stop myself multiple times from heading over there and dragging him home with me, but I have to try to get his parents to see the truth of what they're doing. Fin being there at Re-Souled until we figure things out is a last resort, solely because if there's a chance of some kind of understanding with his family then I'd be crazy not to try. Existing in a world without his family's support is no life at all.

It's five o'clock when Poppy's mum, Isla, arrives with my mum. They've been out all afternoon buying fabrics and sparkles and ribbons and I practically crash tackle them to the ground when they waltz through my bedroom door and dump the bags on my carpet.

June and Poppy have been sewing and cutting and sewing for the last two hours since we got home from school and now that Isla and Mum are here we can finally wrap these babies up and get ready for our ambush.

"You sure you know what you're doing?" Isla asks, as Thelma snuggles up next to her and demands an under-the-chin rub.

"Nope," I say, pulling out sheets of sequins and rainbow-hued fabrics from the bags.

Poppy grins.

"June grab that end," I say, folding out the fabric and flattening it with my palm.

We spend the next few hours tailoring our costumes to perfection. I'm absorbed in sewing and sticking, but still every few minutes my mind wanders back to Fin.

I know it's sappy and cheesy and I bet that even my mum considers it "young love" and *whatever*, but none of that makes this feeling I have for him any less intense. Love is the only word I have for it. What other reason could I have for spending my afternoon crafting these over-the-top outfits?

✳

It's nearly seven o'clock when we hear a knock on the front door. It takes a moment for it to register because everyone who matters is already in my room.

Mum looks up and shrugs and Isla puts down the giant "WE LOVE OUR KIDS" sign that she's been making out of a sequin-and-ribbon montage.

"I'll get it," Mum says as she steps over Thelma and closes the door behind her.

I hear the fly screen creak open and a simple "Oh" come from behind the door. There's a muffled conversation happening, but I can't make out what's being said.

Can you hear? I mouth to Poppy who shakes her head *no*. June and Isla do the same so I crawl towards the door and put my ear up against it.

From where I'm sitting it's next to impossible to work out who's on the other side of the door – thanks to Thelma's epic snoring – so I slowly open the door a little.

"It was a bad idea to come here."

It's a woman's voice and it sounds familiar.

Fin's mum is at our front door.

"No, I really don't think it was," Mum says. "There's a reason you're here …"

There's quiet for a beat and I wonder if Mrs Whittle has left.

"Do you … would you like to come in? For tea?" Mum says. "Something stronger even? You look like you could use it."

I hear Mrs Whittle half laugh and half sigh and I want to give my mum a fist bump for being so damn cool.

"No … I should go. I just … honestly, I'm not a bad person," Mrs Whittle says, and I can feel every nerve in my body stand on end.

"I'm sure your son doesn't think you're a bad person either," Mum says. "But I know that boy shouldn't be there. He needs his mum to tell him he's not a bad person, too. That he's loved. That –"

"I have to go," I hear Mrs Whittle say.

There's a moment or two before I hear the fly screen shut and Mum lets out this long, hum-like sigh.

"I know you're there, Rye," she says, and I open the door as she walks through and sits on the rug next to Thelma.

"What was that about?" Isla says, her glue gun poised mid-air.

"A distressed mother trying to deal with her homophobia, ignorance and fears." Mum sighs. "Something she's clearly never been quite brave enough to challenge before." She seems mad, which is odd because I didn't get that vibe a minute ago when she was talking to Mrs Whittle.

"Did she listen at all?" June asks.

"Who knows." Mum looks to the ceiling and shakes her head. "I will never understand parents who are not there for their children."

I hear the catch in her voice. Mum is crying.

I walk over and put my arm around her. "Stop being a big baby," I say, planting a kiss on her cheek. "Come on. We have stuff here that needs finishing. These bad boys won't stitch themselves."

*

When I wake up the following morning, I can smell coffee, Mum's carrot cake waffles and incense. It's unbelievably comforting. Like a hug.

I sit up and wipe the sleep from my eyes before stretching and heading out into the front hallway.

I'm about to follow my nose into the kitchen when I notice Thelma is scratching at something underneath the fly screen. She's had this obsession with the door mat ever since we got it. I'm convinced she considers it a threat, but when I bend down to lift her up and away from her mortal enemy I notice a square of white paper tucked just through the space between the floor and the door.

Two words are handwritten on the front: Rye & Karen. I open the paper and read:

Please come for dinner tonight. We'd really like to talk.
Charles and Sally Whittle.

I barely make it to the kitchen before I'm waving the paper in Mum's face and we're both completely hysterical like it's a letter from the Queen.

*

By seven o'clock – when we are finally standing outside the Whittles' house, Mum clutching a bottle of wine like it's a grenade and me with my best pressed shirt and jeans that have been ironed four times over – I feel like I'm about to collapse.

"You okay?" Mum asks.

I nod, taking a slow breath in and holding it for five like my meditation app tells me.

When Elliot opens the door, I finally breathe out to the count of seven.

"Hey," he says with a smile.

"Hi," I say. This happy-go-lucky vibe doesn't match how I'm feeling but I'm open to it. If Elliot is mellow, then I'm assuming we're not being entirely thrown to the wolves.

We're led inside and I take a look around. There are a few photos on the walls of Elliot and Fin as kids and I can't help but grin. Fin was *such* an adorable baby. He still has the same eyes and smile, and his nose is still cute as a button.

When we get to the kitchen Elliot takes the wine from Mum and pours her a glass as Mr and Mrs Whittle join us.

The atmosphere is more jittery than the NASA control room during the *Apollo 11* disaster, but I stand up tall and wait for someone to speak.

Elliot keeps glancing between everyone and Mum seems like

she's ready to chug the entire glass of wine in one go when Mrs Whittle's eyes light up.

"Wine!" she says. "I'm glad you – I was going to offer, but –"

"Brought some," Mum says, with a tip of her glass to let Mrs Whittle know it's all good.

"Here, Mum, Dad," Elliot says, handing them each a glass.

"Thank you, that's thoughtful of you," Mr Whittle says.

Mum smiles graciously, and I look at Elliot. I'm silently pleading with him to say something to keep the conversation moving.

"Rye, would you like a coke? Water? Juice?" is his best effort.

"Water, please," I say as Mr and Mrs Whittle lead us through some double doors and into the dining room.

When we're all seated Elliot helps keep the painfully awkward conversation going with anecdotes about his time in the tropics and the amazing people he met.

Mr and Mrs Whittle listen politely, even though they must have heard it all before. Every once in a while, I feel like they're about to say something.

Until eventually: "And there was this one guy I met in the rainforest who was –"

"I'm sorry," Mr Whittle says, cutting Elliot off mid-sentence.

Everyone sits still and I wonder who exactly he directed that apology to. I have a feeling it's not about interrupting Elliot's story.

"I'm going to cut to the chase here," he says, looking down at his plate. "I'm having doubts about whether sending Fin to this programme was such a good idea."

Silence. Everyone, including Mr Whittle himself, seems shocked by his change of heart.

"That's a start," Mum says, eventually.

I attempt a nudge under the table but miss and kick Elliot in the shin. He's grinning. I can tell he enjoys the experience of another adult standing up to his dad, but this whole thing feels beyond excruciating to me.

"We asked you to come tonight because ..." Mrs Whittle starts but then looks down at her plate and rolls her napkin. She seems to reboot her thought process a few times before settling on what to say. "Fin is ..." She sniffs and I can tell this is agony for her. I wish I could feel some sympathy but every time I begin to, I think of Fin stuck in that camp and my mood turns to rage. "We love our son."

Mum nods. "I don't doubt that."

"We just want what's best for him and this lifestyle he's choosing is a lot for us to under–"

"Wait one second," Mum says, holding up her hand. "Excuse me, but being gay is not a lifestyle choice. Did you choose your sexuality, Mrs Whittle? No. We simply are who we are."

Elliot grins, not bothering to hide his amusement at mention of his mum's love life.

"I ... Well, I know, but –"

"So, if you know, what makes you think Fin can choose? More to the point, why on earth should he?"

Slam dunk from Mum.

Mr Whittle sits up taller in his chair. "We invited you tonight because we are afraid. Afraid of making any more mistakes. I didn't realise ... I had no idea ... No idea that ... people have actually died." He swallows, obviously still shaken by the news that Re-Souled really is as catastrophic as we've been telling him. Then he continues. "We want Fin to be happy and if this is his choice then we –" He stops talking at a single blow from Mum's stone-cold glare. "If this is who he is …"

Mum's glare softens to a small smile of approval.

"… then we want to show him," he says, as Mrs Whittle squeezes his hand, "that we don't want to lose him. Even if, even if he's –"

"We're here for Fin," Mrs Whittle says firmly, interrupting her husband. "We're willing to work on this –"

Mum claps and grins like a fourth grader. "Now *that's* the kind of attitude I'm talking about," she says, downing her wine in triumph.

Mr Whittle sits back a little in his chair. He seems wrung out, but proud of himself. I guess in some weird way, I'm a bit proud of him too. Angry as a whole swamp full of crocodiles still, but I know it takes a lot to admit you're wrong.

"Right," Mum says, all business and ready for action. "You need to get on the phone to that camp director and tell them you're coming to collect your son."

Mr Whittle's brow furrows and the fluffy feeling I had in my tummy a moment ago vanishes as quickly as it came.

"I tried," he says, his voice low. "He wouldn't come to the phone last time I called. Apparently he's refusing to leave."

"Mr Whittle, with all due respect, that's bullshit," Mum declares, and I nearly lean across the table to take the wine glass away from her, but screw it. She's right. It is bullshit.

"What can we do?" Mrs Whittle asks. She sounds genuine and I can tell she's on board with getting Fin out of there, and probably has been long before Mr Whittle caught up.

"I'll try calling them again," he says.

I clear my throat and think of the best way forward.

"There's no way Fin would ever choose to be there," I say. "But we've promised to get him out, tomorrow night,"

That was the best way forward, Rye? Seriously? Insert eye roll here.

Mr and Mrs Whittle look at one another.

"We've had a plan since we realised you'd sent him there. And with your help it'll be a whole lot easier for Fin when he gets out."

My heart is beating up against my chest and I catch Elliot's eye. I can tell he's excited and nervous all at once.

"We never should have sent Fin to that place," Mr Whittle says again, drawing his hand down over his face in a gesture of utter weariness.

I take a breath and steady myself. "It's not me you need to say that to," I say. "It's Fin."

There's a silence that seems to last for eternity before anyone breaks it.

"What can we do?" he asks at last, his face pale.

Plenty, I think. "Was there anything Fin used to do as a kid?" I ask. "Anything cute that he'd know only you guys would remember? A family joke or memory?"

Mr and Mrs Whittle look to Elliot who smiles back.

"A few things actually," Mr Whittle says, his eyes brightening a little.

"A ton." Mrs Whittle smiles.

Elliot grins and starts scrolling through his phone. "I'd be happy to *Cher* them with you."

43

Fin

This so-called chapel is dusty and dismal even as the sun rises on a new day. I roll over and smush the lumpy pillow I found in a supply closet over my face, reminding myself that this isn't for ever. Soon, I'll be out of here.

Someone's unlocked the door, so I leave the stuffy chapel and head to the main building, taking deep gulps of fresh air as I go. It's sunny, but even the surprising warmth on my skin does nothing for my mood.

My plan for the day is to retain as many details about this place as I can, to write everything down as evidence. The thought makes me shudder, but Re-Souled is my mission now. Game over.

I take another bite of my toast, gulp down some coffee and am standing to leave when Greg enters flanked by Taylor.

"*Good morning,*" he says to the room, in that fake friendly tone of his.

He gets a few desultory *Morning*s for his efforts, but not from me.

"How did you sleep?" Greg goes on, clearly throwing that one to me and my overnight stay. "I trust you're well-rested, Mr Whittle, as I have an individualised therapy session lined up for you."

I don't blink. I don't speak.

"And, can I remind you all, that this evening the Mountain Song Choir will be joining us. In order to make the most of tonight's ceremony, I advise you to spend time with your prayers. Ask God for the strength to continue on your journey of transformation and healing." He smiles his mild, creepy smile again and I have this daydream where I throw my plate across the room at him. "For tonight, you will renounce your sinful urges and be reborn ready to follow the true path to salvation."

Everyone in the room seems to have frozen. None of us moves, speaks or breathes.

Taylor is standing to one side directing her vengeful icy glare at me and only me. I can't help but give her one of my biggest and fakest smiles in return.

Bring it on.

Another day in paradise.

*

I'm shaking from the inside. Trembling. My throat is tight. I stare in the mirror but I barely recognise myself.

Why did they keep interrogating me like that? On and on, digging into my relationship with my parents when I was a child. Insisting that my attachment to my mum is "unhealthy".

Why did they keep telling me I was damaged?

I step into the shower and turn the water on as hot as it will go. I don't bother with the cold tap. Instead I just breathe and let the water sting my body.

I refused to answer them, shut my eyes, did everything I could to block out their endless words, but something inside me shifted today and fear seeped in like tar.

And now I'm scared. Really scared. Not of an eternity in hell. But that I'm starting to believe less and less.

I'm scared of a lifetime spent questioning myself.

They told me again and again how lonely and lost I'd be without my family.

They drilled into my fear, asking what made me imagine anyone would stay with someone like me. What would I do when my *boyfriend* deserted me – they spat the word out – as he surely would? Then, when we weren't together, where would I go?

The trembling, the fear is too much. I make the shower pressure stronger and sink, slumped, to the floor as the water pours down, burning my back.

At last, I'm done with crying. I'm numb. Everything is numb.

*

It's nearly dark outside when I'm shaken awake. While I was "spending time with my prayers", I fell asleep in the recreation room. It takes me a second to realise where I am again – this place is so much like a living hell it's hard to tell when you're awake and when you're having a night terror.

When my eyes focus they settle on Clare who is standing next to me, her face haggard.

"It's time for the choir," she announces.

"Urgh, do we have to go," I say, shutting my eyes again.

"Yes," Clare says, impassively.

"Clare, please. I'm not going."

But she sits down next to me. "I don't want to go in there on my own," she says, with an honesty that stabs me right in the gut.

I let out a long, slow sigh and sit up.

"Okay, but I'm not doing a thing. And neither are you. They can't make us get up there and renounce shit," I say, forcing myself to feel badass. Poppy swears like a sailor, but I save it for when I'm really pissed. Like now. I'm really fucking pissed.

*

We make our way along the various gloomy corridors and then head across the asphalt through the double doors to the assembly room. The stage is set up and it is so tacky and amateurish that it looks almost laughable. Someone has stuck up the letters: R E – S O U L E D across the top of the stage curtains but half of the U is faded which means I can't help but read it as RE-SOILED. This whole place has left me feeling so painfully immature that I giggle to myself and then sit towards the back with Clare.

The room smells of dollar-store candles that can't disguise its unbearable, musty atmosphere. I shut my eyes, mentally taking notes, as people arrive, our sorry little band plus some others that Greg must have invited.

Taylor is sat up the front and Greg is off to the side wearing a double-breasted shiny suit he must have found from some eighties dress-up store. It even has proper shoulder pads.

"We're waiting on the choir now," he says, beaming idiotically.

Taylor scans the room. When her eyes meet mine, her lip curls and I throw her another one of my over-the-top grins.

"And I trust we're all clear on how tonight will run?" Greg asks.

Nobody speaks, but he must have gotten the answer he was looking for because he turns slightly to look at the stage.

Time crawls by and I'm wondering how much longer we have to wait before this sad bunch of *Sister Act* wannabes turn up when we hear a van bumble outside.

Greg's eyes light up and I can't help but groan at how painful this entire thing is. Is he for real? Honestly, how can anyone be so invested in this insanity?

The double doors open to reveal a scrappy white van parked directly outside. It sits, solitary, with nothing to distinguish it but a handwritten sign that reads "Let's Party" sticky-taped across the sliding door.

I roll my eyes. This group is clearly about as hardcore as Martha Stewart.

Taylor takes a few steps away from the stage, I'm assuming to let the choir make their entrance, and I look across at Clare who sits nervously, her hands twisted together in her lap. She's been through this before; she knows the choir is the least of our worries this evening.

Greg stares out at the van for a moment and I notice his smile slip and a look of confusion roll over his face.

"Uh …uh," he says, taking a concerned step towards the doors. "Hold on."

He's moving with the caution of someone stepping through a minefield when the van's sound system crackles to life. Some tame hymnal chords are unleashed, followed by what sounds like a gospel choir warm-up.

Greg's face softens as he makes his way back to his post and I turn around to get a look at whatever it is that's actually happening.

From within the van, someone is singing about life being a mystery. The tune sounds vaguely familiar – maybe it's one from church back home – and then the van's door slowly opens. Its interior is dark and I can only see a few robes, all white and holy-looking, people's faces covered with big white hoods.

There's the sound of chanting about how we all must stand alone … a song about someone calling my name?

Wait a sec.

The robed choir file out of the van and towards the stage.

Greg looks like he's about to go into meltdown and Taylor's face is clenched in panic.

And then the choir runs down the aisle and up onto the stage.

One by one they fling their arms aloft and whip off bits of robe to reveal spectacular costumes underneath. It's one hell of a striptease.

Then the final figure storms the stage, flinging away an expanse of pure white robe to reveal himself in glorious, sequined, rainbowed outrageousness.

"Rye?" I gasp, my voice lost in the music as the choir belt out "Like a Prayer" while voguing with enough panache to make Madonna herself proud.

I take in the vision before me and I can't help it. The anguish of the week washes away in a tide of relief and joy. I'm laughing and crying simultaneously. Clare is shell-shocked next to me. I grin at her, then take her hand in mine and squeeze it.

This band *is* hardcore after all. (Martha Stewart did go to prison I guess.)

Rye is pointing at me and I can see Poppy, June, June's parents, Poppy's mum Isla, and Elliot all on stage and raving like fabulous queer lunatics and I'm LIVING for it.

A medley of songs blasts through the hall as they rock out and flip the bird to Taylor and Greg. Those two look like creepy, unwanted twins, stock still with their mouths hanging open in horror. I'm really hoping this is hurting them. A lot.

With a circus-master flourish, Rye takes out a microphone from one of his costume's hidden pockets and flicks the switch.

"Fin," he shouts with no preamble. "Fin Whittle, I love you."

The rest of the choir cheer and *woot-woo* and raise their hands to the sky. OTT, much?

Clare nudges me. "Respect," she whispers with a bright-eyed grin.

"And these Re-Souled idiots don't have a clue," Rye goes on. "Their days are numbered."

The room turns tense and I'm worried that a war is starting to brew. But the Re-Souled crew are totally outnumbered and, almost literally, floored by the spectacle unrolling before them.

"You, Fin Whittle, are PERFECT just the way you are." Rye carries on, pointing one at a time to the guys and girls from my group in front of us. "And so are you. And you. And *you*!"

The, he jumps off the stage like a rock star and strides up to me.

He puts his hands on my shoulders then plants a massive kiss on my lips, sending a shockwave through the hall. Not to mention my love-starved body.

Taylor and Greg are still frozen and I wonder if they've died standing up.

"One more thing," Rye says, taking my free hand. "Hit it!"

The track changes and bass rolls along.

I take a few steps towards the stage as the bass thrums some more.

Cher's voice comes from the speakers.

I grin helplessly and look around the hall. Trust Rye – and his mum – to go full-blown musical theatre on this.

The choir on the stage part and there, in the middle of everyone, is Mum and Dad.

How could I have missed them? I shake my head in disbelief.

Rye grabs my hand.

"We're outta here," he says, tightening his grip on my hand. "Let's go disco."

A chorus of "Turn Back Time" bellows from the stage as I turn to Clare. "Come with us," I say.

Clare blinks, obviously struggling to speak. "I …"

"Clare, come with us," I say again, to which she whispers: "Okay." Softly. The only answer I need.

Everything's chaos. Cher's still going full blast on stage. I can't help but laugh at the sight of Mum and Dad. They've actually started to get into it: their arms are linked with Elliot's and he's belting like he's the real deal.

I rush the stage and wrap myself up in my family, linking arms and grinning fit to burst. Clare and Rye run up alongside us and together, forming one enormous, ridiculous, glittery, rainbow-crazed choir, we sing our way back down the aisle to the van.

Taylor's coming straight for us as we near the exit. "You … You can't just –" she protests.

"Can't what?" June asks, glaring up and down at her.

"Can't what *exactly*?" Poppy echoes.

"This is against protocol," Greg declares, trying to gather his wits. "This is totally unacceptable. You've had your fun, but I really must insist that Mr Whittle remains for his Re-Souled transformation. It's a vital component of –"

"That is enough!" Mum literally growls. She takes a threatening step towards him and Greg's harping comes to an abrupt stop. "What's *vital* is that we get *Mr Whittle* away from you and your toxic propaganda."

Dad's face has turned to stone and he's now moving with the unstoppable authority of an army sergeant towards the van.

"Fin is our son," he says. "And we love him."

Elliot's in the driving seat as we pull the doors shut and the van rumbles to life.

Rye takes my hand and we lurch forward. The music's on and we're still singing as we head off away from this horror show and into the night.

44

Fin

It's been six weeks since our escape from Re-Souled and when the school bell for the day rings I throw my backpack over my shoulder and bolt for the door. I haven't seen Rye properly in the last couple of days. But I know that his mum's been a star, sorting out government support and temporary accommodation for Clare. It's far from ideal, but we're going to make it happen. Chosen family or not, we're on side to get her through this next part of her life.

Not so great is the fact that Re-Souled is still somehow open for business. It baffles me how it can even be allowed to operate in a legitimate way. My time there gives me nightmares and I worry about the kids who are subjected to their poison. Still, I'm managing to put together an article about my experience there, and June and I have set up a campaign to get them closed down once and for all. We're working on it ...

*

But here in Lochport, today, the sky is purple and the air is soft and warm. This is my favourite kind of weather. It makes me feel like everything's going to be okay.

Mum and Dad still have their moments. I'm not going to pretend it's now all sunshine and rainbows – it takes more than six weeks to rethink a lifetime of preconception and prejudice, but they're getting there. Elliot has been amazing. Whenever things get tense or awkward he's sure to jump in with some fun fact about LGBTQI+ youth that he's been researching since we got home. He's started a course and a volunteer placement so he can train to be a youth support worker. It's a job he'll be phenomenal at. After a stint mucking in at an orangutan sanctuary, he can cope with anything. He's pretty awesome, my brother.

I find my way to our spot at Kettle Lake and shake the blanket to throw off the dried leaves before sitting down and taking a deep breath. The lake is salty and perfect and the breeze is just right. For the first time in as long as I can remember I feel genuinely okay. Not great, not phenomenal. There's still a lot I need to sort through. But okay. I feel okay. I *am* okay. That's more than enough for now.

*

When I see Rye making his way through the bush I stand. A cockatoo squawks and flies overhead; my heart feels just like the flutter of its wings.

"Hey," Rye says, wrapping me in his arms and planting a kiss on my lips.

"I've missed you," I say.

"Missed you more."

We sit on the blanket together and he puts his arms around me.

Bliss.

And everything else has been pretty awesome, too. Poppy and June are steady and genuinely happy, so there's no drama there. For now. And we've been going at our own steady, lovey-dovey pace and life is sweet.

The sun is starting to go down as Rye pulls out a flask of chai latte from his backpack.

"So, you know that lyric from *Hairspray* where Tracey sings to Link about being in love with him for ever? Like even when they die and stuff?" I ask, rolling over to look at Rye who now has an expression that reads nothing other than, *What in the fresh hell are you talking about?*

"No, Fin. I haven't seen *Hairspray*, but from that little synopsis it sounds like a horror. Are you sure you're not thinking of *Misery* with Kathy Bates?"

He offers me a sip of chai latte.

"No, it's romantic," I insist. "She's talking about how much she loves him and how they are going to have all these awesome memories together. Forget the weird thing I just said. I meant it to be cute. Definitely came across as much more frightening than I intended."

Rye laughs. "Well, I'd be happy with this for ever," he says, looking at me.

"Me too," I say. "None of this, one day when one of us is old and goes, I want you to move on without me. Nope. My jealousy is strong. Get in the casket with me."

"You're being creepy again," Rye says, with a belly laugh.

"Okay fair," I say, offering him back his flask. "I played up to it that time."

We sit for a while as the sun finally disappears.

"I can't help thinking about Clare," I say. "I so want life to pan out happily for her."

"Yeah," Rye says, gazing out across the water. "Clare's doing good. That counsellor she's seeing is brilliant, she's really helping her process everything."

I sigh in relief.

"And you?" Rye asks, looking at me and taking my hand in his as he brings it to his mouth and kisses it lightly.

"Me what?"

"How are you doing?"

I shrug. "Not too bad," I say.

Rye smiles, his dimples showing.

"Good," I follow up. "I'm good. Now that you're here. And I'm here with you."

He kisses my hand again.

The first few fireflies blink to life and I feel warm and fuzzy inside.

"I couldn't be happier," Rye says as more and more fireflies flicker and hum across the surface of the lake.

I turn to look him in the eye. "I guess there's no need to come here anymore," I say, holding back a smile and attempting to be as serious as I can.

"Umm … sorry?" he says, seemingly offended that I'd even dare suggest such a thing.

"Well, I mean. The fireflies help with feeling worried, right? And … I don't have a whole lot to worry about anymore now, do I?" I say, letting my smile break a little.

He's on to me. I can tell because he nudges me cheekily and looks at me with smiling eyes.

"True," he says. "But it's a pretty good place for kissing …"

He moves in for the kiss and I kiss him back.

The only light around us comes from the thousands upon thousands of warm, yellow fireflies.

Acknowledgements

Firstly, and above all, I want to thank Mum, Dad and Max. Thank you for everything. I would never have dared to dream as big as I do in life if I didn't have such incredible support from you lot. I love you all loads.

Mum, you're my best friend and I love you so incredibly much.

Pearce Jacobs, thank you for showing me what a true love story looks like. I am so grateful to have you in my life and I am beyond excited for the many more adventures ahead. I love you more than I could ever put into words.

Poppy, I know you can't read this because you're, well, a dog, but I wanted to acknowledge how incredibly much my beautiful English Bulldog means to me.

Nan Diane and Granddad Neil, thank you for forever making me feel like your Special Boy. I love you both gazillions. Thank you for everything.

Nan Barbara, you mean the world to me and I can't begin to tell you how grateful I am for you. I love you to bits. Thank you for always making me feel like a somebody.

Geena Davis. You're a dear friend and I love you bucket loads. Thank you so much for everything.

My incredible agents at Marquee, Emma Langley, David Sheridan, Cassie Moore and Emily O'Brien, you're phenomenal.

Thank you so much to Kai Spellmeier for your awesome contributions to the editorial process.

Thank you to Chris Csabs for your time and effort.

And humongous thanks to the incredible team at Black & White Publishing and Ink Road Books. Emma Hargrave, Janne Moller, Alice Latchford, Ali McBride, Thomas Ross and Campbell Brown, thank you for your amazing support from the get-go right the way through the editorial process.

My amazing friends, there's a sprinkle of all of you within this young cast of characters.

Hayley Thomson, thank you for being such an incredible friend from the get-go.

Tanja Edwards, you're a one in a billion friend and a gem of a human.

Sally Curlewis, you're simply wonderful.

Elisa Vitagliani, thank you for always being such a phenomenal friend.

Bundles of love to Uncle Tony, Kate, Laila, Faye, Dillon, Aunty Debbie and Mollie.

Lots of love to Michelle and Paul Hosking. Thanks for raising such an amazing son that I'm proud to call my partner and for making me a part of your beautiful family.

To every young queer kid reading this and wondering if it's possible to write books, be in movies, on TV, perform on stage or tell stories: you can and you must.

Queer representation matters more than anything right now. Go out there and make magic.

"I wanted him to know that someone is here if he needs to talk."

If you've been affected by anything you've read in *Fin & Rye & Fireflies*, if you would like to talk or are worried about someone in your life, there are organisations in the UK who can offer free advice, help and support, and will listen to you in confidence. Words have power. And if you can't always find the words for someone you know, please consider contacting one of the organisations below.

Stonewall Youth
For all young lesbian, gay, bi, pan and trans people – and those who are questioning – to empower and let them know they're not alone.
www.youngstonewall.org.uk

Childline
A counselling service for young people up to age 19.
www.childline.co.uk

Samaritans
Round-the-clock support for anyone who needs to talk.
www.samaritans.org

Mind
Dedicated to better mental health. They can offer details of help and support in your local area.
www.mind.org.uk

Papyrus
An organisation dedicated to the prevention of young suicide.
www.papyrus-uk.org

THE JOURNEY STARTS HERE

As a Young Adult imprint, Ink Road is passionate about publishing fiction with a contemporary and forward-looking focus. We love working with authors who share our commitment to bold and brilliant stories – and we're always on the lookout for fresh new voices and the readers who will enjoy them.

@inkroadbooks